Three Motives *for* Murder

Jewel Imprint: Emerald
Medallion Press, Inc.
Printed in USA

PREVIOUS ACCOLADES FOR MICHELLE PERRY'S
IN ENEMY HANDS:

★★★★★ FIVE STARS
"IN ENEMY HANDS is an exhilarating romantic suspense tale . . ."

—*H. Klausner, Independent Reviewer*

"IN ENEMY HANDS is an exciting suspense that will force you to read it in one sitting. Heart-stopping action, rapid-fire dialogue, and adventure in every chapter propel IN ENEMY HANDS forward in a race to the finish."

—*Romance Junkies*

★★★★ FOUR STARS!
"IN ENEMY HANDS is a well-written, non-stop, action-filled story of good versus evil. The characters are well defined, and there are some excellent, imaginative scenarios that will leave you breathless. The interaction between Dante and Nadia is sizzling and based on love and trust. If you enjoy a good romantic thriller, this is the book for you."

—*Affaire de Coeur Magazine*

"IN ENEMY HANDS is fantastic! It is action packed and deeply sensual and I was on the edge of my seat from the first page to the last . . . Michelle Perry has written a truly captivating and thrilling book with IN ENEMY HANDS. It's a must read for any romantic suspense fan. I can't wait to read it again!"

—*www.joyfullyreviewed.com*

"Ms. Perry delivers another impressive romantic suspense with IN ENEMY HANDS. The action is almost non-stop and both characters are more than sufficiently developed in order for us to understand why they feel and act the way they do. If you are in the mood for a thrilling romance with characters you can't help but adore, then this book is a must read. I'm certainly hoping some of the secondary characters will get their own book in the future."

—*Romance Reviews Today*

"The action is vivid and fast moving — both the violence and the love . . . it was hard to put down."

—*Mysterious Women*

"To say that IN ENEMY HANDS is action-packed is a total understatement! . . . the most thrilling and creative action sequences it has ever been my pleasure to read. Add to the mix . . . sexual tension, a little humor, a lot of danger and one really creepy bad buy and you have the makings of a perfect summertime read!"

—*Melissa Fowler TRRC*

AND FROM HER FIRST NOVEL, *CAIN & ABEL*:

"The romantic suspense of Michelle Perry grabs you and won't let go."

—*Affaire de Coeur Magazine*

"Michelle Perry's writing sizzles! Breathtaking suspense, great characters, and non-stop action make CAIN AND ABEL a fantastic read. Don't miss this debut from a star who's sure to shine!"

—*Tina Wainscott, best selling author of*
WHAT SHE DOESN'T KNOW, *St. Martins Press.*

"An intensely dramatic psychological thriller. An intriguing romantic suspense that will keep you turning the pages!"

—*Best Selling Author of* DEEP BLUE, *Kat Martin*

"Wow. Perry's thriller is edge-of-your-seat intense. Every page adds another layer and you want to put the book down and take a break, but you find you can't. You have to know how the story ends. While fiction, CAIN AND ABEL does resemble life, as you read Jessica's story, escaping from an abusive husband and trying to start a new life, you realize there are women doing the exact same thing at this very moment. This realization adds to the storyline and intensifies the emotions.

CAIN AND ABEL is a masterful thriller!"

—*www.inthelibraryreviews.net / Sharyn McGinty*

DEDICATION:

For Ronnie Wayne, my partner in crime.

Published 2007 by Medallion Press, Inc.

The MEDALLION PRESS LOGO
is a registered tradmark of Medallion Press, Inc.

If you purchased this book without a cover, you should be aware that this book is stolen property. It was reported as "unsold and destroyed" to the publisher, and neither the author nor the publisher has received any payment from this "stripped book."

Copyright © 2007 by Michelle Perry
Cover Illustration by Adam Mock

All rights reserved. No part of this book may be reproduced or transmitted in any form or by any electronic or mechanical means, including photocopying, recording, or by any information storage and retrieval system, without written permission of the publisher, except where permitted by law.

Names, characters, places, and incidents are the products of the author's imagination or are used fictionally. Any resemblance to actual events, locales, or persons, living or dead, is entirely coincidental.

Typeset in Adobe Garamond Pro

Printed in the United States of America

10 9 8 7 6 5 4 3 2 1
First Edition

ACKNOWLEDGEMENTS:

Special thanks to Rebecca Miller, Lori Saltis, Theresa Gaus, Quinton, Chase & Selena Perry, Tammy Layne, Cat Brown, Barbara Hughes, Nicole Service, Patsy Phillips, Karla Brandenburg, Marie DisBrow, Caryl Harvey, Eric Wright, Eric Kriegel, Frank Meredith, Rebecca Coleman, Jennifer Colgan, Angie McElroy, Judith Fox, Kristen Quinn, Skye, Patricia Myers and the Yarworth clan, Kathy Nunley, the Scissoms, the Perrys, Krystal Bean, Treva & Robert.

Extra special thanks to the Medallion team, especially my patient editor Helen Rosburg.

And Audioslave for my mood music, *I am the Highway*.

CHAPTER 1

BRADY SIMMS SAT QUIETLY WHILE THE MAYOR AND county sheriff argued. The stiff collar of his dress blues made his neck itch, but he felt the eyes of the town council members upon him and tried not to fidget. So far, he hadn't been asked to comment.

How had he let Mike talk him into this?

Brady wasn't sure he wanted to be tied to this town, but the thought of putting chief of police on his resume was tempting. He wouldn't find this opportunity in a larger town.

In two weeks, he would be twenty-three, the minimum age to apply to the FBI, but he knew he was probably years away from an appointment. Despite the minimum listed, the average age of new agents was twenty-nine. Anything he could do to add to his work history might shave a few years off that.

"He's too young, Mike. You can't put a kid like that in charge of your police department." The sheriff, Pete Richards, hitched up his pants and paced in front of the handful of citizens who'd gathered in the cramped city hall for the special meeting. His beefy face reddened when Mike smiled.

"Sheriff Richards, we're lucky to have a man like Simms." Mike tapped the bulging folder in front of Councilwoman Clark. "I think his record speaks for itself."

"You have to have five years police experience—"

"He has that," Mike said.

"Dispatching doesn't count."

"Read your rule book. It counts."

The sheriff glanced at his nephew, who perched on the front row in the audience section. "Joe has eight years on-the-job experience as a deputy."

"But he doesn't live in Coalmont, and he doesn't have his bachelor's degree."

"The late chief Lowrie, rest his soul, would expect you to appoint someone with the experience to carry out the job."

Uh-oh, Brady thought.

Mike frowned and pushed away from the table. The tall, skinny mayor towered over the short, fat sheriff. "Gus Lowrie trusted Simms implicitly. I have a copy of the recommendation he gave Simms for his FBI application. I believe if he were here today, this is the choice he'd make. Also, promotion should be within the department. Since Roscoe Noone doesn't want the job, Simms is the next in line of succession."

"Nowhere in the book does it say that promotion should be within the department," Sheriff Richards said.

"If you want to get technical—no, it doesn't. That is my personal opinion. But it does say that all officers—including the sheriff—are required to pass a physical test every two years. How long has it been since your last physical, Pete?"

"Gentlemen..." Councilwoman Clark shot Mike an admonishing look. "The council has reached a decision."

She nodded at Brady, and he stood to face them.

"Officer Simms, this is an impressive file. I'll hit the high points for the audience." She flipped through the papers. "Brady Simms began taking college credit classes while still in high school. At the age of twenty, he graduated Summa Cum Laude from the University of Tennessee at Knoxville with a dual major in Criminal Justice and Accounting. He's been working toward a master's in Criminal Justice while simultaneously working as a deputy for the city of Coalmont. He completed police academy certification and also has a certification from the National Forensic Academy. His I.Q. has been measured at—" She paused and lifted an eyebrow. "—147. That's genius level, folks."

Mike walked over to stand beside Brady. He winked at Brady and clamped an arm around his shoulder.

"After careful consideration this week, the board unanimously backs Mayor Wilson's motion to hire Officer Simms as the police chief of Coalmont. We believe you will be a great asset to the town of Coalmont and can only hope the FBI doesn't steal you away from us anytime soon. Now, is there any further business?"

When no one spoke, she banged her gavel. "This meeting is adjourned."

The sheriff stalked out of the city hall with his nephew in tow, and most of the onlookers dispersed with them. Brady and Mike walked over to shake hands with the council.

"Thanks, Bea," Mike said, and grasped Councilwoman Clark's hand.

"You're welcome." She smiled at Brady. "I'm going to miss Gus. I was so saddened to hear of his heart attack, but I agree with the mayor. This is what he would've wanted. I've heard him speak of you many times. 'Boy Wonder', he called you."

Mike grinned. "I thought that was Joe's nickname."

She gave an unladylike snort. "I wouldn't trust Joe Richards to take care of my garbage pick-up, much less my town. Which is what he'd probably be doing, if his uncle wasn't sheriff." Glancing at her watch, she said, "I have to run, but congratulations again, Brady. Make us proud."

"Yes, ma'am."

He and Mike were the last to leave. They walked into the warm July night, and Mike locked the door behind them.

"Well, Genius, we got you in. I bet old Gus is laughing right now. Did you see Richards's face?" Mike rubbed his hands together. "Just wait. I think I'll start spreading the rumor that we're prepping you to run for sheriff next year."

Brady groaned. "No, please. He's still technically my boss."

Mike's smile faded. "Yeah, but Coalmont is yours. He doesn't have a lot of business here. Don't let him root you out. He'll be pulling some power plays, I'm sure, but hold your ground. I expect you to be as big a thorn in his side as Gus was. Speaking of which—" Mike dug a set of keys out of his pocket. "—you have a new ride, Chief."

Brady looked over his shoulder at the gleaming white Ford Explorer. A lump rose in his throat when he pictured Gus behind the wheel, singing along with his Merle Haggard tapes.

"I had my boy detail it for you today. Do you have any personal stuff in the patrol car?"

"No."

"Good. I'll drive it back to the station for you."

"Thanks."

"Don't mention it."

Brady smiled. "No. I mean thanks for everything."

Mike surprised him by giving him a quick hug. "You're welcome. Now get to work."

Brady slid into the leather seat that gleamed with a fresh coat of Armor All. The smell of the glass cleaner almost masked the cherry scent of Gus's cigars.

He jumped when the CB crackled to life.

". . . didn't copy, Mary Ann. Where did you say Brady went?"

Brady fumbled the mike out of its holder and keyed it. "I just got out of the town meeting. What's going on?"

"Turn to my favorite channel."

Roscoe wanted a private conversation. It took Brady a moment to find the switch in the dark. "Okay. I'm here."

"First of all, how did the meeting go? Am I talking to the new chief?"

Brady grinned. "You are."

"Yee-haw. Glad I'm not stuck with that dip Richards." Roscoe cleared his throat and chuckled. "Well, Chief, you ain't gonna believe this, but you're getting broken in right and proper. We've got a 187 at Miller Subdivision."

Brady blinked and hesitated before he keyed the mike again. "You're kidding me."

"Wouldn't kid about a homicide. Now you know why I didn't want the job. You've been chief for what—"

"Ten minutes."

"—ten minutes. Ten minutes on the job on a perfect July night, and Coalmont has its first murder of the year. It's some kind of cosmic thing, like when you drop your car insurance to liability only and the next day you total the thing—"

"Where are you?" Brady asked. He'd be sitting there all night if he let Roscoe launch into one of his theories of the universe.

"Third house on the right entering the subdivision. Thought I'd give you a heads-up before I put in the call to dispatch. I was working another call, a drunk and disorderly, when a girl came running down the sidewalk, screaming her head off."

"So . . . it's a domestic situation?"

"No. She told me—ah, you'd better just head over. I gotta log it with dispatch too."

"I can be there in five."

Brady flipped on his lights and roared out of the parking lot.

Four minutes later, he slowed when he entered the subdivision. This was the kind of place where kids were left to their own devices. It had been dark for an hour now, but still children played kickball in the street.

He hit the brakes when a little girl with matted blond hair darted in front of him. She couldn't have been older than five. Her wan face looked dirty and sad in the amber glow of the streetlights, and Brady wondered if her parents knew—or cared—where she was right now.

One of the lost ones, Gus would've said. As methamphetamine became an increasing problem in this area, they saw more and more of these lost children.

When he rolled down his window, she sprinted toward one of the houses. A boy of about ten emerged from the shadows of the porch and took her arm. Although Brady couldn't hear their muffled conversation, he appeared to be scolding her. With a sigh, Brady rolled his window back up and cruised around the block until he spotted Roscoe's squad car. Its blue lights danced across a ramshackle brown house with dangling green shutters.

Roscoe appeared in the doorway, then hopped off the sagging porch to meet him. The gray-haired deputy wore no sign of his usual good humor.

"Who is it?" Brady asked.

"I haven't gotten an ID on the victim yet, or talked to the witness. Thought I'd better secure the scene first."

Brady started across the yard. "Who does the house belong to?"

"Mildred Bright, but she rents it to a ..." Roscoe paused to glance at his notepad. "... Natasha Hawthorne."

Brady felt like he'd taken a hit in the solar plexus. He lurched to a stop, and Roscoe collided into his back.

No, no, no.

This whole night was some crazy, stupid dream. This wasn't happening.

Brady ran.

Roscoe yelled something, but Brady couldn't stop. He bounded up the steps and through the doorway.

The corpse slumped in a recliner. Even though half his head was gone, Brady recognized him immediately.

Brady covered his mouth with his hand and squatted, trying to regain his equilibrium in the crazily swaying room.

Roscoe entered behind him, banging the screen door.

"His name is Bobby McBee," Brady said.

"Friend of yours?"

"No."

Brady glanced at the wooden cane lying beside the faded blue recliner. His chest hurt, and it was hard to push out the question. "The girl . . ."

"What?" Roscoe asked.

A TV blared canned laughter into the cramped living room, and Brady struggled to raise his voice over it. "Is the girl okay?"

"Yeah. She's with the landlady."

Sirens screamed down the street, and Brady forced himself to stand, though his legs were shaking.

Sheriff Richards appeared in the doorway. "Simms," he barked. "What are you standing in?"

Brady glanced at his shoes, then followed the yellowish stream to the seeping carton of Tropicana. "Orange juice."

For the first time, he noticed the groceries scattered in the doorway. The sheriff slipped in a puddle of cola and inadvertently sent a can of peas skidding across the cracked linoleum floor. It rolled to a stop against Bobby's recliner.

The sheriff caught himself—just barely—and huffed, "You and Roscoe get out of here. You're contaminating my crime scene."

Brady wiped a hand over his mouth and replied, "Actually, it's my crime scene until the state gets here. You can assist, but you can't push us out."

The sheriff grunted, but didn't say anything else as

he strode toward the body. "So, what makes you think it's a homicide instead of suicide?"

Roscoe cleared his throat. "Other than the lack of a weapon, we have a witness who says it was."

The sheriff leaned to peer at the corpse. "Ayuh, I know this one. Nothing but trouble."

Brady glanced at the body. For once, he and the sheriff could agree on something.

"Hey, men." Ian Kirby stuck his head in the doorway, and Brady lifted his chin in acknowledgment at the Tennessee Bureau agent. "What do we have here?"

Roscoe briefed him, and Kirby nodded. "Okay. I'll get busy in here."

"I'll question the witness," the sheriff said.

"I'm going with you." Brady moved past the sheriff before he could object.

Kirby slapped Brady on the shoulder when he passed. "I hear congratulations are in order, Chief."

Brady smiled. "Word travels fast."

"That it does, my boy. That it does."

The sheriff grunted behind them.

"Mildred's house is the yellow one at the end of the block," Roscoe called.

Brady stalked toward the house with the sheriff on his heels. He heard the man's heavy breathing, but made no effort to slow for him. Finally, the sheriff gave up the pace and trailed behind.

Natasha sat on the front steps of the house. An older

woman sat beside her, puffing a cigarette and awkwardly patting her shoulder. Nat glanced up at him, and the sight of her tears stopped Brady cold.

In all the years he'd known her, he could count on one hand the times he'd seen her cry, and every one of those times had been somehow related to that damned Bobby McBee.

Her beautiful green eyes widened in surprise. "Brady," she squeaked.

He heard the sheriff lumbering up behind him, and her gaze shifted. Her eyes grew hard when she looked over Brady's shoulder. "I told you this would happen. I told you the stalker was going to kill one of us."

Brady glanced at the sheriff, then back at Nat. "What stalker?"

She pushed a lock of dark hair behind her ear. "Some psycho has been calling for the past two weeks. First, he only threatened me, but then he started threatening Bobby too."

Brady shifted. Too thin. She looked too thin, and tired. He noted the Quik Mart logo on her shirt, and it saddened him that someone as smart and vibrant as Nat had ended up working at a gas station.

"What, some guy has a crush on you or something?" Brady could write a book on being obsessed with Natasha Hawthorne.

She blinked and stared up at the streetlight. Then she laughed, a sad, hopeless sound that tore at his heart.

"The accident. He said it wasn't fair that we survived."

Brady lifted his eyebrows. "Wh—the car accident? That was four years ago. Why would anyone be coming after you now?"

Nat shrugged. She looked so miserable and small sitting there, so defenseless, that his first impulse was to take her in his arms.

"I—uh, I'm not sure, unless it has something to do with the trial date. The civil case is coming up this month. That's all I can figure. He's been calling, and he vandalized the house last week. If that's not it, I simply don't know."

"Is this person threatening Reed too?"

She bit her lip and stared at her fingernails. "I don't know," she said finally. "Reed doesn't talk to me anymore."

The sheriff grunted. Brady glanced over his shoulder at him and was startled by the hard look on his face.

The memory of Nat's trial forced its way to the front of Brady's mind. The sheriff had testified against Nat and asked for justice for his niece and the other slain teenagers.

Brady rubbed a hand down his face. How had he forgotten that the sheriff was Melanie Cox's uncle? But in a town the size of Coalmont, he'd probably be hard pressed to find anyone who wasn't somehow connected to one of the six teenagers involved in the accident.

Sheriff Richards had dragged his sister down the courthouse steps that day while she'd screamed curses and protested Nat's two year sentence to the juvenile center. Would Richards even try to help Nat if she was being stalked?

The sheriff stepped up and crossed his arms over his chest. "It was probably a drug deal. McBee was no angel."

Brady expected Nat to argue, to defend Bobby as she always had, but she simply lowered her head. Where was the proud girl he'd known?

"What happened this evening?" he asked.

"I got off work around six, then I stopped by the grocery store to pick up a few things."

"Which store?"

"The one on the corner. I don't drive anymore."

"Can anyone verify you were there?" the sheriff asked.

"I paid by check. I guess they can."

"I saw the receipt in the bag. It would have the time on it," Brady said.

Nat shot him a questioning look. "Yes, I'm sure it does. Anyway, I walked home. I yelled for Bobby to let me in because my hands were full. He never came, but I thought I saw him walk by the window, so I yelled again. Finally, I set the milk down and opened the door myself. Bobby was sitting in the recliner. A man in a black shirt and black ski mask stood behind him." She took a great, gulping breath. "He had a gun, pointed at Bobby's head."

The sheriff waved his hand impatiently. "What

happened then?"

"I dropped the bag. Bobby yelled for me to run, and I took off. Oh, God. I left him there. I heard the gun go off, and I knew he was d-dead." Her teeth chattered, though the temperature had to be in the mid-seventies. Once again, Brady fought the urge to go to her.

She lifted a hand to her face, then lowered it again.

Brady caught a glimpse of her raw palms. "Nat, you're bleeding. What happened?"

She stared at her hands. "I tripped when the gun went off and fell down the steps. I scraped my hands on the sidewalk."

"Come with me," Brady said. "Let me clean those up."

"No." The sheriff looked at Brady with gleaming dark eyes. "First you have to test her for GSR."

"What?" Brady demanded. "What on earth for?"

Nat stood shakily. "GSR?"

"He wants me to swab your hands for gunpowder residue."

She gave the sheriff an incredulous look. "Are you serious? You think *I* killed Bobby?"

"About eleven percent of murder victims are killed by an intimate partner. I'm only covering the bases," the sheriff replied.

Fire flashed in her eyes. "Swab all you want. I have nothing to hide. If anybody has reason to feel guilty about Bobby's death, it's you. You didn't even come inside the house when we told you it had been vandalized."

The sheriff dismissed her comment with a wave of his hand. "We'll have to go to the station to do it. Get in the back of my car."

Brady opened his mouth to tell Nat that she didn't have to do anything without a warrant, but then he shut it again. As chief of police, his first obligation was to Bobby, not Nat. Still, he didn't like the way Richards looked at her.

The sheriff took a step toward her, and Brady shook his head. "She's going with me."

Nat shot him a grateful look, and Brady had to turn his head. He was through playing her hero.

"Whatever," the sheriff said, and stomped back to the crime scene.

"Thank you," Nat said quietly. "I despise that man."

Brady pulled the keys from his pocket, and they walked in silence back to the Explorer. It hurt him, to be this close to her and feel so far apart inside. They walked shoulder-to-shoulder, but he couldn't see her for all the past that hung between them.

When they approached the driveway, Nat glanced at the house. Her eyes misted with tears and Brady's stomach clenched with jealousy. Even in death, Bobby had more of her than he ever would. He opened the passenger door and helped her inside.

"I'll be right back," he said, and closed the door.

Brady was really here.

Nat could hardly believe it. So many times she'd wished she could see him, talk to him, but she'd given up that right when she'd gotten out of Cedar Ridge and went back to Bobby. Would Brady ever understand why she'd done it? Did he even care anymore?

For a moment, she watched him talk to a man with TBI emblazoned on the back of his shirt. Then she closed her eyes and leaned against the headrest.

She kept seeing the look of terror on Bobby's face. Even though he'd crushed any illusion of love they'd had a long time ago, he would always be a part of her. He was dead, murdered because of an accident she'd caused. In the end, she had failed him too.

His killer had taunted her on the phone, had told her he planned to kill the survivors, and she'd been tempted to ask him who they were. Bobby, with his cane and his addiction to painkillers, or maybe Reed Donally, who stared at his football trophies from his wheelchair and wished he'd died in the crash? Maybe he'd meant her, and what a joke that was. Her life had ended that night too. Maybe not as suddenly as Jen, Melanie, and Tony's, but in torturously slow degrees.

She heard Brady's door open, but she didn't move.

"Nat?" he said, and she opened her eyes. His hand, which hovered near her face, jerked away.

"I'm okay."

He gave her a long, searching look, then nodded.

When he started the engine, she said, "Wow, you deputies are riding nice these days."

She caught the barest hint of a smile before the interior light flicked off. "Got a promotion. Chief of police."

"Congratulations. I hadn't heard."

"Thanks."

His replies were terse, stilted, and suddenly she simply needed him to talk to her, to say anything. "When?" she asked.

"Tonight."

Tonight. Just when she'd needed him. Maybe someone up there was looking out for her, after all.

Brady surprised her when he swung into the parking lot of the Quik Mart where she worked. He put the Explorer in park and jumped out to extract a black leather bag from the back seat. Climbing back inside, he laid it across his lap and turned to her. "Let me see your hands."

"But the sheriff said—"

Brady grimaced. "Yeah, I know. That's why . . ." He squinted at her in the light. "Dammit, Nat, I'm sorry. I feel like a heel for doing this, but I know how Richards is. We'd better do everything by the book."

"Okay," she said meekly, though she wasn't sure what she was agreeing to.

His long, strong fingers grasped hers and turned up her raw palms. The light glinted off his blond hair and the faint growth of his goatee. Angel hair, she'd called it when they were kids. Shamelessly, her gaze caressed the strong line of his jaw where her hands could not. The boy she'd left behind had grown into a man. Her Brady was gone, and this stranger had taken his place.

A sob rose in her throat as he inspected her wounds, and he gave her a sharp look. "I didn't mean to hurt you," he said.

She almost said something stupid, like "I didn't mean to hurt you either," but she managed to keep her mouth shut.

As if he sensed her thoughts, Brady stared into her eyes.

His eyes. Even though she'd looked into them a million times, they still jolted her. Sapphire ringed the pale blue that swirled around his irises. When he looked at her with those odd, beautiful eyes, she felt like he was staring into her soul.

For a moment, neither of them moved. Nat hardly dared to breathe. It was the first time she'd been this close to him in nearly four years, and she didn't want it to end.

Brady's gaze dropped to her lips, and he leaned toward her. She closed her eyes when she caught the spicy scent of his aftershave and somehow broke the spell. Brady pulled away from her and opened the bag.

He extracted a couple of brown paper bags and a roll of masking tape. Quickly, he snapped one of them open and stuck her hand inside. Nat watched miserably while he taped the end tight around her wrist and followed suit with the other hand. He tossed the leather bag in the back seat and started the Explorer.

"We'll get some ointment and bandages on it after we do the test," he promised.

Nat turned to look out the window, unable to respond. They rode to the county jail in silence. Brady parked by the front and hurried to open her door. His warm hand closed around her elbow as he helped her out, then his hand slid to her lower back while he guided her toward the door. She felt the warmth of his body through her shirt and had to resist the silly, weak urge to lean into him.

When she walked into the station, the brilliance of the fluorescent lights blinded her, and she staggered backward into Brady. His hand closed briefly around her waist when she collided with his hard chest. People stared. She felt stupid and somehow guilty with the paper bags taped over her hands.

"Hey, Tom," Brady said, and the man behind the dispatch desk nodded. "We're going to borrow the sheriff's office for a minute, okay?"

"Sure, Brady. Help yourself."

Brady led her to a small office and motioned to a leather chair in front of the cluttered desk. "Have a seat. I'll be right back."

He returned with a blue box and moved a teetering stack of files to clear a spot on the desk. Opening the box, he laid out what looked like six tubes of Crazy Glue.

Brady glanced at her, then rolled his eyes. "Hang on. Just to be on the safe side . . ." He opened the door and yelled, "Can someone come in here a sec?"

A thin redheaded man ambled through the door. "What do you need?"

"A witness."

While the redhead watched, Brady clasped Nat's right wrist and gently removed the tape. Holding her hand in one of his, he dipped a Q-tip in a vial of clear liquid. This time she felt no sense of warmth at his touch, only his clinical detachment when he ran the Q-tip along the inside edge of her thumb. He swabbed her right hand and dropped the Q-tip inside a thin container. Nat watched him label it with her name and the letter R, then he repeated the procedure with her left hand.

Brady snapped the vials in a plastic case and threw the rest of the kit away. Nat waited with the redhead when Brady again left the room and came back with a first aid kit. By the time he'd finished cleaning and bandaging her palms, the sheriff had arrived. He looked somewhat irritated to find them in his office.

Brady grabbed her wrist and tugged her toward the door.

"Where are you going?" Richards asked.

"I'm taking this GSR kit to the lab."

The sheriff nodded at the redhead. "I can have Stevens here do it."

"Don't want to break the chain of custody." Brady glanced at the man who walked in behind the sheriff, the one in the TBI shirt. "Kirby, I'll have my report ready by morning if you want to drop by and get it."

"Sure thing." Kirby shot a puzzled look at the box in Brady's hand. "Why did you do a GSR test?"

Brady rolled his eyes. "Sheriff's orders."

The ride to the hospital seemed endless, but Nat was glad Brady had taken her with him. After they dropped off the container, she and Brady sat in the Explorer and he asked her a series of questions, this time into a tape recorder. Finally, he clicked it off and jammed it into his pocket. "You can't go back to the rental house. Do you want me to take you to your parents?"

Nat dropped her head. "I-I'm not sure I'm welcome there anymore."

Brady's voice was gentle when he said, "Nat, I know your mom and dad. They wouldn't turn you away."

Tears welled in her eyes and she dabbed them with the hem of her work shirt. "You, uh, don't understand. Things got really bad between Bobby and Daddy after I got out of Cedar Ridge. I haven't been home in awhile."

Brady stiffened. If she'd had any doubt of how irreparably she'd screwed up her life, the hardness in Brady's eyes confirmed it. But then the look vanished as quickly as it had appeared.

"Would you like me to call them?" he asked.

The lump in her throat nearly choked her. As badly

as she'd hurt him, he still protected her. "Would you?" she managed.

Brady pulled out his cell phone and dialed the number. "Hi, Jake. This is Brady. Yeah, thanks. I—" He laughed. "They did? I forgot to tell Dad about the meeting. Look, Jake, I'm calling on business." He glanced at Nat. "Bobby McBee was killed tonight. No, not an accident. Someone shot him. Yes, she's okay. She's right here with me. We're just leaving the hospital. No, I swear to you, she's fine. Do you want me to—okay. Will do. Okay. Goodbye."

"What?" Nat asked when he hung up, unable to make sense of his fractured conversation.

He smiled and squeezed her arm. "He wants you to come home."

Brady pulled out of the parking lot and headed toward their old neighborhood. Nat sat up straight when he pulled onto their block a few minutes later.

He parked at the curb, and they walked to the porch together. Her parents met them at the door. Nat hesitated, not sure what to expect, but her father seized her in a fierce hug.

"Honey, are you okay?" he whispered into her hair, and Nat nodded. He released her, and her mother took his place.

"Baby, I'm so glad you're home," Selena Hawthorne said.

"I am too, Mama."

Her father wiped a hand down his face. His appearance shocked her. He'd aged so much in the past two years.

He caught her stare and smiled. "Come in, come in. I'm sorry. I wasn't thinking."

Brady took a step backward. "No, I . . . I'd better get going." He jerked his thumb at the house next door, where he'd grown up. "Better stop by and see the folks for a minute." He glanced at Nat. "I'll be in touch when we find out anything."

A sense of *déjà vu* struck Nat when she remembered the last time they'd all stood on the porch like this. Bobby had rejected her, but Brady had come to her rescue yet again. With tears streaking her face, she'd clutched Brady's hand while he claimed responsibility for a child that wasn't his.

Her father had knocked him down the front steps.

She wondered if they were all remembering, because they simply stood there for a moment in awkward silence.

"Are you sure you don't want to come in, Brady?" Selena Hawthorne asked, wrapping an arm around Nat's waist. "I've made a fresh pot of coffee."

"Maybe next time." He offered a pained smile. "I'd better go."

"Bye, Brady."

They watched him jog across the yard to his parents' house.

Nat let her parents usher her inside, where her brothers waited. Matt stood to greet her, while his twin Justin watched from the sofa. Her chest tightened when she saw how big they were. They were sixteen now, and they were strangers too.

She opened her arms, and hesitantly, Matt hugged her. She laughed and ruffled his hair. "Oh my goodness! You're taller than me now."

"You've been gone a long time," Justin said.

Her smile faded when she glanced at him. He crossed his arms over his chest and lifted his chin defiantly.

Nat pushed a lock of hair behind her ear. "I—I know."

Her father broke the uncomfortable silence that followed by taking her arm and steering her to the couch. "Well, she's home now," he said with determined cheerfulness. "That's all that matters."

She sat, and her parents flanked her.

"What's going on, Nat?" her father asked. "Do you know who killed Bobby, or why?"

"Yeah," Justin said. "What kind of trouble was he in this time?"

Nat stared at her bandaged hands. "I don't think it was something he did. I think he died because of me."

"What?" her parents asked in unison.

"It started a couple of weeks ago. A man called me at work. He talked about the wreck, said that the wrong ones had lived. He said he was going to kill the survivors. I thought it was a prank or something, because he disguised his voice, so I hung up on him. That night, he called me at home." She looked at her father. "We have an unlisted number."

"He kept calling, nearly every day and night after that. Sometimes he threatened me, sometimes Bobby. A couple of times, I thought someone was following me while I walked home from work."

"Did you call the police?" her mother asked, and Nat gave a humorless laugh.

"One day, Bobby had to go to the hospital for some tests. I went with him. When we came home that night, we found the place ransacked. Someone had spray painted the date of the accident on the kitchen cabinets. I called the sheriff. He came by, said it was probably kids and that there was nothing he could do. He wouldn't even come in to look around."

Anger darkened her father's eyes. "Why didn't you call me?"

Nat blinked, remembering that last shouting match. How she'd had to push between her father and Bobby, and how her father had begged her not to go up until the moment she'd climbed in Bobby's car.

"I knew how you felt about Bobby," she said quietly.

He put his hand on top of hers. "But that didn't change the way I feel about you."

Nat threw her arms around him and squeezed him tight. "I'm sorry, Daddy. I never wanted to hurt you, but I didn't know what else to do." She gave him another squeeze and released him. "I still don't know what to do. In fact, I probably shouldn't be here now. Maybe I should go."

"No, Nat," her mother pleaded.

"You belong with us," her father said.

"Oh, here we go," Justin said, pushing himself to his feet. "Time for the Nat the Martyr routine. If you'll excuse me, I've seen this one before."

"Justin!" their mother said.

Hurt, Nat stood to face him. "I don't want to put you all in danger."

Justin waved off her comment on his way out the door. "Hey, you just do what you want to do, at the expense of everybody else in this damn family."

A moment later, the screen door banged shut.

"I'll go talk to him," Matt said.

"No!" Nat held up her hands. "I'll do it."

She found him in the back yard. He had a five gallon bucket full of baseballs and he pitched them one by one at a target painted on the side of a storage shed.

"You still here?" he asked. "I thought you were cutting out on us again."

"Justin, you don't understand. I'd never forgive myself if any of you were hurt because of me."

"That's a joke." He dropped the ball he was holding and faced her. "If you leave here now, don't you know it will kill them?"

Nat glanced back at the house. Her parents stood in the doorway, watching them.

"You don't understand. This guy came into my house. He murdered Bobby almost in front of my eyes. I don't want to bring him here."

"No, you don't understand. You should've seen Mom and Dad's faces after Brady called. They were so happy that you were coming home. Dad didn't leave the window until he saw Brady pull up in the drive."

"I'm happy to see them too, but—"

Nat flinched when Justin picked up another ball and slammed it into the building.

"Dad had a heart attack the night you left," he said.

The news hit her like a physical blow. She took a stumbling step backward. "What?" she gasped. "Why didn't anyone tell me?"

"He wouldn't let us."

Nat's breath left her in a huff and she covered her face in her hands. "Oh, God," she whispered.

To her surprise, she felt Justin's arms close around her. She buried her face in his shoulder and hugged him back.

"Dad's right," he said softly. "You belong here, with us. Don't leave, Nat. Whatever this is, we'll get through it together."

"What if this guy comes after me?"

"Then he comes. You're safer here, with us. Don't try to deal with this on your own." He pulled back and took her face in his hands, making her look him in the eyes. "Stay."

"Okay."

Arm-in-arm, they walked back to the house. She saw the relief on her parents' faces when she announced she was staying.

"Are you hungry? Have you eaten?" her mother asked, heading to the kitchen before Nat could answer.

"No, Mom—" Nat caught her arm. "I'm not hungry. "I'm just . . . wiped out."

"Okay, baby. Your room is ready. I changed the linens after Brady called."

Nat kissed her father and hugged her brothers before following her mother upstairs to her old room.

Nothing had changed. Not one thing. Nat walked over and sat on her purple bedspread. Tears filled her eyes when she picked up the picture of her and Jen that sat on her nightstand. "I guess I've really made a mess of things, haven't I, Mom?" she said, and her mother hugged her.

"It's going to be all right, honey. Now that you're home, everything's going to be all right."

Nat nodded, but as she stared out the window at Brady's parents' house, one thought kept running through her head.

What have I done?

CHAPTER 2

AFTER A QUICK CALL TO IAN KIRBY, BRADY DROVE back to the crime scene. This whole stalker thing bothered him. Why now, after four years? The old saying about revenge being a dish best served cold sounded fine in theory, but it rarely applied in a case like this. Even with the civil suit coming up, it all felt wrong.

A professor had once taught him there were three basic motives for murder, and all other motives sprang from one of these. Love, money and revenge.

Who had wanted to kill Bobby McBee?

Most everyone who'd ever met him, Brady supposed.

He didn't know anyone who loved Bobby besides Nat, and he might've owed someone money, but from the looks of the rental house, he didn't have any.

Roscoe sat on the front porch, nursing a Dr. Pepper and fanning himself with a rolled up newspaper. He looked up when Brady crossed the yellow crime scene tape and walked across the yard. "Some night, huh, chief?"

"You can say that again." Brady rolled his head on

his shoulders, making his neck pop.

"Egad, don't do that," Roscoe complained with a shiver. "It sounds awful."

"Ah, you big baby." Brady smiled and snapped on a pair of latex gloves. "Kirby told me I could poke around in there, see what I can see."

Roscoe shrugged. "Ain't nothing to see. The place is a dump."

"I have a feeling that we're missing something."

Brady wandered inside. The glow from the single light bulb seemed to soak into the peeling beige walls, but at least someone had turned off the television. Brady walked past the recliner and stepped into a hallway. He opened the door straight across from him and found himself in a narrow bathroom. Inside the medicine cabinet, he found a neat row of pill bottles. All of them bore Bobby's name, prescribed by seven different doctors.

Brady frowned when he tried to remember what injuries Bobby had sustained in the wreck. To be honest, Bobby had been his least concern at the time. He knew Bobby had walked with a cane since then, but he didn't know if his injuries warranted this much medication.

Water struck the discolored sink basin with a disconcerting plop-plop-plop. Brady tried to shut off the faucet, but to his irritation, he only succeeded in making the water drip faster. A hairbrush lay on the sink, filled with strands of Nat's dark hair. Brady started to pick it up, then jerked his hand back.

What the matter with him?

Seeing her had shaken him, left him disoriented. Even now the thought of her tears made his stomach knot. But Nat had never loved him like he loved her. She'd made that abundantly clear when she'd left him for Bobby.

Brady wandered into the next room. For a moment, he thought the place had been trashed. Various articles of clothing were strewn across the floor and bed. Men's clothing. He saw nothing that belonged to Nat. A poster of a heavy metal band hung on the cracked wall. An empty pizza box and a Playboy magazine rested beside the bed.

The bed that Nat had shared with Bobby?

The thought infuriated him. Her parents would've given her anything—*he* would've given her anything—but she had chosen to live in squalor with Bobby.

Brady's irritation turned to puzzlement when he inspected the room. There was no trace of Nat here, except for an old photo of her and Bobby on the dresser.

Brady poked around in the closet, which was packed despite the piles of clothes on the floor. When he shoved aside a row of shirts, he heard the rustle of plastic. He flipped through the shirts, pressing his hand against the front of each until he found the one that made the sound. He undid the first few buttons of the blue shirt and saw the Quik Mart logo on the white bag. Brady removed the hanger, shirt and all, then extracted the bag hidden beneath it.

Inside, he found another assortment of pill bottles, but none of these had been prescribed to Bobby. He didn't recognize any of the patient names. All the bottles were full, and all bore the name of the same doctor. Martin Atkinson.

Why did that name sound familiar?

His cell phone chirped in his pocket, and he fished it out. "Simms."

"Hi, honey."

"Hey, Charity." Brady shuffled through the bottles again. Vicodin. Darvocet. Hydrocodone. Lortab . . . heavy stuff. Maybe the sheriff was right, and it had been a drug hit after all.

"Where are you? You're off duty, right? I thought we'd go out and celebrate."

He frowned and turned the bottle in his hand. "Celebrate what?"

Martin Atkinson. The name bugged him, pulled some memory in the back of his mind.

She laughed. "Celebrate what? Don't play dumb with me, big boy. I've already heard all about it."

Reed! That was it. Martin Atkinson was Reed Donally's stepfather.

Charity sighed into the phone. "I'm talking about your promotion, you goof."

"Huh? Oh, sorry." Brady shook his head. "I didn't mean to zone out on you like that. It's been a busy night."

"Too busy to pick me up? If it's a problem, I can catch a ride with one of the girls . . ."

Brady glanced at his watch. He'd forgotten about her car being in the repair shop. "I'm on my way."

He clicked the phone shut and hurried toward the door. He tossed the bag of pills to Roscoe. "I need to pick up Charity. I found these in McBee's closet. Could you—"

"Tag and bag 'em? No problem."

"Thanks, man."

Charity was waiting on the sidewalk when he pulled into the empty restaurant parking lot fifteen minutes later. Brady rolled down the window and cruised up to her. She laughed when he turned on his blue lights.

He stuck his head out the window and drawled, "Ma'am, you are under arrest."

"Oh, yeah?" She leaned in the window, and he curled a lock of her blond hair around his finger. "What's the charge, officer?"

"It's gotta be a crime to look so cute in that godawful uniform."

Charity peered down at her yellow and red manager's outfit and grinned. Then she grabbed a handful of his shirt and tugged him closer. "You're lucky you're so good-looking, because your pick-up lines suck."

"Umm," Brady said when she kissed him. "So, you forgive me for being late?"

She rolled her pretty brown eyes. "Hmmm . . . I'll

think about it."

Charity pulled back and ran a hand down the gleaming white fender. "Cool ride. Much better than that clunky old cruiser."

She hurried around the side of the Explorer. Brady leaned across the seat to open her door.

"Ooh, leather seats too," she purred as she scooted inside.

He kissed her again. A vision of Nat flashed behind his eyes, startling him. Nat in the silver gown she'd worn the night they'd slept together.

Brady's eyes flew open, and he kissed Charity a little more urgently. She was real, not Nat. Nat was a beautiful illusion, smoke and mirrors, and he couldn't fall for that trap again.

"Oh, Chief!" Charity giggled. "So, tell me all about it!" She bounced up and down in the seat. "I bet Sheriff Richards nearly died."

"He did." Brady gave her a play-by-play, complete with his voice impersonations of Mike and the sheriff. Charity laughed and clapped her hands in delight.

"What did Joe do?" she asked.

Brady grinned. "Poor old Joe didn't look like he wanted to be there anymore than I did. He followed the sheriff out like a puppy."

Charity scanned through the radio stations while Brady coasted to a standstill at the town's one stoplight. She settled on a classic rock station, and Brady grimaced when he heard Janis Joplin belting out "Me and Bobby McGee."

He hated that song.

Nat used to sing that when they were in high school, substituting McBee for McGee. He rolled down the volume. Charity made a face at him and cranked it up again. Irritated, Brady reached over and pressed the power button.

"Geez, okay! You're acting awfully grumpy for a guy who just got a big promotion. What's wrong?"

Brady sighed and pulled away when the light turned green. He didn't want to take out his frustration on her. "I'm sorry, babe. It's only—did you hear about the murder at Miller Subdivision tonight?"

Charity's eyes widened. "Murder? No! You're kidding. Who was it?"

Brady squeezed the steering wheel. "Bobby McBee."

"Bobby? Oh, wow." She cleared her throat. "So . . . I guess you saw her."

Her voice sounded funny, tight, and Brady glanced at her. She stared down at her lap. He didn't bother to ask who she meant. "Yeah, I saw her."

"How did she look? What did she . . . say?"

The last word came out strangled. Brady glanced at her and was stunned to see she was blinking back tears. He hit his turn signal and pulled to the side of the road. "Hey," he said. "What's this? What's the matter?"

When he flipped on the interior light, Charity

flushed and ducked her head. "I just—I know how you felt about her."

Brady's jaw dropped. "Charity, you don't have to worry about me and Nat."

"Geez, Brady." She swiped at the tear streaking down her cheek. "How can I *not* worry about you and Nat? If it hadn't been for that accident, she wouldn't have lost that baby. You'd be married to her right now, raising Bobby's kid."

Brady shook his head. "She would've never married me. She and Bobby would've worked it out."

"But *you* would've married her. You've always loved her. I can't compete with the history you two have."

"You don't have to compete with it."

She still didn't look convinced, so Brady sighed and took her hands. "Look," he said gently. "We haven't been dating that long, and I'm not sure where we're going, but I can tell you this, I'm not going to leave you for Nat. That part of my life is over."

Charity sniffed. "She's probably going to want you back, now that Bobby's gone."

Irritably, he said, "That doesn't mean I want her back. I'm not some little lap dog who comes running every time Nat snaps her fingers."

He'd never raised his voice to her before, and the surprise on her face shamed him. He squeezed her fingers and tried again. "Have a little faith in me. I'm not a kid anymore. I'm a man." He winked. "Plus, I'm a nice guy."

She gave him a tiny smile.

"I'm probably going to run into Nat again while I work this case, so I don't want you to freak out every time I mention her name, okay? Besides, Nat has more to worry about than me right now."

"What do you mean?"

Brady released her hands and rubbed the back of his neck. The accident wasn't something they talked about, because they stood on separate sides of the issue. Charity's older brother, Tony, had died in the crash. Charity's family considered Nat a killer, but Brady couldn't see it like that. Not without the involvement of drugs or alcohol. It had been an accident. A horrible, tragic accident.

Both Charity and Melanie's families had protested Nat's sentence of two years at the juvenile center as being too light. Brady still thought it too harsh. They resented the fact that Nat was alive and couldn't see that she was scarred too.

Hesitantly, Brady told Charity about the stalker.

"Oh, that's awful! Even poor Reed?"

"I don't know. I'm going to talk to him tomorrow. What I can't figure out is why now, after all this time?"

Charity shrugged. "Did you know the civil trial is coming up this month? Mom met with the lawyer yesterday. She spent the rest of the evening in Tony's room, crying."

Brady pulled her into his arms and kissed the top of

her head. He felt a little guilty for the stable home he'd grown up in. Charity's mother had nearly gone crazy after Tony's death. Her father had been in prison for the past two years for nearly beating a man to death in a barroom fight.

Charity wrapped her arms around him and squeezed.

"So, we're good?" he said.

She pulled back and smiled. "We're good."

He started the Explorer and pulled back onto the road. In a few minutes, he parked in front of Charity's apartment building.

"You want to come up?" she asked.

"I've got to go back to the station, work up the report to give the state guy. Can I get a rain check?"

"Okay." She leaned over to finger the nameplate on his uniform. "Are we still on for tomorrow night?"

Brady's mind went blank.

"Remember? Howard and Kristi are coming over for dinner . . . " Charity prodded.

"Oh, yeah." With some effort, Brady smiled. He liked Charity's best friend, but Kristi's boyfriend was a different story. "Do you need me to pick up anything?"

"Maybe a bottle of wine?"

"It's a date."

Brady stayed in the parking lot until she got her door unlocked. She gave him a little wave and slipped inside. His mind returned to the case as soon as he put the Explorer in reverse. He had to find out if some stalker had killed Bobby.

He had to know if Nat was in danger.

NAT SLIPPED INTO BRADY'S DARKENED BEDROOM. Though she knew the house was empty, she made no sound while she quickly undressed. She slid the silver gown over her head, then folded her jeans and blouse into a neat pile and laid them on his dresser.

Taking a seat by the window, she waited.

The bright glare of his headlights flashed through the window when he turned in the drive, and she jumped up to turn on the CD player.

The soft strains of Etta James singing "At Last" filled the room, just like the first time. Her heart pounded while she waited on him to climb the stairs.

He threw open the door. His long, lean silhouette filled the doorway, but he said nothing. He flipped on the light.

Nat screamed when she saw the black ski mask and realized it wasn't Brady at all. He took a step toward her. Light glinted off the revolver in his hand.

"What are you doing here?" he asked.

"I was waiting . . . on Brady," she gasped, and backed toward the bed.

The stalker laughed. "He's already here."

He pointed to the bed with his gun, and Nat

reflexively looked over her shoulder. Brady sat propped against the pillows, covered in blood.

Half his head was missing.

Nat woke up wheezing, gasping for air. Her lungs felt like two large stones in her chest. Consciousness came to back to her in degrees, as did her breath.

"A dream," she whispered, and squeezed her eyes shut. "Oh, Brady."

Terror still twisted her stomach. Her hands ached from gripping the sheets, but she couldn't let go. For a moment, she had no idea where she was, then she remembered.

Home. She was home.

She untangled herself from her sweaty sheets and swung her legs over the side of the bed. Nat reached for the lamp, but decided to pull the blinds instead. Streaks of rosy pink and yellow painted the eastern sky outside her window. She stared over the hedge at Brady's old bedroom window.

The big oak tree was still there. While they were growing up, she'd come and gone through his window as much as she had his front door. So many times he'd been there for her, and never asked anything in return. Steady as the sun.

So many years she'd wasted because she'd been too blind to see that Brady was in love with her. She'd been stupid back then, looking for adventure, looking for a spark.

Looking for that golden Prince Charming.

She'd been dazzled by the flash of Bobby McBee and thought he was the one, but he was fool's gold. Prince Charming had been under her nose the whole time. Brady was pure. The love he'd felt for her was pure, and now she'd lost it forever.

Nat walked to her closet, wondering if some of her clothes were still inside. When she'd gone with Bobby, she'd taken only what she could cram in a duffel bag. She wouldn't have blamed her parents if they'd thrown the rest of her things away.

But they hadn't. Rows of clothing hung inside. Nat retrieved a pair of jeans and thumbed through the shirts. Her hand faltered when it brushed against a white baseball jersey with red pinstripes that belonged to Brady. Number two, his lucky number. How had it gotten in here?

She pulled it off the rack and pressed it to her face, but it no longer held his scent. She stared at it for a moment, then threw it across her shoulder on top of her jeans. After rummaging through her dresser to retrieve some underwear, she padded down the hallway to the shower.

The hot spray washed away some of the residue of her dream. Nat felt much better after she toweled her hair dry and dressed. Careful not to wake anyone, she slipped downstairs to make breakfast for her family.

It cheered her to simply set foot in her mother's clean, bright kitchen. Nat hummed to herself as she retrieved a skillet from the cabinet. Soon, the room filled with the warm, familiar scents of scrambled eggs, sausage and gravy. Nat removed a row of crisp, brown toast from the oven and placed it on a plate. After carrying it to the table, she poured herself a cup of coffee and wandered into the living room.

Maybe some new information about the investigation would be on the morning newscast. She searched the room for the remote and, not finding it, walked over to the entertainment center.

The neat rows of home movies in the cabinet caught her eye. Her mother was a camcorder fanatic. Nat scanned the titles and smiled when her gaze lit on one labeled "Nat and Brady Birthday Parties Ages 1-7" in her mother's graceful handwriting. Their birthdays were only a day apart and their parents had always thrown their parties together.

She removed it from the row, turned the television on, and pushed the tape into the VCR. The tape hadn't been rewound. A five-year-old version of herself chattered to the camera, then spun to show off her satin Wonder Woman outfit. Nat sat cross-legged on the flowery sofa and tried to remember what they'd called her gold rope. The golden lasso of truth, or something like that. She watched her onscreen self trying to tie up her daddy with it.

Nat took a sip of coffee and nearly spit it out when a pint-sized Brady slid into the frame, his Superman cape fluttering behind him. She giggled, then laughed outright when she and Brady and a kid in a Batman costume chased the dog around the yard.

"Now that's a sound I've missed," her father said from the doorway, and Nat twisted to smile at him.

"What, the sound of Patches yelping?"

Jake laughed. "Well, that too. He was a good old dog. You and Brady put him through a lot." He walked to the sofa and Nat scooted over to make room for him. "What I meant was the sound of your laughter."

Nat laid her head on her father's shoulder. "To be honest, I can't remember the last time I've laughed, either. It makes me feel guilty, to laugh when Jen can't laugh anymore, or Tony or Mel."

Her father wrapped his arm around her. "Honey, you can't think like that. It was an accident. You can't keep punishing yourself. You nearly died in that wreck too."

Maybe she should have. Maybe that was why she felt hollow inside, except for that dull, relentless throbbing she could never seem to ease. But she couldn't very well tell her daddy that, so she changed the subject. "I made breakfast."

"Smells good. Did you eat?"

"Not hungry."

"You should eat."

"I will," she promised. "In a little while. Right now

I want to watch this."

The tape ended about half an hour later, about the time her father left for work and her mother took the boys to school. Nat rewound it and got up to replace it in the cabinet. She looked over the other titles and frowned when she noticed one labeled "Nat's graduation". She'd never seen that one, never known it existed, although she should've known her mother would've taped that.

She punched the tape in the VCR, and tears filled her eyes when Jen appeared, beautiful and sparkling in her gold honors robe. She hovered just outside Nat's bedroom door, but turned to face the cameraman.

"Hiiiii, Justin." She gave him a coy smile and crooked her finger for him to come closer.

She slowly unzipped the robe while the cameraman advanced and presented him with her back. Pursing her lips over her shoulder like a Hollywood siren, she dropped the robe a few inches to reveal a bare shoulder. Then she spun around and jerked the gown open like she was flashing him. They both laughed when she revealed the pink dress underneath.

"You tease," Nat's brother complained in his squeaky, pre-teen voice. "I knew it was too good to be true. Where's Nat?"

Jen smiled and pressed a finger to her lips. "Shhh," she whispered, and eased open the door. The camera zoomed in on Nat and Brady, lying on top of her purple bedspread, kissing.

The morning after they'd made love.

Nat swallowed hard over the lump in her throat. The Nat on the screen wore the same shirt she had on now.

"What do you think Nat should pay me, so I don't give this tape to Dad?" Justin asked loudly, and the couple on the bed jumped. The screen did a shaky dance and then the camera showed the area under Nat's bed as apparently she and Brady attacked. She heard Justin beg them to stop tickling.

The doorbell rang and Nat glanced toward the front door with irritation.

Where was that stupid remote? She wanted to see all of this.

The doorbell chimed again, longer this time, and she scrambled to answer it. She leaned to peer through the peephole and saw Brady standing on the welcome mat. Hurriedly, she combed her fingers through her hair and opened the door.

His blue eyes widened when he looked at the shirt. Then he glanced away.

"Good morning," she said.

"I need to ask a few more questions," he said briskly, as if wanting her to understand he was here on business and business only.

"Sure. Come in." She swung the door wide and moved back to let him enter, but as Brady walked to the living room, Nat remembered that she'd left the tape playing. She nearly shoved him in her haste to get inside first, but it was too late.

Brady froze in the doorway, his eyes riveted on the television. The Brady on the tape had abandoned his torture of her little brother in favor of tickling Nat.

Nat stood rooted to the floor while she watched the couple on the screen kiss. "Brady, I . . ." she began, and turned to face him.

Brady didn't say a word. He didn't have to.

His fury was evident in his posture, in the hardness of his face. The fierce look in his eyes caught her off-guard. For an instant, he looked wild. Desperate. But then the expression was gone, replaced by a cool mask. Nat moved toward the VCR, and he caught her wrist.

"Leave it," he said. "This won't take long."

Flustered, she nodded and sat on the sofa. He sat on the other side of the room, as far away as he could get from her.

"I found some pills—"

"Oh, Bobby's pain medication? He had a lot of stuff. I can call the pharmacy and get a printout of his regular meds if you need it."

"What about the pills in his closet?"

"What pills?" Nat asked, but before Brady even said it, she knew. Bobby had been coming up with extra money lately. It didn't take a genius to figure out where he'd gotten it.

"I found a bag of pill bottles in the closet. None of them were prescribed to Bobby, and they all came from

Dr. Martin Atkinson. Do you know him? Is he someone Bobby went to regularly?"

Nat shook her head. "The name sounds familiar . . . but no, he wasn't one of Bobby's doctors." She ticked them off on her fingers. "There was Dr. Garvey, Dr. Bean—"

The doorbell rang again.

"I'm sorry. Let me get that."

Brady nodded, and Nat hurried to answer the door. It was Bobby's sister, Dara.

Nat threw open the door, ready to tell her this wasn't a good time, but Dara burst into tears before she could say a word.

"Nat!" she cried, and flung herself into Nat's arms.

Nat had always liked Dara, had been around her most of her life. Holding the shaking teenager, she decided Brady would just have to wait a minute.

"Come in, honey," she said.

Dara stumbled past her, dabbing at her eyes with a wad of tissue. When they entered the living room, Nat noticed Brady watching the screen. He jerked his head around when he heard them coming.

"Brady, this is—"

"Bobby's sister," he supplied. "I don't remember your name, but I'm sorry for your loss."

Always a gentleman, Nat thought, while he stood to shake Dara's hand.

"I have to tell you something," Dara blurted. "It's about Bobby, something he told me last week . . ." She cut her gaze to Brady.

"Brady is a friend," Nat told her, though she wasn't sure it was true anymore. "He's trying to find out who killed Bobby, so if you know anything that might help him with the case—"

"This doesn't have anything to do with the stalker, other than the fact that Bobby was so worried about him. I think that's why he told me." She took a gulping breath. "It's about you."

Nat started to tell her to wait, to let her tell Brady she'd answer his questions at another time, but it was too late. Dara started talking fast.

"I love you, Nat. You've always been good to me, and I know you were good to Bobby, even though he wasn't good to you. I know he yelled at you and stuff, and I know he hit you—"

Nat sensed Brady's head snap around, but she refused to meet his stare. Heat flooded her face.

"Dara—"

"I wanted to tell you last week, but Bobby threatened me. And he was messed up a little, so I don't know if what he was saying was true, but if it is, you need to know—"

"Honey—"

"It's about the accident. Like I said, he was a little doped up, but I think he was telling the truth—"

"Dara, what is it?" Nat asked, a little abruptly.

"He said you weren't driving that night."

CHAPTER 3

NAT GAPED AT DARA, UNABLE TO MAKE ANY SENSE of what she'd just said. "He said . . . what? I don't . . . I don't understand . . ."

Her legs went rubbery, and Nat stumbled. Brady lunged at her and caught her around the waist. Her face pressed against his chest while he guided her backward and gently pushed her into the nearest chair.

Nat watched in stunned silence as he led Dara to the sofa and sat beside her. He took the teenager's hand and said, "Hon, you need to be very clear about what you're saying. What exactly did Bobby tell you? Start at the beginning of the conversation."

Dara shot her a searching look, but Nat couldn't move the slack muscles in her face. Brady tipped the girl's chin with his fingers, making her look at him. "What did Bobby say?"

"He said, 'Someone's going to kill us because of that stupid accident, and the crazy thing about it is that the one who caused it all is dead.' I asked him what he meant, and he gave me this weird smile. He told me he didn't know how Nat got belted behind the wheel, because when they left that party, Tony Franklin was driving, and Nat was in the passenger seat with Jen."

Could it possibly be true? But how could Bobby have let her suffer like that? Why?

A strangled sob rose in Nat's throat, a mixture of grief and anger. She felt Brady's worried gaze, but her eyes were glued on Dara. Bobby's sister cried harder.

"I wanted to tell you what he said, but Bobby told me I'd better not if I knew what was good for me. He said soon he'd get money from the insurance company and he'd buy you a nice place to live. He'd take care of you, and it would be all right."

Nat shut her eyes.

For money, Bobby had let her live in anguish. For money, he'd thrown her to the dogs. That, and the fact that he knew she'd never stay if she broke free from the heavy chains of guilt she carried. All the misery he'd put her through. All the things she'd lost because of him . . .

"What else did he say?" Brady asked.

Nat opened her eyes.

"That's all, I swear." Dara wrung the tissue in her hands. "Nat, I'm so sorry. It's eaten at me all week. I wanted to tell you, but I was afraid."

"It's okay," she heard herself say. She held open her arms and the teenager scurried from the couch to hug her. "Thank you for telling me now," she whispered into Dara's hair.

Dara pulled away and swiped at her eyes. "I have to go. I'm supposed to go with Mom to tell Grandma about Bobby, but I couldn't wait any longer talk to you."

She let Brady walk Dara to the door. Nat rubbed a hand down her face and pushed herself to her feet. She stared at the television screen, where the gold and purple robed graduates were accepting their diplomas one-by-one.

Brady reappeared in the doorway. The pained look on his face made Nat's eyes burn with tears. He shoved a hand through his blond hair.

She jumped when he slammed his fist against the wall.

"I will regret not killing him myself for the rest of my life," he said.

"Do you think . . . is there any chance it could be true?" Nat cupped her hands over her face, then pointed at the television screen. "I don't remember that day. Any of it. The last thing I remember is . . ." She faltered, and looked away.

"What?" he asked quietly.

She forced herself to look at him. "Making love to you."

Brady sucked in his breath. Nat brushed a hand across her cheek and tried to smile, but her tears came faster. Harder.

"It's like I went to sleep in your arms . . . and woke up in hell."

Brady's heart lurched. The raw pain in her eyes seared him to the bone. For once, he shoved aside the warning voice in his head and strode across the room to take her in his arms.

Nat clung to him like a child. Her arms circled his waist, and she buried her face against his chest. Great, shuddering sobs wracked her body, and her tears burned him through the thin fabric of his shirt.

Brady held her just as tight, pressing his face in her damp, dark hair and stroking her back. "I don't know if it's true, but I promise you I'll find out."

Hatred for Bobby McBee boiled through his veins like poison. When Bobby and Nat first began dating, Brady heard rumors about the drugs, about the other girls. Nat heard them too, and he figured it was her business if she chose to ignore them, but if he'd had any inkling that Bobby hit her, he wouldn't have cared what Nat thought. He would've torn Bobby limb from limb.

The front door slammed, and Nat pulled away from him. "Mom," she whispered, and lifted the collar of her shirt to swipe at her red, swollen eyes.

As her mother's footsteps approached, Nat faced him, turning her back to the doorway. She didn't want her mother to see her crying, he realized.

"Hi, Brady," her mother said cheerfully.

He lifted his chin in greeting. "Hi, Mrs. Hawthorne."

"Is everything okay?"

"Yeah."

"I'll be with you two in a second. Let me get this ice cream put up."

"She's gone," he whispered, when Selena Hawthorne disappeared around the corner.

"I don't want to tell them any of this until we find out if it's true."

"Nat, they need to know. Your father needs to tell your lawyer."

She sighed. Her shining eyes appeared two shades brighter. "I guess you're right. I . . . just didn't want them to get their hopes up for no reason."

Brady clasped her hands in his. "Look, I'm going to see Reed this morning, to find out if anything's going on with him, and maybe ask his stepfather about the pills. Then I'm going to dig through the accident files. If anything's there, I'll find it."

"Thank you," she said, and brushed a feathery kiss on his cheek.

The sweet sensation of her lips on his skin made him ache. He inhaled the soft smell of strawberries that drifted from her hair . . .

Brady flushed. He had to get out of there before he did something stupid. He broke away and headed for the door.

"Bye, Mrs. Hawthorne!" he yelled, and bolted down the steps before she could answer.

He probably sprayed gravel when he roared away from the curb, but he couldn't help it. Brady drove half a mile down the road, then pulled over beside a tobacco field. For a moment, he simply laid his head on the steering wheel and tried to get his bearings.

He had to be the biggest idiot walking the planet.

After all this time, he didn't understand why the sight of Nat's tears provoked such savage protectiveness from him. How the feel of her body against his made him want to fall on his knees and beg her to love him.

She'd been his first kiss at age twelve, his first lover a few years later, but he'd always been second choice for her.

"It's not enough," he said aloud.

With a sigh, he started the Explorer and pulled back onto the highway. He picked up the CB mike. "Hey, Roscoe. I'm going to be out of pocket for a little while. If you need me, call my cell. Dispatch has the number."

"10-4 boss."

He didn't want to broadcast where he was going in case the sheriff was listening. Reed Donally lived in Monteagle. Although located only fifteen minutes from Coalmont, Monteagle was technically two towns away from Brady's jurisdiction.

He'd visited the Donally estate a time or two when he was in high school, but he'd forgotten how big it was. Brady cruised up the winding asphalt driveway to the stately brick home and parked beside a gray Mercedes. After retrieving a new notebook from the glove compartment, he hurried up the front steps.

The door flew open before he could lift his hand to

knock and Brady found himself nose-to-nose with a wild-eyed woman clutching a fireplace poker. He stumbled backward, thinking he was about to be attacked, but she glanced at his uniform and lowered her arm. "It's about time," she growled. "I called you forty minutes ago."

Brady made an effort to close his open mouth. "Ma'am?" He blinked. "Mrs. Donally?"

What happened to you? he almost asked.

The ex-beauty queen looked like she'd spent a season in hell. Sharp worry lines etched her face, and gray streaked her disheveled hair. Far from the sleek, sexy outfits she'd worn when he and Reed were in high school, she now sported a ratty pink jogging outfit.

"It's Mrs. Atkinson now." She narrowed her eyes. "Bradley, is that you?"

"Brady. Yes, ma'am. If it's not too much trouble, I'd like to speak to Reed."

"You're not from the county?"

"No, ma'am. I work for Coalmont. What happened?"

She blew out a breath and ran a hand over her hair. "I'm sorry I snapped at you, but now really isn't the best time."

Rachel Atkinson started to shut the door, and Brady reached out to keep her from slamming it in his face. "Please, Mrs. Atkinson. It's important."

She rubbed her forehead, then sighed. Finally, she held the door open and motioned him inside the spacious entryway. He followed her to the adjoining living room, but stopped in the doorway when he saw the spray of glass. A sheer white curtain billowed from the broken window. A red brick lay in the center of the mess, with a piece of paper attached to it by a rubber band.

Reed's mother leaned against the wall and hugged herself while she stared at it. "Something has to be done," she whispered. "I can't take this anymore."

Brady gingerly stepped over the broken glass and leaned to peer at the paper. He recoiled when he saw it was an obituary notice.

Reed's obituary notice. It was dated the day after tomorrow.

He glanced at Rachel Atkinson, and she began to cry.

"Reed didn't hurt anyone," she gasped while she dabbed at her eyes with her shirtsleeve. "He was a victim in this mess too."

Brady stood. "How long has this been going on, Mrs. Atkinson?"

"A couple of weeks, and that ignorant sheriff hasn't done a thing about it. Why would anyone do this to Reed? He's a—" She froze and looked over Brady's shoulder at the opposite entranceway.

Something squeaked behind him, and Brady turned to watch Reed wheel himself inside the room.

A bitter smile curved Reed's lips. "It's okay, Mama. You can say it. He's a cripple. Why does anyone want to hurt poor, crippled Reed?"

"No, Reed! That's not what—"

Ignoring her, he said, "What are you doing here, Brady? I assume it's business, since I no longer have any friends."

Brady felt a stab of guilt, even though he and Reed hadn't run in the same circles in high school. Reed had been the super jock . . . king of the prom . . . captain of the football team. The only time they'd ever spent together was the semester he'd tutored Reed in senior English, and maybe a time or two when he interviewed Reed for the school paper. Brady was surprised Reed even remembered his name.

Seeing Reed was almost as much of a shock as seeing his mother. It was hard to put his finger on the reason why, because Reed didn't look all that different physically, but . . .

Faded

Maybe that was the wrong word, but that was what popped into Brady's head. Reed looked faded, like an image on a television set with a bad picture tube. It wasn't simply the absence of his tan, although there was that too. The blue eyes that gazed at him were flat and uncaring. Even his hair seemed wrong. In school, its strange color had hovered between blond and brown, defying classification into either group. Now it seemed too dark, like the stubble dotting his pale face.

"See something green, man?" Reed asked, his eyes narrowing. "I asked what you were doing here."

Brady forced his gaze away and gestured at the brick.

"I came about this. To see if you were being threatened too."

Reed gave a resigned nod and seemed to relax. "Yeah, I figured Nat and Bobby had to be getting a piece of this action. So, they're getting phone calls too. Vandalism . . . right?"

Brady glanced at Rachel Atkinson, then back at Reed.

"What?" Reed demanded.

"Bobby McBee was murdered last night," Brady said.

A flicker of panic crossed Reed's face, but it was quickly replaced with a scowl when Rachel Atkinson began to wail.

"Mama," he said, then louder, "*Mama!*"

Her sobs died abruptly at the harsh bark of his voice. The room fell eerily quiet.

Reed gestured at the broken glass. "Do you know for a fact that his murder was connected to this?"

"No," Brady said.

Reed jerked his head impatiently. "See, Mama. It may not have anything to do with this at all. Bobby was always in trouble."

Brady caught the pleading look Reed shot him and said, "Yes, Mrs. Atkinson. It may be unrelated, but I have to follow every lead right now."

The faint sound of sirens drifted through the broken window and Reed rolled his eyes. "Have no fear, the sheriff is here. Come on, Brady." He wheeled his chair around. "We'll talk upstairs."

"But what if the sheriff needs to speak with you?" his mother asked.

"He doesn't want to hear what I have to say," Reed replied.

He disappeared through the doorway, and Brady followed. Reed waited at the elevator. When the door slid open, he rolled himself inside and held the button until Brady squeezed in beside him.

"So, Bobby's dead, huh?" Reed mused. "What happened?"

Brady told him about the gunman, and Reed shook his head. "You know it's probably dope, right? He was always messing with that crap."

"Probably," Brady agreed. "Like I told your mom, I'm only trying to cover the bases."

"You really think someone's that pissed we survived?"

Brady shook his head. "I don't know. It seems like a stretch to me. I mean, it's been four years now. I can see how someone might come after the driver, but why you and Bobby? I can't see someone trying to kill you simply because you lived."

Reed laughed, and a chill snaked down Brady's spine when he realized how much it sounded like Nat's laugh. Hollow. Empty.

The elevator door swung open and Reed wheeled himself into the hallway. "I survived—I'll give him that—but he can't accuse me of living, man. Living and surviving ain't the same thing."

Brady followed him down the hallway and into a room that was half the size of his entire apartment. Trophies and athletic pictures filled one whole wall. Brady flushed when Reed caught him staring at them.

Reed looked embarrassed too. "Glory days. I should probably throw that crap away, but it brings back good memories. I wasn't half-bad, you know?"

Brady pointed at a picture of Reed hoisting the high school championship trophy over his head. "You were incredible," he said. "That last drive, I thought they had you guys pinned on the two yard line, then I see you break out of the pack. Jim Perkins was supposed to be the fastest defensive player in the state, and you left him in the dust."

Reed laughed. It sounded so genuine, so happy, that it might've surprised them both. Reed gestured toward the small card table in the corner and Brady pulled up a chair.

"I don't know if I ever told you how much I appreciated the write-up you did in the paper. Mom kept three or four copies. You made me sound like Superman or something."

Brady grinned. "You were."

A sad smile flickered across Reed's face and he gestured at the chess board in the middle of the table. "Do you play?"

"A little. I'm not very good, though."

"I bet I can take you down in eight moves. You go

first."

Brady made his first move and glanced back at Reed. He was staring up at a prom picture of himself and the pretty blond cheerleader he'd dated senior year, Mandy Jarvis.

"For sure, I should throw that one away," Reed commented, then made his move. "She came to visit me a few times, but I could tell she didn't really want to be here. She wouldn't look at me. Kept staring at something over my shoulder and finally I asked her, 'What the hell are you *looking* at?'" Reed laughed softly. "She never came back."

Reed's pain . . . his loneliness . . . was tangible. Brady didn't know what to say, so he simply made his next move.

"Hey, maybe I should call Nat, now that Bobby's out of the way. Might even get some action. She's used to banging crippled losers, right?"

Brady jerked his gaze away, and Reed laughed.

"Oh, man!" he said, slapping his armrests. "Don't tell me you're still jonesing for her after all this time."

"No, I—"

Reed waved him off. "Don't bother to deny it. You should've seen your face just then. But it's cool. I don't blame you. Nat's hot. Maybe the only hot girl in our class who ever shot me down." He shrugged. "But if she'd turn down two guys like us for that scumbag McBee, forget her. Right?"

Reed's eyes widened. "Oh, wait just a minute! I remember something. She didn't always shoot you down, did she? I hit on her at the party that night, but she told me she was with you." He grinned. "I backed off after that. You were always nice to me, man. If it weren't for you, I'd have never passed that stupid English class."

Brady leaned forward. "What do you remember about the party?"

"Ah, not much, you know? I was pretty drunk. I remember Jen locking her keys up and calling Nat to bring her spare, and I remember Nat showing up in her new car. She let a few kids test drive it, and I sat with her and Jen while we waited on them to come back. I passed out while I was with them and don't remember another thing until I woke up in the hospital."

Brady moved his knight and wondered if he should tell Reed what Bobby's sister said.

Not yet, he thought.

"So, what happened?" Reed prodded. "With you and Nat?"

"I don't know. Bobby McBee happened, I guess." Brady changed the subject, asking Reed a few questions about the stalker. His story was much the same as Nat's.

"Check," Reed said absently, as soon as Brady made his next move. Brady made another move and Reed grinned. "Check-*mate*."

With a sigh, Brady conceded defeat. "You got me."

"You got that right. You want a beer or something?"

Brady glanced at his watch. "Nah, I'm on duty. And I really have to get going."

Childlike disappointment covered Reed's face, but he nodded. "Well, it was good seeing you."

"My number's in the book," Brady said when he stood. "Give me a call if anything else happens, okay?"

"Will do."

Brady walked toward the door, but stopped and turned around when Reed called his name. "Yeah?"

"Come back and see me sometime," Reed said, then began resetting the chess pieces.

Downstairs, Brady saw no sign of Rachel Atkinson or the sheriff, so he showed himself out. The sheriff's Bronco sat behind his Explorer, but Brady thought he could get around it. He opened the door to the Explorer and a hand shot out to slam it shut again. Brady turned, and found himself staring into the sheriff's angry face.

"What are you doing here?" Richards asked. "Last time I checked, Coalmont was twelve miles back that a-way."

Brady drew himself up straight. He knew better than to let Pete Richards think he could intimidate him. "I'm following up a murder investigation."

"Aw, crap, boy," the sheriff muttered, and spat a stream of tobacco near the Explorer's back tire. "Don't read more into it than it's worth. You're wasting your time here. McBee's murder ain't got nothing to do with that accident. You said yourself, nobody would wait four years if they was gonna do this. I guarantee you, it's a drug deal."

"Don't you think we owe it to Natasha Hawthorne and Reed Donally to make sure of that?"

The sheriff gave him a saccharine smile. "Well, now, that's why I'm here, son. You just get yourself back to Coalmont. Write a traffic ticket or two and let me handle this."

Like you've handled it so far? Brady almost added, but didn't.

Ignoring the smirk on Richards's face, he dug his keys out of his pocket and climbed inside the Explorer. He deftly backed around the sheriff's Bronco and turned around in the driveway. When he checked in the rearview mirror, he saw the sheriff walking back toward the house.

Brady screeched to a stop when a bright red BMW swung off the main highway onto the paved drive, nearly sideswiping him. Brady looked in the mirror and saw the brake lights flash as it roared past, then the driver threw it in reverse and backed to where Brady sat. They both rolled down their windows.

"What's going on?" the dark-haired man asked. "My wife . . . my stepson . . . are they okay? I was at the club when I got the message to come home."

Martin Atkinson. Brady couldn't believe his luck.

"Uh, they're fine, sir. Someone threw a brick through the front window, but the sheriff is with them now."

Exasperation crossed the man's face and he slapped the steering wheel with his open palm.

Brady studied him. From his fancy white shirt to his manicured nails, Martin Atkinson gave off an air of wealth and authority. He didn't look like someone who would associate with the likes of Bobby McBee. But then again, neither did Nat.

Atkinson reached for his keys. "Well, thanks, son. I guess I'd better—"

"Wait!" Brady said. "Actually, I was here to see you about something else. Do you know Bobby McBee?"

Atkinson frowned, revealing tiny pockmarks on his tan cheeks when he replied, "He was one of the kids involved in the accident with Reed, wasn't he? Yes, I've met him."

"Have you seen him professionally? Was he a patient of yours?" Brady knew he was overstepping his bounds. Atkinson didn't have to answer, but he did anyway.

"I saw him twice, I think, but then I referred him to a specialist who I thought more capable of handling that type of nerve injury. What's this about?"

"Bobby McBee was murdered last night. I found—"

"Dear God!" Atkinson exclaimed. "Do you think it has anything to do with this . . ." He waved his hand. ". . . person who's harassing Reed?"

"I don't know, sir, but I'm looking into it. The reason I needed to speak to you was because of the prescription bottles I found in Bobby's closet. There were seven of them, all prescribed by you."

"I never wrote Bobby McBee a prescription. I'm sure of it. It was a consultation only."

Brady fished the list of names from his pocket. "They weren't prescribed to Bobby. Do you recognize any of these names? Lester Davis, Mike Brannett, Justin Thomas, Lee Matthews, John Green, Andy Wilson . . . Frank Arp?"

Atkinson drummed his fingers on the leather steering wheel and finally shook his head. "I'm sorry, I don't think I know any of those people, but if you'll give me a copy of the list, I'll have my secretary check."

Brady handed him the list through the window. "Take this one. I have another. Any idea how all these men ended up with prescriptions from you?"

"What kinds of drugs were they?"

"Pain killers, mostly. Lortab, Vicodin . . ."

Atkinson shook his head in disgust. "I'll tell you how they got them. I had a prescription pad stolen a couple of months ago. The prescriptions were forged."

"Did you report it?"

"Of course I reported it. To that moron of a sheriff. Any idea what drugstores they were filled at? He was supposed to notify the surrounding ones."

"One of them was Radcliff Pharmacy, in Gruetli-Laager. Sorry, I don't remember the others."

"I can see how it might be hard to catch in another county, but Gruetli is ten minutes away. You said he's up there, right?" Atkinson gestured toward the house.

Brady nodded, and Atkinson reached for his keys. "I think it's time the sheriff and I had a little talk. If he isn't interested in pursuing this, I'm calling in the state investigators. I'll have my office contact you, Officer. . ." He frowned and peered at the insignia on the Explorer's door.

"Simms. My name is Brady Simms. I'm the new chief at Coalmont."

Atkinson nodded. "Nice to meet you. Sorry about Gus. I played golf with him a time or two. Good man. I always tried to talk him into running for sheriff. I don't know whether Richards is corrupt or inept, but I don't appreciate either quality in a sheriff."

He drove off without another word and Brady watched the BMW disappear over the hill before he pulled onto the highway. He would get a good reaming for the hornet's nest he'd just stirred up, but it was worth it to picture Richards's face when Dr. Atkinson got hold of him.

Brady drove back to the station and nodded at the dispatcher. "Hey, Mary Ann. Did I miss anything exciting?"

She rolled her eyes and snapped her gum. "That depends. Do you consider Jesse Floyd decking Matt Hubey exciting?"

Brady sighed. Hubey and Floyd both had to be in their late sixties. A minor land dispute back in the spring was escalating into a feud to rival the Hatfields and McCoys.

"What was it this time?" he asked.

"Hubey's goats were in the road again. Floyd ran over one of them and threw the carcass in Hubey's driveway. Hubey came out and got to mouthing, then Floyd decked him. The two old coots rolled around in the yard, slugging it out, until another neighbor intervened."

"Is Roscoe there?"

"Yeah, he's there."

"Have him tell them we'll throw them both in the clink for 48 hours if it happens again." Brady winked at her. "In the same cell."

"Oooh," Mary Ann said with a smile. "I like it."

She was hollering for Roscoe on the radio when Brady shut his office door behind him. He moved to the dented black filing cabinet by the window and started searching for the accident file. Luckily, Gus's filing system was top notch. Within seconds, he pulled the fat manila folder and sat behind the desk to look it over.

The accident report lay on top. Brady scanned the page for the reporting officer and his heart sank when he saw Reuben Layne's name at the bottom. The retired officer was both honest and methodical, the type of man who didn't make many mistakes.

Brady scanned the report, but didn't find anything he didn't already know. He flipped the page. The sight of the glossy accident photos hit him like a slap in the face.

Bile rose in his throat when he stared at the image of a bloody, unconscious Nat slumped over the airbag. The black safety harness was clearly visible against her white shirt.

He studied the pictures of his classmates, trying to look at them objectively, but the sight of their twisted bodies filled him with horror. Even Bobby's, who had been ejected from the car and landed against a massive oak. Reed Donally had been pinned in the backseat. Jen hung halfway out of the passenger side window, her gray eyes staring sightlessly at the sky.

Tony Franklin lay just outside the car, curled on his side like a sleeping infant. His right leg hung at an odd angle behind him. Brady closed the folder and slipped into the adjoining bathroom to splash his face with icy water.

He walked back to the desk and sat on the edge while he flipped through the phonebook. His hand shook when he dialed Reuben Layne's number.

"Hello," a gruff voice answered.

"Hi, Mr. Layne. My name is Brady Simms. I don't know if you remember me—"

"Sure I do!" he boomed. "Gus's Boy Wonder. What can I do for you, son?"

"I was wondering if I could meet with you. I have some questions about a case you covered, the accident on graduation night four years ago."

Reuben sighed into the phone. "Whoo boy, I don't

guess I'll ever forget that one. I've got to testify in court this month about it. Where do you want to meet?"

Brady hesitated and glanced back at the folder. "How about at the scene of the accident? You can walk me through it."

"I can be there in ten."

Brady hung up the phone and reached for the file. He remembered the blind hope on Nat's face, and tried to tell himself he was only doing what was right, that he would do it for anybody, and that he simply wanted the truth to come out, even if it meant Nat was driving.

But the truth was, he prayed all the way to the scene he'd find something, anything, to prove her innocence and erase the despair from her green eyes.

NAT BENT TO TIE HER SHOE, THEN DID A FEW MORE stretches before loping into the woods at the edge of her parents' property. Fall was her favorite time of year, and, although it was only the middle of July, the sweet, woodsy scent of it already hung in the air. She breathed deeply and increased her pace, jogging along the four-wheeler trail her father and brothers had worn in the forest floor.

She took comfort in running. It always helped clear her head and relax her. She'd first started running at the juvenile center. Some days she'd run for hours, run until she was exhausted and could barely limp back to her room, simply to take the edge off the mindless day-to-day routine of that horrible place and chase away the guilty that haunted her.

But today was different. It was probably wrong to think it, but God, it just felt good to be alive. To think there was a chance she wasn't responsible for anyone's death, and that maybe there was still a chance for Brady and her, after all.

The pain in his eyes had stunned her, but it had also given her hope. If he was over her, he wouldn't care what Bobby had done to her. He wouldn't have held her, and he wouldn't have promised to help her.

Would he?

Just the thought of the way his arms felt around her was enough to make her cry. In his arms, with his scent surrounding her, she'd felt safe, protected. Resting her cheek against his chest, she'd found a solace she hadn't felt in years.

Nat made the circle and was approaching the spot where she'd first entered the forest when the masked man stepped out from behind a tree, directly in front of her. He hefted a big stick over his shoulder.

There was no time to slow, no way to dodge. Nat careened helplessly past him. The stick struck the middle of her back, knocking the wind out of her, and sent her sprawling onto the forest floor.

CHAPTER 4

BRADY LEANED AGAINST THE EXPLORER AND watched the gray-haired investigator climb from a rusty blue pickup. "I really appreciate you meeting me like this, Mr. Layne." Brady transferred the accident folder to his left hand and offered the other to the investigator.

While they shook hands, the investigator said, "Call me Reuben. And it's no problem. For the first few months, retirement was nice, but I've been getting antsy lately, missing the job." He pulled off his faded John Deere cap and scratched his head. "So, are you working with the defense, helping them get ready for the trial?"

"Actually, I'm not working with anyone. I'm following up on a statement that was made in my presence this morning." Brady hesitated. "Did you hear about the McBee murder last night?"

"Yeah, I—oh, wait a minute!" Reuben's eyes widened. "He was one of the kids from the wreck, wasn't he? I didn't put it together."

"Yes. It seems someone was threatening the three survivors. I'm not sure whether it's connected to the murder yet, but I was interviewing Natasha Hawthorne this morning when McBee's sister came over. According to her, McBee told her last week that Natasha wasn't driving on the night of the accident, that Tony Franklin was."

"What?" Reuben frowned and shook his head. "I don't know how he could say that. I was the first officer on the scene. The Hawthorne girl was the only one wearing a seatbelt and she was strapped behind the wheel."

"Do you think someone could've staged the scene?"

"Not one of the passengers, that's for sure. Upon my arrival, all the occupants of the Camaro were either deceased or unconscious. Frankly, I'm surprised any of them made it. It was as bad a wreck as I've ever seen, and I worked with the D.O.T. for fifteen years before becoming an investigator. Plus, you gotta look at something else. If anyone staged it, they had to do it quick. A witness reports that he helped put a drunken Reed Donally in the car at ten minutes after one that morning. He was sure about the time because he had to be at work at two. The party was breaking up and some of them were meeting at the local Pancake Hut for breakfast. I was on the scene twenty minutes later."

"Okay." Brady sighed. "Let's walk through it anyway. Did you come upon the accident yourself, or did someone call it in?"

"It was a 911 call. I was the nearest available unit." Reuben flipped through the stack of pictures. He removed one of the highway and showed it to Brady. "Immediately

I saw the marks on the road."

"Skid marks?"

Reuben shook his head and walked down the white line. "Yaw marks." He stopped and glanced down at the photos. "The driver lost control of the car about right here, long before they reached the curve. Yaw marks happen when a vehicle travels in a curved path faster than the tires can handle. The car was no longer moving parallel to the road, but the wheels were still turning. Once the adhesion limit of the tires is reached, the tires begin to sideslip, leaving visible marks on the pavement. Yaw marks are always curved. We estimated the speed based on the radius of that curvature, and by using a drag sled to establish the road's friction coefficient. When I plugged that number into the formula to calculate speed, I figured that Camaro was traveling approximately 92 miles an hour when it hit this first cedar guidepost."

Reuben rested his hand on the guidepost and stared down at the pictures again. Brady thought about Nat's speeding tickets in the months prior to the accident. She'd gotten two in the same week. But she'd changed after she'd found out about the baby, had tried to take better care of herself. Surely she wouldn't have barreled down this narrow road at 92 miles per hour, even if she'd been showing off her new car. Would she?

Brady turned at the sound of the car coasting to a stop behind them. A frowning Roscoe shut off the engine and climbed from the squad car.

"You get Hubey and Floyd under control?" Brady asked, and Roscoe's scowl deepened.

"Finally." Roscoe scratched his sunburned ear. "I told them I had better things to do than to babysit two cantankerous old coots like them. Do you believe they started to turn on *me*?"

Roscoe shot a curious glance at Reuben, who nodded in greeting. "Hey, Rube. What are you doing?"

"He's helping me go over the Hawthorne case," Brady answered for him. He briefly told Roscoe about Dara McBee's statement. Roscoe's bushy brows shot up, but oddly enough for him, he didn't have any questions other than "Can I tag along?"

"Sure," Brady said, then nodded at Reuben. "Go on."

"Okay. So, the car crashed through this guidepost, traversed the embankment . . ."

Reuben huffed as he trotted down the hillside. Brady and Roscoe hurried down the grassy slope behind him. They pushed their way through the brush into the clearing.

". . . then the car struck the perpendicular embankment, vaulted into the air. It landed over there by that creek, then flipped to a stop right here, coming to a rest on its rooftop."

Brady glanced up at the road. Even if the headlights on the Camaro had still been functioning, he didn't see how a passerby could see this spot from the road. It had been too dark, the embankment too steep, and the car had traveled too far. To test his theory, he jogged back up the hillside. The summer sun beat against his back, plastering his uniform against him, but he felt a glimmer of hope when he stared back at the thicket. He couldn't see either of the men below, and couldn't imagine anyone being able to see a black car.

He skidded back downhill and rejoined them. "Was all this brush here before?" he asked Reuben.

"Yeah, maybe not as thick, but it was here."

"Did the 911 caller say he'd witnessed the wreck? I know there were no witnesses listed in the report."

"No, dispatch said the caller had noticed the broken guidepost and saw a light down there."

"Were the Camaro's lights on when you got here?"

Reuben frowned, gazing over Brady's shoulder. "No. It was eerie. Foggy. The motor was dead and I remember how utterly quiet it was. I used my flashlight beam to trace the skids through the brush. I saw the Franklin kid first."

"You know what I think?" Brady said. "I think this caller witnessed the accident. I don't think he saw any lights from the road. Maybe he staged the scene."

"But why?" Roscoe asked. "Why would anyone do that?"

"I don't know, but I bet if I can find that caller, we could find out." Brady's mind raced over the possibilities, then he groaned. "911 calls. How long are they kept in archives?"

"In most places, 60 days and then evaluation." Reuben

winked. "But you are fortunate in the fact that Grundy County has the most obsessive compulsive sonofagun I've ever met in the records office. If anyone still had them, it'd be Mole. Have you ever met Mole?"

"No, I . . ." Brady looked at Roscoe. "Mole?"

"His office is in the courthouse basement. He's in charge of archives and maintaining the evidence log book. Can't believe you haven't met him yet."

"Is there any chance he'd still have tapes from four years ago?"

Reuben laughed. "Mole probably has bellybutton lint from four years ago, so I can imagine him having 911 tapes. Like I said, he's a compulsive sonofagun. A packrat. It's worth a try. But I gotta tell you, son, I think you're grasping at straws."

But Brady barely heard him. "May I?" he asked, and gestured at the file. Reuben handed it to him and he flipped through the reports. "So, you did a blood test on the airbag."

"Yep, and it was saturated with Natasha Hawthorne's blood. No one else's."

"Of course it was," Brady murmured. "She was lying against it. What about saliva? Did you have the bag tested for saliva?"

Reuben frowned, and Brady realized he'd better watch his step. Reuben Layne was a thorough investigator and would resent any hint that he hadn't done his job right. But Reuben looked more thoughtful than annoyed.

"I didn't see the need," he said, rubbing his chin. "So, you're thinking, when the airbag came out . . ."

"Pow," Brady said. "It would hit the driver right in the face. Surely there would be a saliva deposit. Of course Nat's might also be on there, since she was slumped across the bag, but if we found Tony Franklin's there, it might cause reasonable doubt."

He could get Nat's lawyer to subpoena the bags and do their own test. He knew that evidence should still be around.

"The Hawthorne girl's boot was found in the driver's well," Reuben said. "It's in one of the pictures."

"But look at Tony's injuries," Brady said. "It says his right leg was crushed, his foot nearly severed. The way the car was caved, the front driver's side sustained most of the damage from the impact. Don't you think it's possible he got that injury behind the wheel?"

"He could've gotten it sitting on the console too. That's an awfully small car for six people to cram into."

"I can't see a guy as big as Tony Franklin sitting on the console. It would've been easier to cram in a seat with Jen, or to have her sit on the console. She was tiny."

"Let me get this straight," Roscoe said. "You think someone happened to be behind Natasha Hawthorne's car, saw the wreck and then ran all the way down here, pulled that big Franklin boy from the driver's seat—"

"If he wasn't belted in, he might've been ejected," Brady interrupted.

"—put Natasha Hawthorne behind the wheel, and just to make it look good, strapped her in?"

Brady caught the look Roscoe and Reuben shot each other, and he knew how crazy he sounded, maybe even a little desperate, but he was on to something.

He just knew it.

Nat's mouth filled with blood and dirt, gagging her. Shale bit into her palms when she tried to force herself up, but then her attacker was on her back, driving her into the ground. He jerked her arm up roughly behind her, making her cry out as he hauled her to her feet. Nat stumbled and allowed herself to be tugged along until she could clear the cobwebs from her mind.

When he started downhill, she abruptly went slack, throwing him off balance. She heard his muttered curse near her ear and snapped her head back, catching him dead in the face. They tumbled down the incline.

The impact of their landing nearly knocked the breath from her again, but she forced herself to her feet at the same time he did.

He went for his waistband and her heart skipped when she saw the handle of the gun sticking out of his holster. She pivoted and struck his hand with a flying roundhouse kick. The gun went flying into the bushes.

While her assailant howled and clutched his wrist,

Nat grabbed his shoulder. She caught a glimpse of startled brown eyes before she drove her knee up as hard as she could.

The blow was off mark, but close enough to give her a few seconds. She sprinted through the forest. He couldn't know these woods as well as she did. She ran until she felt like her lungs would explode, and was almost to the clearing when she tripped over a rock. The pain that jolted up her leg was hot, stunning. Nat clutched her ankle and fought the nausea that rose in her throat.

A crashing in the woods behind her made her scramble backward into the brush. Briars tore at her hair and poked through her clothing as she tucked herself into the blackberry thicket. She only prayed she wouldn't disturb a resting copperhead.

She caught a glimpse of black when her attacker ran past. He knelt a few feet from her, clutching his knees and gasping for breath. How she wished he'd take off that mask!

The rumble of approaching ATVs made him stand up straight. Nat watched as he bolted back into the woods.

She stumbled out of her hiding place, into the path of the four-wheeler riders. The first rider swerved to avoid her, and the second braked to a stop so close to her that she reached out to touch the battered red cooler strapped to the front rack to regain her balance when her ankle threatened to give way.

A couple of roughnecks with coolers and shotguns. Nat had never been so happy to see anyone in her life.

"Honey, what happened to you?" the bearded rider asked.

"This man . . . he attacked me. I—" Nat horrified herself by bursting into tears.

"Was he armed?" the man asked as he fished a couple of shotgun shells out of his pocket and put them in his gun.

"He, uh, had a gun, but I kicked it away. I don't know if he had another."

Chivalry might be dead in some parts of the world, but it was alive and well in Middle Tennessee. Local men took care of their own. The men quickly devised a plan.

"Dave, get this gal out of here and call the law. I'll see if I can find him. Which way did he go?"

Nat pointed in the direction she'd last seen the attacker, then the grizzled man on the first four-wheeler had her by the elbow. He helped her onto the ATV and climbed on in front of her.

"I've got a cell phone," he said. "In that bag behind you."

Nat twisted to retrieve it from the zippered bag. She punched in Brady's cell phone number, but hung up when she got his voice mail. Then she called the Coalmont police department and had a short conversation with the dispatcher, who assured her she'd track Brady down.

"Where do you live?" the man asked, and Nat pointed toward the clearing. He nodded and started to turn when she said, "No, wait! Could you go back that way? He dropped his gun and I'm afraid he'll double back to get it."

She directed her rescuer to the place where she'd fought, and together they searched for the gun.

"Here it is!" she said, and reached for it.

"Don't touch it," he commanded. "Might be prints on it."

"He was wearing gloves . . . I think." Nat rubbed her head.

"Well, better safe than sorry." He removed his Jim Beam tank top and gingerly lifted the gun, barrel first. He folded it in the black material as carefully as if he were diapering a baby, then pinned it to the front rack with one of the straps.

"Now let's get you home," he said.

BRADY SHOOK HANDS WITH REUBEN. "THANK YOU FOR your time. I appreciate you meeting with me like this."

"Anytime. Good luck, son." The investigator gave a little wave before climbing into his battered pickup and driving away.

The radio on Brady's hip crackled to life. The tone of Mary Ann's voice immediately put him on alert when she called out his name. Brady hurried to the Explorer because the reception would be better on that radio. Roscoe ran around to the passenger side to listen.

"Go ahead, Mary Ann," Brady said. "I'm here."

"A girl just called for you. She sounded real upset, said she was attacked in the woods behind her house. She said 'tell him it's Nat.' Do you know who I'm talking about?"

Brady swallowed hard over the sudden lump in his throat. "Yeah," he rasped. "She okay?"

"Seemed to be, but she asked me to send you over there."

Roscoe started out of the Explorer, but Brady shook his head and jammed his keys in the ignition.

"But the squad car—" Roscoe protested.

"Leave it. We've got to move." Brady called Mary Ann from his cell phone and told her to send Deke out for the car.

"Brady, I'm worried about you," Roscoe said hesitantly. "You ain't acting right, and I'm afraid it's gonna catch up with you."

"What are you saying, Roscoe?" Brady shot him a quick glance. "You don't think I'm doing my job?"

"Naw, I'm afraid maybe you're getting too involved. I seen the way you looked at that girl. I saw how you acted just now. I'm telling you, I think you need to back off this one."

"Back off?" Brady asked, surprised and a little angry. "What do you mean, back off? A girl's life is at stake here, Roscoe."

"I'm talking about this accident stuff. I know you want to believe she wasn't driving, but you're stirring up a hornet's nest. Do you have any idea what the sheriff will do if he finds out you're poking around with this case? One of those girls was his niece."

Brady snorted. "I'm not worried about the sheriff."

"Well, you should be. I wouldn't put it past him to trump up something against you, maybe get you fired. Don't laugh. I've seen it happen before. And what do you think your chances of getting into the FBI would be if he manages to smear your record?"

His words made Brady blink. Would the sheriff go that far?

Just as quickly as the thought occurred to him, he realized it didn't matter. Not when Nat's life was at stake.

"Why would he do that, unless he has something to hide?"

"Maybe he does. Maybe he doesn't, but I can tell you how he'll react. That Hawthorne girl has served her time. You ain't gonna change that. So what if the insurance company has to pay out some money? Let it be done and over with. You're better than this town, Brady. Don't ruin your whole life over something like this."

Brady gripped the steering wheel with white-knuckled hands. "I can't believe you said that."

"I believe if Gus were here, he'd be saying it too. He loved you, Brady, and he respected you, but he used to tell me to look out for you. He'd say, 'that boy's got a good head on his shoulders, but his heart's too tender. It'll get him in trouble if he don't watch it.' I think that's what's happening now."

"This doesn't have anything to do with my heart," Brady snapped. He wished now that he'd let Roscoe take his own car. "It has to do with right and wrong, and if I start blurring the lines simply because I don't want to get the sheriff riled up, then there's not much point in my being here, is there?"

Roscoe opened his mouth, then shut it again. They rode in silence the rest of the way to Nat's house. Nat's mother stood in the front yard with a girl Brady didn't recognize. He threw the Explorer in park and hurried over to them.

"Where's Nat? Is she okay?" he asked.

"She . . . I . . ." Selena Hawthorne's eyes filled with tears and Brady's stomach dropped.

The girl laid a hand on Brady's arm. He stared into her doe-like brown eyes and felt somehow reassured, even before she spoke. "Nat called. She said she'd twisted her ankle, but she was all right. We're waiting on her."

"Where is she? I thought she was here."

"She was running in the woods behind the house. She said some guy on a four-wheeler is bringing her in. He let her use his phone." The girl smiled. "I'm Alisha, by the way. A friend of Nat's from Cedar Ridge."

Brady's gaze had drifted over her shoulder toward

the back of the house, but it snapped back to her at the mention of the detention center. His face heated when she laughed.

"I'm harmless, I assure you."

"I wasn't—" He bit off his protest when she lifted an eyebrow. He *had* been wondering what she'd done to end up in the detention center. She was pretty enough to be a model, with smooth skin the same shade of brown as her eyes.

Brady smiled and held up his palms in surrender, then offered his right hand. "Let's start over. I'm Brady Simms."

"The famous Brady. We meet at last," Alisha said.

Before he had a chance to ask her what she meant, he heard the roar of a four-wheeler in the distance. Brady led the charge around the side of the house.

The sight of Nat's pale, blood-streaked face stopped him in his tracks.

THE SHOCK AND CONCERN IN BRADY'S BLUE EYES MADE her want to cry again, but Nat fought back her tears. She was tougher than that, and she was tired of crying, anyway. She'd shed enough tears in the last four years to last a lifetime.

Brady ran over to the four-wheeler. "What happened?" he asked as he tipped up her chin to inspect her busted mouth.

She told him the story while he inspected her wounds. His hands were everywhere at once, as if he had to see for himself that she was okay. It might not have meant anything, but she wanted to believe he still cared what happened to her, and not only because of his job. His mouth pressed into a grim line when he gently lifted the hem of her tank top and inspected the abrasion on her back.

"Can you take me to the scene?" Brady asked Dave.

"You can take the twins' four-wheelers," her mother told Brady and Roscoe. "I'll get the keys for you."

"Let me take you inside, Nat," Brady said, and she shook her head.

"I'm going with you."

Brady looked like he wanted to protest, but then he nodded. Her mother returned with the keys, and he and Roscoe strode to the outbuilding to get the ATVs.

Nat stayed on the four-wheeler with Dave. Alisha gave her a reassuring wink and climbed on behind Brady when he stopped beside her.

Roscoe sat on the other ATV by himself. "Mrs. Hawthorne?" he said, and looked at her mother. Selena shook her head.

"I called Jake. He's on his way home, so I'm going to wait here for him. Nat, you and Alisha should stay here too."

"No, Mama. Maybe Dave's friend caught the

attacker. I want to go with them."

Dave led them back to the place where Nat had hidden from the attacker. His friend waited for them on the path.

"I saw him. Thought for a minute I was going to catch him, but he had a motorcycle hidden by Chet Meeks' fence." The redhead took off his Budweiser hat to scratch his head. "He just flat outran me from there. You okay, girl?" he asked Nat.

Somehow she managed a smile, though it made her face hurt. "Thanks to you and Dave."

While Brady asked them a series of questions into a tape recorder, Alisha walked over and wrapped an arm around Nat's shoulder. "Sit on the four-wheeler," she commanded. "You look like you're going to faint."

That drew a sharp look from Brady, so Nat let Alisha lead her to the green Honda. She perched on the seat and listened as Brady resumed questioning her rescuers. Finally, he clicked off the recorder.

"Okay, if I can get that gun . . . thanks." Brady carefully unwrapped it and returned Dave's shirt. "You guys are free to go. Thanks for your help."

"Yes, thank you," Nat murmured when they walked by.

They nodded, and Dave said, "Hope they catch him, Miss."

Brady waited until they were gone to turn on her. "Dammit, Nat. What did you think you were doing, running out here by yourself?"

His tone irritated her. A headache throbbed behind her eyes and her reply came out harsher than intended. "I'm not in jail anymore, Brady."

His face tightened. "You were never in jail."

"Not far from it." She rubbed her forehead. "I went for a run in my back yard."

"There are too many four-wheelers cutting through these woods to get to the lake. Run in the evenings, when you can get one of the twins to run with you."

"Can you tell us anything about your attacker, other than he was dressed in black with a black ski mask?" Roscoe asked. "About how big was he?"

Nat frowned. "He was about the same height as Brady. Maybe a little taller, and probably thirty or so pounds heavier."

Roscoe's pen halted in mid-stroke and he glanced up at Nat. "Now, hon," he said, and Nat grit her teeth. Her daddy was the only person in the world who could get away with calling her "hon.'

"You say this guy was bigger than Brady? I find it hard to believe that a slip of a girl like you could take down a man that size."

"Maybe I could show you," Nat said sweetly.

"Oh, God," Brady mumbled, and Alisha stifled a giggle.

Nat slid off the four-wheeler and limped toward the place where she'd been knocked down. Brady quickly stepped between her and Roscoe.

"That won't be necessary," he said.

"I'm okay," Nat assured him. "Maybe I'll remember something if we re-enact it." She lay on the ground without waiting on his answer, and told Roscoe to pull her up by the arm.

"Don't worry. I won't hurt you," Roscoe said.

Her body felt battered and sore, but she went through the motions. Within seconds, Roscoe lay flat on his back, holding his nose and staring up at the sky.

Alisha grinned when Nat dusted herself off. "Not bad for a skinny white girl," she offered.

Nat laughed, remembering the first time Alisha had said that, during Nat's first week at Cedar Ridge. After Nat was threatened by another resident, Alisha took it upon herself to make sure her new roommate could defend herself. They had sparred in the rec room for several minutes before Alisha slammed her on the mat. Alisha had helped her up and said, "Not bad for a skinny white girl."

Nat had felt pretty proud of herself until Alisha added, "But skinny white girls ain't what you gotta worry about in here."

Alisha had been right about that. Even now the thought of Maria Alvarez's empty black eyes gave Nat a chill.

"I learned from the best," she said with a wink, and climbed back on the four-wheeler. Brady frowned when Nat slid back to give him room to get on. She knew he didn't want to be close to her, but maybe she could change that. She'd wasted so much time, punishing herself for something she might not have done.

He swung his leg over the four-wheeler and reached to start it. Nat pretended not to notice how he stiffened when she wrapped her arms around his waist.

She rested her cheek against his broad back and closed her eyes as the warm sun beat down on her face. She wished she could hold him like that forever, but all too soon they were back in her backyard.

Brady climbed off the four-wheeler and, wordlessly, he scooped her in his arms. He carried her up the steps to where her parents stood waiting at the back door.

"I'll wait on you out here," Roscoe called, and Nat's father reached for her.

"Take me to the couch," Nat said quickly, before Brady could hand her off.

Brady surprised her when he smiled. "It's a little late for the helpless female act, Boom Boom."

But he did as she asked. Selena held open the door and he carried Nat inside. He deposited her on the couch and tried to answer the stream of questions from her father while he examined her swollen ankle. Nat closed her eyes at the feel of his warm hands on her bare skin.

"I think it will be okay, but maybe you should go to the doctor and have it x-rayed, just in case," he said.

"It'll be fine." Nat opened her eyes. "Thank you, Brady. For everything."

He nodded, and stood to leave. He stopped in the doorway and frowned at her over his shoulder. "I mean it, Nat. I don't want you going anywhere by yourself. If you want to run, make one of the twins go with you."

Nat gave him a little salute. "Aye, aye, Chief."

"See you, *hon*," he said, and grinned. He ducked the throw pillow she tossed at his head.

Her parents showed him to the door and Nat punched Alisha's arm. "Did you see that?" she whispered. "He smiled at me. Maybe it's not too late for us."

"Maybe?" Alisha snorted. "Girl, that man is as crazy about you as you are him, he just doesn't want to admit it yet. You'd better get in there and claim what's yours before someone else gets him. You're lucky they haven't already. Men like that don't stay single long."

༻•༺

Brady's phone started chirping as soon as he opened the Explorer's door. Roscoe pulled it off the holder and handed it to him. Brady was still a little punchy from being so close to Nat. He fumbled the phone and had to scoop it off the floorboard.

"Hey, babe," Charity said cheerfully, and Brady's face flooded with heat. For some reason, he felt like a kid with his hand caught in the cookie jar.

"Hey," he managed over the lump in his throat.

"Would you mind stopping by the store and picking

up an extra pack of rolls before you come over tonight? I've started cooking, and I need to mop before they get here."

"Sure. No problem."

"You're a doll. Well, I'll let you get back to work. See ya."

"See you," Brady said, and clicked the phone off.

"You okay?" Roscoe folded a piece of Big Red gum into his mouth. "You look funny."

"I'm fine."

"So, what are you going to do now . . . about all this?"

"First, I'm going back to the station. I'm going to dust the gun for prints, run the numbers and then see if I can catch Mole in."

"Twizzlers."

"What?" Brady glanced at the deputy, who winked.

"Mole likes Twizzlers. If Gus ever needed a favor from him, he'd stop at the Piggly Wiggly and buy a pack. With as much digging as you're asking him to do, you might want to buy a case."

Brady sighed. Oh well, he had to stop by the store anyway.

The station was quiet. Brady dusted the gun himself and found nothing. Then he turned on the computer and logged the serial number in the database. He leaned back in his chair and rubbed his eyes.

The computer blipped when the program found a match.

Brady frowned when he saw that the gun was registered to Jim Foster, a small town hood who was in jail for trying to rob the Texaco station a few months back. He scrolled down the page and froze when he saw that the gun beside him was the one Jim had used in the robbery.

It was supposed to be in the evidence room in county lock up.

CHAPTER 5

BRADY LEANED BACK IN HIS CHAIR AND STARED AT the screen. Then he pushed away from the computer and grabbed the gun. Somebody had some explaining to do.

The drive to the county jail passed in a blur. Brady twisted and turned the pieces of the puzzle around in his head like sections of a Rubix cube, but he still couldn't make sense of it. The sheriff had to be in on it. But why? And why now?

Maybe the sheriff knew Nat wasn't driving that night and was trying to save the settlement his sister expected from the insurance company. The only possible reason for the attacker to want Reed Donally dead was because he was afraid Reed might know something that might be damaging in court. That is, unless he really was crazy.

Brady double parked and hurried inside the jail. Joe Richards, the sheriff's nephew, stood with his back to Brady, talking to Ian Kirby by the coffee pot. Ian lifted a paper cup in greeting. Brady nodded, but strode past them to the evidence room.

Without preamble, he leaned against the counter and told Wayne Tolbert, the deputy behind it, he wanted to see the gun from the Foster robbery.

"What do you want that for?" Tolbert asked with a yawn. "That's been awhile back. Might take some time to dig it out."

"You'd better get to it, then," Brady said brusquely. He wondered if someone had bothered to switch guns or if the deputy would find an empty box.

Ian Kirby wandered in. "Hey, Brady." He slurped the last sip of coffee from his cup and crumpled it. He tossed it over the counter and grinned sheepishly when he missed the blue garbage can on the other side. "Oops."

Distracted, Brady forgot to smile. Kirby propped on the counter next to him and said, "Not being nosy, but is something wrong here? You look like you're a thousand miles away."

"I was going to call you anyway," Brady replied. "You know that girl who witnessed the McBee murder? Someone attacked her today."

Kirby's social face disappeared, replaced by the cool investigator mask. He pulled out a notebook and started firing questions at Brady.

Brady detailed what Nat told him about the attack, growing more agitated as he talked. He made an effort to keep his voice down. "And there's something else . . ." He fell silent when Tolbert returned.

The deputy's ruddy face flushed even redder when

he saw Kirby standing there. "Uh, Brady . . . the gun ain't back there. Probably the prosecution still has it."

Brady laid the gun on the counter. "It's right here." He glanced at Kirby. "The Hawthorne girl's attacker dropped this. I want the TBI to help me find out why a gun that's supposed to be in county lockup ended up at my crime scene."

"What are you thinking?" Kirby asked.

Tolbert pushed through the swinging gate and headed to the main office. Going to get the sheriff, no doubt. Brady ignored him and focused on Kirby.

"I have something to tell you, but I was waiting to get more evidence first."

"Tell me now. Maybe I can help." He put his notebook away. "As a friend."

Brady lowered his voice. "I have reason to suspect that maybe Natasha Hawthorne wasn't driving the night of the accident. Right now, I have nothing, but I think it was set-up. What's more, I think the McBee murder, the threats against Nat Hawthorne and Reed Donally—"

"Whoa, whoa!" Kirby held up his hands. "Back up. Who's Donally?"

"The other survivor from the crash. He's been getting death threats, the same as Nat, but I think someone is trying to throw us. I don't think the motive is revenge. I think it's money. Insurance money from the civil case."

Kirby tugged at his ear. "Sorry, I don't think I follow—"

"The sheriff's niece was killed in that accident."

Kirby's eyes widened. "You don't think—"

"What would you think?" Brady raked a hand down his face. "I'm following up a lead. Maybe I'll have something for you soon."

"Make it solid, Brady. That's a serious accusation."

"Believe me, I know."

They fell silent when the sheriff barreled through the doorway. "Gentlemen," he said breathlessly. "Something I can help you with?"

"You can tell me how a gun that's supposed to be in lockup ended up at an attempted murder scene," Brady said, watching his face for a reaction.

The sheriff's expression remained inscrutable. "I have no idea, but before you start blaming my boys, you gotta know that all the departments in Grundy County have access to that room, including yours."

Brady bit off a retort when Joe Richards appeared over his uncle's shoulder. His nose was swollen and both eyes were black at the inside corners.

Rage rumbled through Brady, shocking him with its force. Ian Kirby must've seen it on his face, because he blocked Brady before he could launch himself at Joe.

"What happened to your nose, Joe?" Brady yelled over Kirby's shoulder.

The puzzled look the sheriff shot Brady appeared so genuine it made Brady falter.

"I got clocked trying to separate two drunks at Blue

Lounge last night. What's it to you?" Joe said, but he backed from the doorway, out of Brady's sight.

"You have any witnesses?" Brady asked, and the sheriff's eyes narrowed.

"What's this all about?" he asked.

"Natasha Hawthorne was attacked this morning. The man who assaulted her had a gun from this room. She said she head-butted her attacker and might've broken his nose."

The sheriff pushed Ian Kirby out of the way like a rag doll and stood face-to-face with Brady. "Looky here, boy," he said, blasting Brady with a burst of hot, sour breath. "I don't know what you think you're getting at here, but I'm warning you, you'd better be very careful about what you say."

Brady poked the sheriff in the chest. "And I'm warning you . . . if anything happens to Nat Hawthorne, it won't be business and it won't be the law. It'll be personal."

"Easy, Brady," Kirby said, and shoved between them once again. He glanced over his shoulder and said, "Sheriff, I think you and I need to have a little talk with the bureau. I assume you'd rather we went into your office and did it privately?"

The sheriff grunted and stalked toward his office without another word.

"Keep it cool, Brady," Kirby whispered. "You don't have anything yet, so don't blow it, okay?"

Brady nodded, but when he followed Kirby out

of the evidence room, one look at Joe Richards's face sparked his fury again. Images of Nat, broken and bleeding, flashed through his mind. How differently things could've turned out today.

Joe wouldn't meet his eyes. He hurried into the bathroom and Brady heard the click of the lock twist behind him.

Brady left the jail and drove to the nearest grocery store. Taking Roscoe's advice, he bought all the Twizzlers they had. He laid them on the Explorer's passenger seat and headed toward the sprawling brick courthouse on the corner.

"Hey, Chief."

"Hey, Glenda." Brady nodded at the county clerk.

She looked at the box in his hand and laughed. "Going to see Mole, I gather."

Brady forced a smile. His head pounded and he felt a little queasy. "How'd you guess?"

She rolled her eyes. "Old Mole's all right. Just a little . . . odd."

"How do you mean?"

She opened her pink lipsticked mouth, frowned, then shook her head. With a wave of her hand, she said, "You're about to see for yourself, hon."

The elevator doors dinged open and Brady pressed the button to take him to the basement.

He'd expected a dark, dingy room stacked to the ceiling with dusty files. When then elevator doors swung open, he had to shield his eyes against the bright glow of the fluorescent lights.

Black dots danced in front of Brady's eyes and it took him a moment to focus on the short, curly-haired man behind the desk.

He shot Brady an annoyed glance and asked, "Can I help you?"

Brady glanced at the long, neat rows of files and felt a glimmer of hope. He felt a little stupid standing there with his boxes of candy, so he laid them on the desk. He felt even more stupid when Mole glanced at them and lifted an eyebrow.

"I'm Brady Simms. The new—"

"—Chief at Coalmont," Mole interrupted, waving his hand. "Yeah, yeah. I know who you are. What I don't know is what you want."

"I need a 911 tape."

"Date, place, and time," Mole said.

Brady rattled off the information. To his relief, Mole didn't blink when he told him it was four years ago.

"I don't know if I have it or not. That's pretty old. Is it an ongoing investigation?"

"No, but it's being reopened. The criminal case has been decided, but the civil case is coming up next week."

"I'll look it up for you and give you a call. How's that?"

Brady hesitated. "I was hoping you could do it now."

"I can't do it now." Mole slapped a thick folder in front of him. "Got this many requests in front of you."

"Maybe you could show me where the tapes are and I could look myself." Brady could tell those were the wrong words as soon as he saw the look on Mole's face.

"Nobody back there but me . . . ever. But I'll get to you tomorrow, maybe the next day. Take it or leave it."

Brady sighed. "I'll take it. But please hurry. It could be a matter of life and death."

"Yeah, yeah, and so's my getting my supper. I have a life outside this room, you know."

Brady glanced down at his watch, surprised.

Charity. He was late for supper at Charity's.

"Uh, thank you. I appreciate it," he told Mole and hurried back to the elevator.

He was nearly twenty minutes late by the time he got back into Coalmont, so he didn't bother going home to change out of his uniform. After a quick call to check in with the dispatcher, he bounded up the steps to Charity's apartment.

She swung open the door at his knock. Her dark eyes flashed at him and he knew he was in trouble.

"Bread, wine?" she asked curtly, and it took him a moment to realize what she was talking about. He'd forgotten to pick them up.

"No," he admitted, and thought for a second she was going to slam the door in his face.

"I'm sorry," he said. "It got busy, and I forgot."

She sighed and grabbed his hand. "Come in. Guess it will be sweet tea and Wonder Bread, then."

Brady shuffled inside her tiny apartment and nodded at Kristi and Howard, who were sitting on the couch. Kristi returned his wave, and he took that as a good sign.

"Sorry, guys," he said. "I got caught up in a big case and lost track of time."

Charity shot him a sharp look and he saw the jealousy on her face.

"And what is a big case in Coalmont?" Howard asked. "Helping Farmer Jones herd runaway cows?"

Brady gritted his teeth. He wasn't in the mood for Howard's thinly veiled snobbery, and he wasn't in the mood to defend himself to Charity either. "Actually, it's a murder investigation. I've been at the courthouse, looking up records." Brady sank into the chair beside the couch.

"Wow," Howard mused. "A murder. What was it, one of those redneck squabble things?"

"No." Brady leaned back in this chair and wished for this night to pass quickly.

"Come on, Kristi," Charity said. "I'm starving. We can gossip while I throw the salad together."

Brady sent her a pleading look, but she merely smiled. She knew he hated being left alone with Howard, but she was too mad to care.

Luckily, conversation with Howard didn't require a lot of talking. In fact, Brady could usually get by with a few mumbled "uh-huhs" and maybe a nod or two when Howard paused for air.

He was talking politics now, a subject that bored Brady in the best of company. He smiled and nodded, but his mind went back to Nat's case. While he mulled over the possible motives, something Howard said filtered through his thoughts.

"What did you say?" he asked, and leaned forward.

"What, about the senator's plane crash? I said they still haven't found the black box, but I doubt they ever will, it being in the middle of the ocean and all."

Black box.

The idea hit Brady like a lightning bolt. He sprang to his feet, ignoring Howard's startled look.

"Excuse me," Brady said. "I'll be right back."

He nearly ran to Charity's bedroom and booted up the computer she kept in a corner of the room.

"Please, please, please," he whispered as he typed a query into an internet search engine. His face broke into a huge smile when he saw the results.

This could be it.

Nat's Camaro had been equipped with an event data recorder under the center console. Attached to airbag modules, the EDRs were still new enough four years ago that probably no one had thought to check it. EDRs record information about the crash such as speed at impact, whether or not brakes were applied, and whether or not anyone was wearing seatbelts. If his hunch was right, he bet the EDR would show none of the Camaro's passengers were wearing seatbelts that night.

Brady dug his cell phone out of his pocket and called Nat.

"Hello?" Her voice sounded sleepy and smoky and he had to push an irreverent thought from his mind.

"The car, Nat. Where's the car?"

"What?" She yawned. "Brady, is that you?"

"Yeah, it's me. Where is the Camaro?"

"I don't know. Daddy knows, I think—"

"Find out. I'll be there in a minute." He hung up without waiting on her response. Next he called the office and asked the dispatcher where the closest EDR reader was. After a couple of minutes of searching, she came back to him with a Chattanooga address. Brady hung up the phone and turned. He found himself staring into Charity's furious face.

"First you show up late, you don't bring what you're supposed to, and then you ditch Howard to play on the computer. What's your problem, Brady?"

His problem. Looking into Charity's dark eyes, he saw his problem right away. Not once in his grand quest to save Nat had he thought about the implications of his investigation.

By absolving Nat, he would be implicating Charity's brother.

He hadn't thought of Charity at all.

Indecision tore at Brady. He should tell Charity what he suspected, should brace her for what he thought was coming, but the practical side of him whispered "wait." Wait until he knew for sure. Or maybe it was the cowardly side of him, because he dreaded the fight that was to come.

He grasped her shoulders and gave them a little squeeze. "Honey, I'm sorry," he said. "I know I've been caught up in this case lately—"

She jerked away and presented him with her back. "Caught up in Nat, you mean."

"No," he said. "No."

Brady wrapped his arms around her waist and pulled her to him. He buried his face in her blond hair. "Don't be mad at me, but I have to go," he whispered.

She exhaled in protest and tried to pull away. Brady wouldn't let go. "The sooner I get this case wrapped up, the sooner things can get back to normal between us."

"And you'll be able to walk away from Nat?"

Brady made her turn to face him. "Yes."

He wanted Charity to see that he meant it. After this case, he'd have no reason to see Nat again. The thought caused mixed feelings of relief and dread, but he knew things could never work between them. He couldn't live through that hurt a second time around.

Charity sighed, then lay her head on his chest. Brady stroked her hair.

"Go. Do what you need to do. I trust you," she said.

He kissed her forehead and she pushed away, offering him a faltering smile. "Oh, and before I forget . . . your mom called. She didn't want to bother you at work, but she wanted us to come for a cookout tomorrow if you could. What do you want me to tell her?"

"What time is it?"

"She said around noon."

"Tell her we'll be there. Pick you up around a quarter till?"

Charity nodded, then walked him out of the bedroom. Kristi and Howard sat on the sofa.

"Guys, I'm sorry, but I have to run. Howard gave me an idea about the case I'm working on and I need to follow up."

Howard's chest swelled and his face lit with a self-important smile, even though Brady knew he had no idea what he was talking about.

Brady returned the smile, but it felt tight and pinched on his face. No matter how hard he tried, it simply wasn't in him to like this guy. "Thank you, Howard," he said.

"Sure thing. Glad to help you work it out."

Charity kissed him goodbye at the door and the trusting look in her eyes cut Brady to the quick. When this investigation was over, he wondered if he'd lose her too.

Nat changed out of her nightclothes into shorts and a T-shirt and pulled on her sneakers. Her right ankle and foot were a little swollen, so she loosened the laces. She groaned when she looked in the mirror. What a wreck.

After yanking a brush through her tousled hair, she hobbled down the hall to her mother's bathroom. Borrowing some of the makeup that lay on the counter, she dabbed a little concealer underneath her eyes and swept blush on her pale cheeks.

Nat winced when she traced a line of strawberry lip gloss over her swollen bottom lip, then gave herself a critical look in the mirror.

Not great, but presentable. She limped downstairs to the living room, where her parents and the twins were watching a movie on television.

"I thought you were going to bed early," her father said.

"I was, but Brady just called. He's on his way over and wants to know where the Camaro is."

"It's at Clint Rooney's junkyard."

Nat sat on the couch beside her brother Matt. "You think it's still there after all this time?"

"Yeah. I thought it best if we kept it there until all the trials were over. I know Clint. He wouldn't have let anybody touch it without asking me first. Do you have any idea what Brady wants with it?"

Nat shook her head. "Nope. He didn't say, but he sounded like he was in a hurry." The doorbell chimed and she smiled. "Guess he was."

Matt jumped up to answer it. He returned a moment

later with a rumpled-looking Brady trailing behind. Matt sat on the floor by their mother's feet, but Brady didn't take the empty seat on the sofa beside her. He stood in the doorway, looking a little ill at ease. His eyes sought her out, but then looked away when he found her staring at him.

"I'm sorry to come by so late, but I've thought of something that might help our case. Do you know where the Camaro is?"

"Clint Rooney's junkyard," Nat answered. He nodded but didn't look at her.

"What are you thinking, Brady?" her father asked.

"There's a device in most of the newer model cars with airbags called an event data recorder. EDR. I checked the internet to see if that particular model had them, and it did. Nat's car has one underneath the center console."

"I've never heard of them." Her father leaned forward. "So, what does it record?"

Brady ticked the items off on his fingers. "Vehicle speed at time of impact, brake status, throttle position . . . lots of things. But the biggie for us is it records seatbelt status. I always thought it was strange that Nat was the only one wearing a seatbelt, but I thought maybe she was being careful because of the baby . . ." Brady flushed, and this time Nat looked away. It still hurt to think about that baby, the little girl or boy who would be starting preschool this fall if it had lived.

"You think no one was wearing seatbelts," her father

stated.

"I think it's worth checking out. And another thing . . . I think you should call your lawyer and get him to run another test on the driver side airbag. They've already analyzed the blood, but I want you to get a forensic biologist to check it for saliva. When the airbag inflated, it popped somebody right in the face. According to the report, there was blood all over the place, but I think the saliva would be more contained."

"Brady, you're amazing," Nat said, and the blush on his cheeks deepened.

"I'm heading to the junkyard now, so if you wouldn't mind giving Mr. Rooney a call to let him know I'm coming . . ."

"Sure. Let me grab a phonebook," Jake said, and hurried out of the room.

He was back in a moment, cradling a cordless phone to his ear while he rechecked the number. "He's not answering."

Brady cleared his throat. "I think I'll head over anyway. Maybe he'll be back by the time I get there."

Nat stood. "Wait up. I'll go with you."

"No, that's okay," Brady said quickly.

"I know Clint, and it'll save you a phone call when we get there."

"I don't mind a phone call." Brady gave her a pointed glance, but she ignored it and walked past him into the hallway. It hurt that he so obviously didn't want to be with her, but she wasn't going to let him push her away anymore. They needed time alone. Time to think. Time to talk. Time to fix what was broken between them.

Nat placed a hand on the doorknob and risked a glance back at him. His handsome face was troubled.

"Don't be a pill, Brady. Come on," she said with more casualness than she felt. Wandering outside without waiting on an answer, she walked down the driveway to the Explorer. Nat sat in the passenger seat without waiting for an invitation and hid her smile when Brady climbed in the driver's side a moment later. As he turned the key, she placed her foot on his dash and retied an errant shoelace. She smiled again when he sneaked a glance at her leg. He still felt it too. She knew he did. Brady scowled when he caught her stare and riveted his gaze to the rearview mirror as he backed out of the driveway.

Nat eyed his wrinkled uniform. "I'm sorry you're out so late because of this. Have you even been home yet? Have you eaten, because Mom made chili and—"

"I'm fine," Brady said curtly. "Look, I've had a rough day, and I'm not in the mood for chitchat."

"Okaaay." Nat rolled her eyes. "It's not like my day has been all hunky dory either. But I get it. You don't like me, and you don't want to talk to me."

When he didn't bother to answer, she crossed her arms over her chest. "I just thought we could try to work this out. I need to talk to you about Bobby—"

Brady shot her an incredulous look and made a

harrumph sound in the back of his throat. "I can assure you, the very last thing I want to talk about is Bobby McBee. And there's nothing to work out. I'm here. I'm doing what I can to help you. Let that be enough."

His words stung her. Nat's voice trembled when she said, "I wish you didn't feel that way."

Brady erupted. "How do you expect me to feel? I loved you. I wanted to marry you, and you left me for that . . . *scumbag*. What's worse, you made me believe you felt something for me too."

Nat stared at him, a little stunned by his fury. "I did—"

"Stop it!" Brady growled.

"If you'd let me explain—"

"If you had anything to tell me that would've made a difference, you should've said it four years ago. I don't want to hear it now."

Nat turned her face to the window, trying to hide the tears streaming down her cheeks. For what felt like an eternity, neither made a sound. Nat furtively wiped her eyes in the darkness.

Finally, Brady sighed. When he spoke again, his voice was quiet. Resigned. "Don't do that."

"Do what?" she asked, and even thought her voice sounded normal.

"Don't cry. I'm sorry. I don't want to hurt you, Nat, but I don't want to get hurt again, either."

"I didn't mean to hurt you."

"It doesn't matter. You did. It took me a long time to get over you, but I moved on."

Nat wanted to ask him what that meant, but they'd reached the junkyard. Brady put the Explorer in park and turned off the engine. He opened the door and stalked toward Clint's trailer without her.

She slowly climbed out and leaned against the front fender while he pounded on the door. After several moments, he turned back to her and shrugged in defeat. "Guess I'll have to come back tomorrow."

"Let's go look for it." Nat walked toward the gate to the junkyard and Brady sprinted to catch up.

"I don't think we should go in there. It's trespassing."

"Clint won't mind. I remember where it's at."

At least she hoped she did. Rows of cars stretched out endlessly before them, lit in the glow of the amber streetlights. Nat made her way down the middle, to where she thought she remembered seeing the wreckage of her car.

When she walked by the crumpled remains of a Ford Taurus, she heard it. The low growl caused the hair on her arms to prickle. A hulking black shape emerged from the shadows a few yards in front of her.

Her heart did a crazy stutter in her chest when the Rottweiler stepped into the light. His head lowered and his lips drew back in a snarl, revealing astonishingly long incisors that gleamed in the light. His ears flattened against his head.

Nat tried to call Brady's name, but all that emerged was a strangled whisper as her lungs emptied.

The dog charged.

CHAPTER 6

"GET ON TOP OF THE CAR!" BRADY SHOUTED.

Nat obeyed him instinctively. She threw herself on the Taurus and scrambled up onto the roof seconds before the big dog struck the hood. His claws shrieked across the metal when he slid back down. Immediately, he threw himself at the hood again.

"Shoot it, Brady!" she screamed.

"I can't see it," he yelled back.

Nat could barely see the dog at the edge of the shadows. Brady shouted at it from somewhere behind her, but it seemed intent on her. She tensed when it tensed, anticipating its attack.

Something hit the side of the car like a wrecking ball. The movement caught her off-guard and Nat nearly toppled over the side as the weight of a second dog rocked the car.

"There's two of them!" she cried.

She heard a dull thump-thump behind her and dared a glance over her shoulder at Brady, who was jumping from car to car, moving toward her.

"I'll distract them and you run for the gate," he shouted.

"I can't. My ankle . . . I can't run."

He swore under his breath. "Move two cars back. There's a stack of them three high."

Brady seemed to have the dogs' attention at last. He stood on the hood of a twisted Grand Am, dangerously close to the snarling beasts. Nat's breath caught in her throat when one of them threw itself at the car.

"Move!" Brady shouted, and scrambled up the car as the dog clamored after him.

Nat launched herself at the car behind her and cried out when she landed on her sore ankle. The dog still on the ground raced toward her. Moving faster than seemed possible for such a big animal, it sank its teeth into her sneaker and jerked her down the hood with one savage yank.

She kicked at the animal with her injured foot and screeched when a white-hot jolt of pain darted up her leg. The dog never hesitated. It jerked its massive tan and black head back and forth so violently she thought it was going to rip her foot from her leg.

Her shoe popped off, startling them both. The dog did a back flip over the hood. Fueled by terror, Nat took advantage of its momentary confusion to jump to the stack of cars behind her. She hooked her hands around a twisted bumper. The metal groaned and shook when she scaled the pile.

"Are you okay?" Brady shouted.

"Yeah." Nat squeezed her eyes shut while the dog stood on its haunches, trying to snap at her feet. At least she hoped she was okay. She didn't know if the cars were moving or if it was just her head spinning. Nat screamed when the dog landed a particularly brutal blow, but when she opened her eyes, she realized it was Brady. She latched onto his arm and tried to pull him up with her. He yanked his feet up just before they were caught in a pair of snapping jaws.

Brady's arms closed around her while they huddled atop the stack of cars. The blood roaring in Nat's ears deafened her, but she felt Brady's heart thumping against her shoulder when she leaned against his chest.

The humor in his voice surprised her when he said, "Well, here's . . . another nice mess . . . you've gotten us into, Stanley."

Nat giggled, then made a stab at sounding indignant. "Me? This was your road trip, Ollie." She poked at his holster and glared up at him. "Why didn't you shoot the stupid dogs?"

"Because I didn't want to risk shooting *you*, then there's the fact that we're trespassing. I didn't want to shoot a man's dogs on his own property if I didn't have to."

Nat glanced down at the hulking creatures. "Those are not dogs," she muttered. "They are the hounds of hell."

One of them still snarled and snapped, but the other lay beside the cars, contentedly chewing on Nat's sneaker.

"Those were my favorite running shoes," she whined.

"You're lucky you still have a foot to run on. Let me see that ankle."

Nat winced when she moved her leg from underneath her. The Rottweiler lunged in the air, snapping at her foot when it passed over its head. Nat jerked, and Brady's arm flew back to her waist, steadying her.

"Easy," he whispered, his breath stirring her hair. "It can't get to us up here."

He gently tried to wriggle her shoe off, but her foot was so swollen he had to pull hard to get it to budge. He inspected her ankle, gauging her face for reaction while he poked and prodded.

"I don't think it's broken, but we'd better swing by the emergency room on the way back."

Nat raised an eyebrow. "So, you're assuming we're actually going to get out of here?"

Brady's mouth quirked. "Well, yeah. Sooner or later."

Nat closed her eyes. Now that she didn't seem to be in imminent danger of becoming a doggie snack, she liked where she was, right beside Brady.

The slight breeze carried the sweet, musky scent of Brady's cologne mingled with his sweat. It stirred her senses, reminding her of the night they'd made love, of how he'd felt, how he'd tasted. His hand still rested on her bare ankle and suddenly his touch seemed to burn. She wanted more. She wanted everything.

Nat watched the throbbing pulse in his neck for a moment before she pressed her mouth to it.

Brady groaned and made a feeble attempt to push her away. "Nat, don't," he said.

"Don't you like this anymore?" she whispered and trailed her lips along his jaw line. The faint growth of his stubble tickled her lips while she made her way to his ear. He groaned again when she caught his earlobe between her teeth.

"Don't," he said again. "Stop."

"Don't stop?" she teased, and laughed softly. She unbuttoned the first two buttons on his shirt and slipped her hand inside to caress his warm chest.

Brady caught her wrist. "Nat, there's someone else."

The words hung in the air, but for a moment, Nat could make no sense of them. Brady was hers. He'd always been hers. He couldn't belong to someone else.

She couldn't really have lost him.

Nat gasped and jerked her hand away. She buried her face in her hands, hiding behind a wall of dark hair. She didn't want to see him. She didn't want him to see her. She couldn't look in Brady's eyes and listen to him say he was in love with someone else.

His hand cupped her shoulder and she jerked away.

"Nat, I—"

"Who is she?" Nat demanded while hot tears scalded her eyes. "Do you l-l-love . . ." Her tongue stumbled over the word and she couldn't force it out.

"You chose Bobby," he said defensively. "What did you expect me to do?"

He was right, she knew he was right, but that didn't make it hurt any less. She felt like throwing herself to the damn dogs.

"What's going on out here?" someone bellowed, and she and Brady both jumped.

"Over here!" Brady shouted.

Nat glanced over her shoulder to see Clint Rooney stalking in their direction, a shotgun in his hand. The dogs ran to meet their owner, sniffing at his hands and acting as harmless as kittens. Clint shone a flashlight first on Brady and then on her.

"Jake Junior, is that you?" he asked, calling her by the nickname he'd called her since she was a little girl.

"Yeah, it's me." She swiped at her eyes and attempted to sound light. "Nice beasts you have there, Mr. Rooney."

"My boys didn't hurt y'all, did they?"

"We're fine," Brady said.

"You can get down. They won't bother you now that I'm here."

Brady climbed down first. The dogs tensed beside Mr. Rooney.

"Timex, Rolex, down," he said mildly, and they immediately sat.

Brady laughed, and Nat wondered what he found so funny. Brady reached out his hands for her and his blue eyes sobered when they searched her face.

"Timex. Rolex. Watchdogs, get it?" he said lamely, but he looked away when fresh tears sprang to her eyes.

Nat ignored his hands and started climbing down the old wrecks. Brady caught her around the waist and swung her down anyway.

"Sorry we were trespassing, Mr. Rooney," he said. "I'm Brady Simms, police chief at Coalmont. We need to get something off Nat's car."

"No problem. I'm only sorry I wasn't here sooner. You been, uh, hung up there long?"

"Not too long," Brady said.

He glanced at Brady's gun. "Thank you for not shooting my dogs."

Nat took a limping step toward Mr. Rooney, needing to put a little distance between her and Brady.

"Jake Junior, what happened to your shoes? And why are you limping?" the junkyard owner asked.

"I hurt my ankle this morning and there's my shoe." She pointed at the tattered sneaker one of his "boys" had just picked up.

Mr. Rooney shifted his toothpick in his mouth and grinned. "You want it back?"

Doggie drool gleamed off the white leather in the moonlight and Nat made a face. "No thanks." She tossed the good shoe to the other dog. "Here, have one too."

She didn't look at Brady when she tucked her arm in Mr. Rooney's. He patted her hand when they started walking and warned her to watch out for broken glass. Nat answered the polite inquiries about her family and asked after his, but inside she was dying.

Was Brady's lover a brunette? A redhead? Was she someone like Brady, or someone more like herself? How had they met? What did they talk about? Did he love her? Did he *need* her?

The questions raced through her head in a dizzying jumble. Clint Rooney stopped and Nat found herself standing in front of the twisted wreckage of her car. While she stared at the twisted, rusting metal that had once been gleaming and black, she wondered how any of them had gotten out alive. Tears threatened to spill again when she thought of Jen, one of the sweetest people she'd ever known. It wasn't fair someone like Jen had died, and someone as worthless as herself had lived.

Brady pushed inside the driver's seat, no easy feat since the front of the car had been nearly smashed into the cab, and started working on the center console. Vaguely, she heard him tell Clint what he was looking for, but she wasn't really paying attention. Taking care not to get too far from Mr. Rooney, she limped around the side and peered in through the broken rear glass.

Foam protruded from savage tears in the leather upholstery. Dark crimson streaked the yellow and Nat hugged herself when she realized it was blood. Reed's blood . . . Bobby's . . . maybe even her own.

Suddenly, none of this seemed to matter. So what if she wasn't driving? It was still her car. Still her fault.

"Got it," Brady said, and held up a dented gray box. When he withdrew from the front seat, he paused to inspect the driver seatbelt. He pulled it out and it snapped back like new.

They thanked Mr. Rooney, who walked them back to the gate. Nat flinched when she stepped from the cool grass of the junkyard to the sharp gravel. She stifled a laugh when she saw the "Beware of Dog" sign she'd missed earlier. Amazing how much trouble you could get into when you didn't pay attention.

She climbed into the Explorer and laid her head against the seat.

Brady got in the other side and closed his door. "Are you okay?" he asked softly.

"I'm fine." Nat gestured at the box in his hand. "When do we find out what's on that thing?"

"I was hoping tonight. There's a reader in Chattanooga. I was planning on going right now, but I'll take you home first if you want—"

"No, go on. Chattanooga's only forty minutes from here." She squinted at him. "That is, if you're not sick of being stuck with me."

"Nat—"

"Never mind." She waved her hand. "I retract that statement on the grounds I'm tired and I don't want to fight with you. I'm just going to rest my eyes."

"Do you want to stop by the ER and check out your ankle?"

Nat shook her head no. Brady flipped on the radio and scanned the stations before stopping on her favorite oldie's station. Tears burned behind her eyelids while she listened to Sam Cooke beg his lover to return to him.

She had so many questions to ask Brady, but she wasn't sure she could bear to hear the answers to them tonight. An eternity passed before the Explorer turned and rolled to a stop. Nat kept her eyes closed, feigning sleep.

She felt Brady's gaze, then his touch as he brushed a lock of hair out of her face.

"God help me," he whispered. "How am I supposed to forget about you?"

Nat froze and that stupid spark of hope in her chest flared to life again. His hand lingered in her hair for a moment, then she heard his door slam shut and the door locks click in place.

She did doze while she waited on him to return and nearly screamed when he opened the door.

"Sorry," Brady said.

Nat sat up and pushed her hair behind her ear. "What did they say?"

Brady sighed. "They said call back tomorrow afternoon. Apparently, only one guy in the place can read the results and he won't be back until tomorrow at three.

"Oh." Nat twisted to stare at the imposing brick building, but she turned back when Brady touched her bare knee. She glanced down at his long, tan fingers and Brady snatched his hand away.

He looked flustered when he said, "Let's get you to a hospital now and have that ankle checked out."

"Really, it's fine. Just take me home."

They didn't talk much on the way home, and Nat figured it was probably for the best. She laid her head back against the headrest and stole glances at Brady from the corner of her eye.

She hoped whoever he was seeing could appreciate what she had.

When they reached her parents' house, lights still blazed through the living room window. Nat refused Brady's offer to help and limped up the yard. Her father met them on the front porch. He cast an alarmed glance at her bare feet.

"Where are your shoes?" he asked.

Nat made a face. "I'll tell you tomorrow. I'm wiped out." She pasted on a smile and turned to Brady. The sight of him underneath the streetlight, looking so rugged and handsome, was enough to steal her breath.

"Thanks, Brady. See you later."

The corner of his mouth twitched and he stared down at his shoes. "See ya Stanley."

Nat smiled and limped into the house. She shut the front door behind her, leaving her father and Brady talking.

After a quick shower, she didn't bother to dry her hair before collapsing on the bed.

Nat slept late the next morning, unusual for her, and might've slept all day if her mother hadn't banged on the door to tell her Alisha was there.

"Tell her to come up here," Nat yelled, then groaned

as she sat up. She hadn't been this sore since the accident. Her muscles protested when she swung her legs over the side of the bed and tested her ankle.

Not too bad. She could walk.

She was rummaging through her closet when Alisha strolled in, eating an apple.

"You look like crap," her friend said unceremoniously and flopped across the foot of the bed.

"Gee, thanks," Nat mumbled.

Nat skinned out of her nightshirt and pulled on a red halter top and pair of denim shorts. She groaned again when she looked into her dresser mirror.

Pathetic. Getting worse all the time. She knew better than to go to bed with wet hair. It stuck up in wild clumps and odd bumps all over her head.

"So . . ." Alisha grinned. "You gonna tell me what happened or not? I tried to call you last night, but your mom said you were out riding around with Brady. Fred and Daph, searching for clues."

"Yeah, well, the dogs we ran into sure weren't Scooby and Scrappy."

Alisha snickered when Nat told her what happened. Then she covered her mouth and laughed again. "Sorry, but you can get into more trouble than anyone I know. So, what happened then? You and Brady on the car. He had to talk to you, right? Did you tell him how you feel?"

Nat sat on the edge of the bed and stared down at her hands. "He didn't give me the chance. He told me he was seeing someone else."

"Oh, honey!" Alisha said, her eyes wide and sympathetic.

Nat blinked back tears and looked away when Alisha squeezed her hand.

"How serious are they?"

"I don't know." Nat sniffled and rubbed the bridge of her nose. "But Brady doesn't do anything halfheartedly. I can't imagine him being casually involved with someone."

"But you don't—"

"Girls!" Nat's mother rapped on the door and stuck her head inside. "Sorry to interrupt, but I wanted to make sure you invited Alisha to the cookout."

Nat frowned. "Cookout?"

Selena crossed her arms over her chest. "Remember, I told you yesterday morning?"

"Sorry . . ."

"Eliot and Kelly are having a cookout in . . ." She glanced at her watch. "Half an hour. They invited all of us and Alisha, you're invited too. When Eliot does one of these things, he invites the whole block. I'm going downstairs to finish up the potato salad, so you girls hurry up. Nat, see if you can do something with that hair."

Nat stuck out her tongue and her mother laughed before she shut the door.

"I can't go." Nat buried her face in her hands. "Eliot and Kelly are Brady's parents. He'll probably be there with his girlfriend."

"All the better to check out the competition," Alisha said, and Nat peered at her.

It was tempting. To see Brady with this woman, to see how they acted with one another.

"Will you go with me?" she asked, and pulled her hair back in a ponytail.

Alisha smiled. "I got your back, girlfriend."

BRADY ARRIVED AT CHARITY'S EARLY, HOPING TO MAKE amends. He needed to spend time with her, to reconnect, because all the time he'd spent lately with Nat had left him disoriented and confused. He needed to keep reminding himself what was real and who he could trust. Nat had already proven it wasn't her. Still, every time he closed his eyes, he remembered the feel of her lips on his neck and her throaty laugh when she said, "Don't stop?"

God, but he hadn't wanted her to stop. He'd dreamed about her last night, and had woken sweaty and shaken. And feeling so damn desperate for her. Now, looking into Charity's trusting brown eyes, he felt like a jerk.

"So, how did it go? Learn anything new?" she asked and motioned him toward the couch.

"Don't know yet." Brady kissed her cheek before flopping onto the plush white cushions. "So, what did

Howard and Kristi have to say after I left?"

Charity picked a piece of lint off his T-shirt. "Kristi said you looked tired. She's afraid you're working too hard. And Howard . . ." She waved her hand. "Howard talked about what he usually talks about—Howard."

Brady grinned. "So sorry I missed that."

Charity rolled her eyes. "Liar."

"Well, I'm sorry I missed dinner with you." Almost on cue, his stomach rumbled and they laughed.

"When's the last time you ate?" she asked. "I could get you something . . ."

"Sometime yesterday morning, I think, but I'm saving myself for Dad's barbecue chicken. Which reminds me . . . do you mind if I invite someone to come to the picnic with us?"

He caught the wary look in Charity's eyes before she replied, "Sure."

Brady picked up the phonebook, then dialed the Donally house. Someone picked up on the second ring but didn't say anything.

"Hello?" Brady said.

"Who is this?" Rachel Atkinson demanded.

"Uh, it's Brady Simms, ma'am. Can I—"

"Did something else happen?" she screeched, and Brady winced at the blast in his ear.

"I just called to talk to Reed," he evaded. He felt guilty about not telling her about the attack on Nat, but the woman didn't sound like she could handle any more bad news. Better to tell Reed first and let him handle it.

The line fell silent for a long beat and Brady almost thought she'd hung up on him when she yelled, "Reed, telephone!"

Brady heard the click of the extension when Reed picked up. He said, "Got it, Mom," and then gave a muffled hello.

"Hey," Brady said. "What are you doing?"

"Brady!" Reed sounded pleased. "Ah, you know, man . . . doing cartwheels, running marathons, that sort of thing. Same old, same old . . . hey, can you hang on a sec?"

"Sure."

"Mom, you can hang up now," Reed said with a trace of annoyance.

Immediately, the phone clicked, and Reed sighed. "Sorry, man. The stalker called again this morning, and Mom's flipping out."

Brady frowned. "Nat was attacked yesterday while she was out jogging."

Charity's head whipped around. Brady glanced at her as Reed exhaled into the phone.

"Is she okay?" Reed asked.

"Yeah, she managed to fight him off."

"Don't tell Mom, okay? I don't know how much more of this she can take."

Brady forced himself to sound cheery. "That's why I'm calling. How would you like to get out for awhile?

Dad's having a barbecue and I'll be glad to swing by and pick you up. Your mom is welcome, too, if she wants to come."

"Really? That would be great. Are you sure your dad wouldn't mind?"

"I'm positive. Can you be ready in half an hour?"

Reed laughed. "You kidding? I'm so sick of this place. I'm ready now. Get me out of here, man."

Ten minutes later, Brady pulled up to the sprawling house. He was glad he'd brought his car, which would be easier to help Reed into than the Explorer. Charity moved to the back seat while Brady went to ring the doorbell.

He leaned closer when he heard the raised voices coming from the other side of the door.

"Fine. Okay!" Reed shouted and threw open the door.

Brady stepped back.

"Sorry, man." Reed wiped a hand down his face and looked over his shoulder. His mother stood in the living room entrance with her arms crossed over her chest.

"Hi, Mrs. Atkinson."

She acknowledged Brady's greeting with a slight dip of her chin, and Brady glanced back at Reed. "So . . . are you ready to go?"

Reed scowled at his mother and jerked his head. She disappeared through the doorway, but Brady bet she hadn't gone far.

He saw the frustration in Reed's blue eyes when he

said, "Sorry to get you out here for nothing, but I can't go. I appreciate the offer, but Mom's pitching a fit."

"Do you want me to talk to her?" Brady said quietly. "Like I said before, she's welcome to come too."

Reed shook his head and ran his hand over the dark stubble on his chin. "Naw, man. You can't talk to her when she's like this. She's afraid to leave the house. I'll just take a rain check, okay?"

Brady smiled and clamped a hand on Reed's shoulder. "Sure. Maybe I can stop by soon, kick your butt at chess."

Reed snorted. "That'll be the day. But yeah, I'd like to see you try."

He shut the door. Brady stared at it for a moment, wishing he could do something. Then he realized he could. He had to find Bobby's murderer before he hurt Nat and Reed.

"WHOA, WHOA, WHOA!" ELIOT COMPLAINED WHEN NAT limped across the yard with Alisha and the rest of her family. "What's happened to my best shortstop? I was hoping we'd get up a game later."

"I twisted my ankle. Guess I'm on injured reserve," Nat answered, and stretched to kiss his cheek. "Good to see you."

Brady's father hugged her and kissed the top of her head. "Good to see you too, hon. I've missed you."

"Where's my hug?"

Brady's mother walked up beside them. "Hey, babe," she said, and held open her arms.

The sweet, familiar scent of her perfume reminded Nat of all the times she and Brady had sat in this woman's lap and listened to stories of princes and princesses and faraway lands. Nat wished for those days again, days when she still believed in happily-ever-after.

While her family mingled with the neighbors, Nat sat in a lawn chair, sipping a Coke and listening while Brady's dad regaled Alisha with tales of her childhood exploits.

"Be right back, ladies," he said while he set a plateful of cooked burgers on the table. "It's time to reload."

"Is Brady coming?" Nat asked, trying to sound casual.

Eliot Simms shot her an all too knowing look. "Yeah, hon. He should be here anytime."

No sooner had he disappeared into the house than the black car turned into the driveway.

Nat's heart gave a funny little flutter when Brady jumped out and strolled around the side to open the passenger door. She gasped when she recognized the tall blonde who stepped out.

"You've got to be kidding me," she muttered and jumped to her feet.

Nat gulped down the last of her soda and slammed the can on the table before she limped toward the car.

"Oh, no," Alisha said. "What's the matter? Where

are you going?"

Nat glanced back at her friend. The force of her anger surprised her. She'd prepared herself to see Brady with someone else, but not her. Not ever.

"Brady may never be mine again, but I'll die before I let that bitch have him."

"Oh wow, you got the Cuda fixed!"

Brady's head jerked up at the sound of Nat's voice.

"What's *she* doing here?" Charity hissed, as a smiling Nat headed straight for them. Alisha trailed behind.

Nat ran her hand along the gleaming black fender, and Charity gave an outraged gasp when Nat opened the driver door and climbed inside.

"What do you think, Nat?" his father called from the across the yard. "It only took us, what, eight years to rebuild it?"

"It's beautiful!" Nat yelled back at Eliot, who strolled over to join them.

Alisha asked his father something about the car, but Brady scarcely heard her over the pulse pounding in his ears. Charity tensed beside him and he had the feeling that all hell was about to break loose.

Brady didn't know where to look. His gaze flitted from Nat's grinning face to Charity's scowling one before finally landing on Alisha, who shot him a sympathetic smile. His dad seemed somehow oblivious to the developing firestorm.

"Hey, Brady," he said. "Why don't I get Jake to watch the burgers and we'll take the girls for a spin?"

Charity growled low in her throat and stalked toward the house. Brady stared helplessly at her retreating back.

"The keys are in it, Dad. Help yourself," he said, and chased after Charity.

Instead of joining the crowd that spilled from the side of the house to the back, Charity headed for the front porch. Brady caught her arm before she turned the corner.

"Charity," he pleaded. "Don't do this."

"Me?" She glared at him. "You didn't tell me *she* was going to be here."

"I didn't know. But she is, and we are. I can't control who my parents invite." Brady grasped her shoulders and she reluctantly met his gaze. "I'm here with you, not her. Let that be enough."

Charity stared into his eyes for a long moment, then exhaled. "Okay. Okay, but don't expect me to talk to her. I want nothing to do with that witch."

Brady wrapped his arm around her shoulders and she leaned into him. Her arm encircled his waist and they walked back to join the crowd. His car was gone.

They made small talk with his mother, and Brady had just begun to loosen up when his father pulled back in the driveway. Nat emerged from the passenger seat, laughing. He met her gaze for an instant, and her smile faded. For some stupid reason, Brady felt guilty when she looked away.

Brady tugged Charity along while he mingled with the guests, taking care to keep a safe distance between her and Nat. Just when he thought he was going to make it through the afternoon intact, Brady let himself get distracted. Mr. Watkins from down the street pulled him aside to complain about the high school kids playing music at the park after dark. Brady listened to him rant, and didn't realize until it was too late that his mother and Nat were only a table's length away.

"Nat, honey, you need to stay off that ankle," he heard his mother say. "You're limping."

"It's okay," Nat assured her. "I put ice on it after Brady and I got back last night, and it's not even swelled now."

"You were with her last night?" Charity asked loudly, and snatched away the hand Brady had been holding.

Conversation died around them and people stared.

Brady glanced at Nat over Mr. Watkin's shoulder and saw the horrified expression on her face. Her hand flew to her chest and inadvertently drew his gaze. Brady's eyes narrowed when he saw the tattoo peeking around the strap of her tank top, a tattoo that hadn't been there four years ago when they'd made love. He saw the B clearly, and the graceful curve of the y on the other side. Hatred erupted inside him, scalding his heart with bitterness. He couldn't believe she'd had that bastard Bobby's name engraved on her after all he'd done.

Brady almost forgot Charity was standing there until she snapped, "Answer me. Did you ditch my friends and me to be with her last night?"

Without a word, Brady turned and stalked toward the house. This time it was Charity chasing behind. She slammed the door behind them when they entered his mother's kitchen.

"Don't run from me!" she said.

Brady turned. Surprise flashed in her eyes when he shouted, "I've had *enough*!" He advanced on her and she backed into the door. "I'm working on a case, and there are times I have to see Nat. If you don't think you can trust me to get two feet out of your sight, then let's end this now."

"What?" Charity gasped.

"I'm tired of defending myself. Either you trust me or you don't. It's up to you. I've never given you a reason to doubt me, but if you can't trust me, we need to call it quits."

"But—"

"No buts. Either walk now or don't ever jump me about this again."

"You want me to break up with you, so you don't look like the bad guy," she accused. "You're looking for a reason."

Brady clenched his fists at his sides and tried to calm himself before he put one of them through his mother's wall. "No, I'm not. But you're making me feel like the bad guy already. I've told you a hundred times. I'm with you, not Nat. I don't want us to break up, but I'm sick of being interrogated."

For a long moment, neither of them spoke, then she whispered, "Okay."

"Okay what?"

"I trust you."

Brady held open his arms and she flew into them.

"I don't want to break up," she said.

"I don't want to break up either," Brady said into her hair. But he thought about the investigation and wondered if they could survive the fallout if he proved her brother was driving the car that night.

Standing there in his mother's kitchen, he nearly told her everything. Maybe he should have. But he thought about the skeptical look on Reuben Layne's face and decided to wait until he knew for sure.

Why should he put them both through hell before he knew the truth?

NAT SMEARED A SPOONFUL OF MAYONNAISE ON A BUN and wondered if she should try to find Brady and apologize. He probably thought she was a first class witch, but she hadn't meant to get him in trouble, not when he was trying so hard to help her. Yes, she'd let her temper get the better of her when he'd arrived with Charity, and she shouldn't have ridden in his car, but she honestly hadn't meant to rat him out about their trip to the junkyard. How was she supposed to know he hadn't told Charity?

She felt someone behind her and started to scoot down the line when Charity said, "Stay away from Brady."

"Or you'll what?" Nat asked quietly, as she speared a slice of tomato. "Make my life miserable? I seriously doubt there's anything you could do to make it any worse."

"And whose fault is that?"

Charity glanced furtively over her shoulder, as if to make sure no one heard. Probably looking for Brady, Nat thought, and wondered where he was.

"You killed my brother. You killed Melody and Jen. Do you think you deserve to be happy?"

Nat set down her plate and looked at Charity.

Brady hadn't told her. Charity obviously had no idea he suspected her brother had been the driver.

Instinctively, Nat knew she possessed the weapon that could destroy their relationship, especially if the news came from her.

And she couldn't use it.

She wanted Brady back, but she couldn't use the fact that he was trying to help her against him. If and when Brady felt the need to tell Charity, he'd have to be the one to do it.

Nat pushed a lock of hair behind her ear. "I loved your brother. I loved Jen. They were two of my best friends. I hadn't known Melody that long, but I would never have hurt any of them on purpose. It was an accident. Whatever happened that night was an accident."

"An accident," Charity sneered. "How fast did the prosecutor say you were going? Wasn't it around 90 miles an hour? That's no accident. I wish they'd charged you with murder."

Leaving her plate behind, Nat started to walk away. To her irritation, Charity trailed behind her.

"Did you know Brady has applied for FBI?" she asked.

"No."

"They do background checks on everyone around him. Do you really think it would look good for him to have a girlfriend with a criminal record?"

Stung, Nat replied, "My juvenile records are sealed."

"You think so? You don't think it will all come out with this investigation about Bobby?"

Alisha walked over and moved between them. "Is everything okay here?"

"Yes," Nat answered, looking at Charity. "We're all finished here."

BRADY SAT AT THE KITCHEN TABLE, NURSING A SOFT drink. He told Charity he'd come back outside in a few minutes, but honestly, he felt like hiding in here the rest of the afternoon. He'd finally gotten his life back on track after Nat left, but in a matter of days, it had been ripped apart again. He didn't know what to do, or what to think, and he most certainly didn't know what to feel.

He was involved with a woman who couldn't trust him and in love with one he couldn't trust. Brady laughed. Maybe he should forget both of them and start writing country songs.

He couldn't get the image of that tattoo out of his mind. What was so damn special about Bobby McBee that Nat had never been able to get away from him, even after all he'd done? What was so special about *her* that Brady couldn't do the same?

Someone touched his arm and he jumped. His mother smiled at him.

"I said, what's so funny?"

"Not a thing, Mom. Not a thing." Brady chugged the rest of his Coke and leaned back in the chair. "I didn't hear you come in."

"What's the matter, girl trouble?" she asked as she opened the refrigerator. "Do you want to talk about it?"

"Yes to the first one, no to the second."

She laid two packs of hotdogs on the stove and sat in the chair beside him. "Are you sure? I'm a really good listener."

Brady picked up her hand and kissed it. "I know you are. But it's too complicated. Too stupid."

"Brady," she said hesitantly. "All I want is for you to

be happy. I see the way you look at Nat. I think there was more to her decision to leave than you realize. You were both so young. She'd just been through a devastating situation. Now that she's back, maybe the two of you could talk—"

"No."

"Okay, I'll butt out." She smiled and gave him a wink. "In a minute."

Brady groaned and she smoothed his hair from his forehead like she'd done when he was a kid. "I don't mean to sound like I don't like Charity. I do. But I've always thought you and Nat belong together. We all think that. I remember you telling me when you were five that you were going to marry Nat one day. And even when you were babies . . . I know you already know all this, but it was all so strange. Nat arrived six weeks early. You were nearly three weeks overdue, and Selena and I ended up in the hospital at the same time. I wondered later if maybe you were simply waiting on Nat."

The comment irritated him. Made him realize how foolish he'd been most of his life, waiting on her to love him as much as he loved her, and it simply wasn't going to happen.

Brady cracked his knuckles. "I'm through waiting on Bobby McBee's leftovers."

He heard a gasp behind him and turned to see Nat peering at him through the open window. Her beautiful green eyes filled with tears.

"I . . . uh, Eliot said he's ready for the h-hotdogs," she stammered before she fled.

Brady swore and pushed away from the table. "Nat, wait!"

He burst out the back door, startling Charity and his dad, who stood by the grill.

"Nat!"

Nat was practically running across the yard, headed home. Her brother Matt followed on her heels, asking her what was wrong.

"Nat!" Brady yelled again. "Stop."

To his amazement, she did. She turned on him, her face red with fury.

"Bobby's leftovers?" she demanded. "You think *I'm* Bobby's leftovers? I don't guess your little girlfriend here told you about the time I caught her and Bobby making out under the bleachers at the homecoming game, did she?"

Brady whirled to look at Charity, who gaped at Nat.

"That's right," Nat said tearfully. "You can talk about me like I'm trash if you want, but I think she's the leftovers. At least Bobby came back to me for more."

She poked Brady in the chest with her fingernail. "I want you to remember something, Brady Simms. I might not have always made the best choices, but I've been with two men in my whole life. I doubt your little bleacher slut can say the same."

She turned to walk away again, and this time Brady

let her go.

He couldn't move, couldn't think. Something flashed by him and it took him a moment to process what was happening. Someone screamed Nat's name, but she didn't have time to react, either. Her head turned the instant before Charity jumped on her back and rode her to the ground.

CHAPTER 7

CHARITY SCREAMED OBSCENITIES WHILE SHE grabbed a fistful of Nat's hair and slammed her head into the grass.

Alisha shoved Brady aside and raced toward them. She grabbed Charity in a chokehold and yanked her off Nat.

Nat rolled onto her back and sprang to her feet. "Let her go!" Nat yelled. "She's mine."

"No!" Brady shouted, but Alisha released her hold on Charity and pushed her forward. Charity and Nat circled each other like boxers in a ring.

Although Charity stood half a foot taller than Nat, and outweighed her by probably twenty pounds, Brady knew at a glance that she was the one in trouble. He'd known Nat his whole life, and he'd never seen her so furious. Her green eyes glowed as vividly as the grass stain on her forehead.

Nat distracted her with a left jab, then threw a lightning fast right that connected solidly with Charity's nose. Charity staggered backward and cupped her hands over her face. Blood spurted through her fingers.

"Come on!" Nat screamed. "Come *on*!"

Before Charity could lunge again, Brady caught her around the waist and started dragging her toward the Cuda.

"Let me . . . go!" Charity yelled as she struggled against him.

Brady ignored her and nodded gratefully at Nat's brother Justin when he ran to open the passenger door. Unceremoniously, Brady shoved Charity inside and shut the door. She opened it again and he hissed, "Don't make this any worse. Stay in the damn car."

He shut the door again and this time she didn't try to get out. She popped open the glove compartment and grabbed a handful of paper napkins to press to her gushing nose.

"I'm sorry," Brady told the crowd. He glanced at Nat. "I'm so sorry."

She turned her head.

Brady ran around to his side and climbed behind the wheel. Charity started in before he could back out of the driveway.

"It's not like she said, Brady. I didn't—we didn't . . ."

Brady sighed. "Don't bother, okay? Just don't lie to me."

"What makes you think I'm the one who's lying?" she demanded, her voice muffled through the tissues. "She's only trying to break us up. Did you see the look on her face?"

"I didn't need to see her face." He exhaled and glanced over at her. "I saw yours."

Charity grunted. Tears sparkled in her eyes before she turned to look out the window. "I was young, okay, and stupid. Bobby was just . . ." She shrugged. ". . . Bobby."

Brady didn't ask her what the hell *that* was supposed to mean. He wasn't sure he wanted to know. There had to be something wrong with him, some deep, fundamental flaw he couldn't see. How else could he explain the fact the two women he cared most about had both slept with that loser McBee?

He pulled into the Ace Hardware parking lot. "Let me see your nose."

She dropped the sodden napkins in her lap and turned her face to him. Brady leaned over and cupped her chin with one hand. He tilted her face upward with one hand and gingerly inspected the bridge of her nose with the other. He felt her gaze upon him but refused to meet her eyes.

"Well, it's stopped bleeding," he said. "I don't think it's broken, but you should probably get some ice on it as soon as you get home."

He dropped his hand, but Charity caught his wrist.

"Can we talk about this?" Charity pleaded.

"What's to talk about?" Brady asked, as he tugged away and shifted gears.

"Don't let her do this to us. Yes, I had sex with Bobby . . ."

Brady clenched his jaw and waited for a red pick-up to pass before he pulled onto the highway. "I really don't want to hear this."

". . . but that's all it was, and it was a long time ago. I'm sorry it happened. I would change it if I could. Nat's not sorry for anything."

A headache pulsed behind Brady's eyes, making his left eyebrow twitch. He drove faster. Charity fell silent, watching him.

When he pulled up in front of her apartment, he didn't shut off the engine. "I'll call you later," he said.

"Will you?" she sniffed, with her hand on the door handle.

"Yes. I just want to be alone for a little while. Okay?"

"Okay." She gave him a little wave as she stepped onto the sidewalk and Brady returned it.

He'd told Charity he wanted to be alone, but he didn't. Not really. An idea formed in Brady's mind. He turned the car around and headed out of Coalmont. After calling in a pizza, he decided to call the station.

"What are you doing, calling in on your day off?" Roscoe chided. "You're supposed to be eating barbecue."

Brady's stomach rumbled. "Just making sure you didn't need me, because I'll probably be out of commission until tomorrow."

"Well, I think Mary Ann and I can hold down the fort. It's deader than four o'clock here. Have fun."

"Yeah," Brady mumbled as he hung up. "Lots of

fun today."

A few minutes later, he rang Reed Donally's doorbell.

Several long seconds passed before Rachel Atkinson swung open the door. "Yes?" she said, eyeing the pizza Brady held as if it might be a bomb.

Her haggard appearance again caught Brady off-guard. "I was looking for Reed," he stammered. "Is he around?"

"Of course he's around," she snapped. "Where else is he going to go?" She squeezed her eyes shut and rubbed the bridge of her nose. "I'm sorry. I didn't mean to bite your head off. Things have been . . . tense around here lately."

"Yes, ma'am. I understand."

She gave him a faint smile and motioned him to the elevator. "Reed just got out of the pool a few minutes ago. You remember how to get to his room."

"I think so." Brady grinned. "This is a huge house."

When he pressed the elevator button, Reed's mother said, "Brady, can I ask you something?"

"Sure."

"Why the sudden interest in Reed? Is it because of the investigation?" She frowned and chewed on her thumbnail. "I don't mean to be rude, but I don't know if you understand how desperately lonely Reed is. This has been so hard on him, and hardly anyone visits anymore."

The elevator dinged and the door swung open. Brady stuck his hand out to hold it open.

"Don't get me wrong. I'm glad you're coming, but

please . . ." She pushed her hair back from her forehead with both hands and smiled. "God, this sounds so overprotective . . . but please don't hurt him. Don't make him think you like him and then stop visiting when this case is over. If it's ever over. It would just kill him."

The anxiety in her eyes tugged at Brady's heart. The accident that had devastated Reed had nearly destroyed her too.

"I like Reed, Mrs. Atkinson. We weren't that close in high school, ran in different crowds I guess, but I want to be his friend now."

"Bless you," she whispered, and quickly left the room.

Brady rode the elevator to Reed's floor and wandered down the wide hallway until he found Reed's door. He gave it a soft knock.

"Come in," Reed called.

Brady stuck his head in the door and Reed paused toweling his sandy hair. "You look like hell," he said conversationally. "Something happen?"

Brady rubbed a hand down his face. "I brought the pizza. I need a friend and a beer."

Reed gave him a broad grin. "Then you've come to the right place, my man. Come on in."

Brady laid the pizza box on Reed's gray bedspread and sat on the end of the bed while Reed retrieved two longnecks from the mini fridge by his desk.

He handed one to Brady and twisted the cap off his. "So, what happened to the barbecue?" he asked, and took a long swig.

Brady snagged a piece of pepperoni pizza and passed the box to Reed. Between bites, he told Reed the story.

"Whooo weee," Reed said when Brady finished. "A real, live catfight, and I missed it." He shook his head. "That Nat was always a scrapper."

"I've never seen her so mad. When she jumped up like that, I was afraid she was going to take Charity's head off."

"So, Charity . . ." Reed frowned at the ceiling. "Charity who? Do I know her? I don't remember any—" His blue eyes widened. "Oh wait! Are you talking about Tony Franklin's little sister?"

"Yeah." Brady took another sip of his beer and watched Reed. Something about the sudden flush of his face and the way he looked away made Brady wonder if Charity had been one of Reed's many conquests too. He decided he didn't want to know.

Reed recovered quickly. He lifted his eyebrows and gave Brady a rueful smile. "So, what are you going to do now?"

Brady sighed. "That *is* the question, isn't it?"

Reed drained the last of his beer and wheeled himself to the refrigerator to get them both a second one, though Brady's was still half full.

Reed winced and shook his head. "The next time I start feeling sorry for myself, and my lack of female . . ." He lifted his eyebrows and grinned. ". . . *companionship*

... I'm going to think of you and be grateful I don't have to worry about that anymore."

"Companionship, huh?" Brady hid his smile behind the rim of the bottle.

"You like that word?" Reed twisted off his lid and tossed it at the garbage can. "Four syllables. Wouldn't my English teachers be impressed?"

Brady laughed. He leaned his head against the wall and closed his eyes. "So, come on, Dr. Donally," he joked. "Let's hear your advice."

Reed cleared his throat. "Ah, okay. I'll play devil's advocate here. Let's talk about Charity. Technically, it wouldn't be fair to break up with her just because she slept with McBee. That was before you, and you took Nat back knowing she'd done the same thing."

"I know. But the thought of it drives me insane. Sometimes I feel like every good thing in my life has been tainted by that bastard McBee."

"I'm sorry, man. I wish Bobby was here right now. I'd kick his ass for you." Reed thumped his fist in his palm and gave Brady a silly grin. "Well, I could run him over with this chair, anyway."

Brady held up his beer to salute the plan. "Appreciate it."

"Back to my analyzing . . ." Reed stroked his chin. "On the other hand, if you don't care about Charity, now might be the perfect time to cut her loose." He held up his hands as if to ward off Brady's protest, but Brady was too busy eating pizza to comment. "I know that sounds harsh, but take it from someone who knows: if there is something you want in this life, you need to go after it before it's too late. So many things I'd do different if I only had one more shot."

"Your life's not over, Reed," Brady said gently.

Reed shrugged and gave him a tiny smile. "The only one I want is."

Before Brady could reply, he slapped his armrests. "But enough about my miserable existence. We were talking about *your* miserable existence. If you want Nat, you need to get over all this Bobby stuff. Bobby's dead. Bobby's not coming back. But just in case there is such a thing as reincarnation, I'll smash every cockroach I see."

Brady laughed, and Reed's grin widened.

"So, what's it going to be?" he asked.

"I don't know." Brady stretched out on the bed and propped his head in his hand. "I don't know if I can be with her and know the only reason she's with me is that she can't be with him."

"I think you and Nat need to have a good, long talk."

"And have her tell me what? That she's sorry she couldn't love me like she loved the guy who cheated on her, who hit her and who. . ." Brady paused, realizing he was about to spill the whole thing.

"Who what?"

He couldn't tell Reed without proof, could he?

Reed made a face. "Ah, come on, man. Don't do

me like that. Mom does that to me all the time. It's irritating."

Brady stared at his hands. If he was going to be Reed's friend, he needed to tell him the truth, or risk blowing the whole thing like he was about to do with Charity. He sighed. "Reed, there's something I want to tell you about the wreck."

Reed's eyes lit up. "Oh, that reminds me. I have something for you too." He opened the drawer on his computer desk and started fumbling through a stack of papers. "Keep talking. I'm listening."

Reed extracted a black notebook and flipped it open. He looked up when Brady didn't speak. "What?"

Brady took a deep breath. "I was at Nat's the other day, doing some follow up questions on the murder. Dara McBee came by. She told Nat that the week before Bobby was murdered, he told her . . . "

Brady hesitated again and Reed laughed.

"Spit it out, man. I ain't got all day." He shrugged. "Well, maybe I do, but—"

"He told her Nat wasn't driving that night. He said Tony Franklin was."

Reed's eyes hardened and his face flushed bright red. "That's bullsh—" He shook his head violently and glanced at the window. "That's not possible."

"Maybe not, but you see why I have to check it out."

"She was found *belted behind the wheel*!" Reed stormed. "How do you explain that, Sherlock?"

"Maybe someone screwed with the scene," Brady said, realizing how stupid it sounded. He wished he never mentioned it.

"Tony and Jen died on impact. Mel died on the way to the hospital. I think I can vouch for Bobby on this one. There was no way in hell either one of us could've staged it."

"But what if someone else did?"

Reed dropped the notebook in his lap and threw his arms wide. "Why? Why would anyone do that?"

"Money. They knew they'd get a lot more money from suing Nat's family than suing Tony's."

Reed absorbed this and shook his head again. "No way, man. It was Nat. It had to be Nat." He toyed with a sliver of paper trapped in the metal spiral of the notebook and stared out the window. Then he lowered his voice. "What does Nat think?"

Brady rubbed the palm of his hand with his thumb. "She doesn't know what to think. She wants to believe it, but . . ." He fell silent when he noticed Reed was blinking back tears.

Reed wiped his eyes with the back of his hand and stared at the blank computer screen. "You know, ah . . . the last time I saw Nat, I cussed her out. She was in the mall with some girl, and she laughed at something the girl said." He frowned. "That laugh pissed me off. Who was she to be laughing, when I was suffering? I was recovering from another surgery that had wiped out all of the progress

I'd made in the last two years, and I'd just spent the last half hour listening to some jerkoff lecture me on the importance of following a bowel program so I wouldn't crap my pants like a baby, and she's out "shopping?"

"What happened?" Brady asked softly.

"I let her have it. I rolled up to her and called her every vile, horrible name I could think of. All the hate, all the pain, all the blackness I'd been feeling just poured out of me." The muscle in Reed's jaw worked furiously as tears spilled down his cheeks. "You should've seen her face. She didn't try to defend herself. She only stood there crying. She said, 'I'm sorry, Reed.' I told her I was sorry too. Sorry I'd lived, sorry she'd lived . . . I'll tell you how bad it was. Mom hates Nat more than anyone, but as I ranted at Nat, she laid her hand on my shoulder and said, 'Reed, that's enough.' But the thing was, when I watched Nat crying, I didn't feel any better. I felt sick. Nat was once my friend, and I said things to her that there was no coming back from. What if she wasn't driving that night? How can I live with that?"

"I'm sure Nat understands. Maybe you could talk to her—"

Reed's bedroom door burst open with such force it ricocheted off the wall and nearly slammed shut again. Brady was reaching for his gun when a furious Rachel Atkinson stalked inside.

Reed gaped at her. "Mom?" he asked. "What is it?"

She ignored him and shook her finger in Brady's

face. "How dare you! How dare you come into my house and fill my son's head with lies. I knew there was a reason you were coming around."

"How did you . . .?" Reed grimaced when he looked at the shelves built into headboard of his bed. Brady followed his gaze and saw the baby monitor, its LCD light glowing bright red. "You're spying on me?" he shouted.

"I'm looking out for you." She pointed at the door and glared at Brady. "Get out. Get out of here right now, and don't come back."

"You can't do that!" Reed said. "He's my friend."

"He is *not* your friend. He's using you. Can't you see that?" Rachel turned back to Brady, who was climbing off the bed. "Get OUT of my house!"

"Brady, wait!" Reed pleaded. "Mom, don't do this."

"I'll call you later," Brady said apologetically, and started toward the door.

"Don't call. Don't come back here," Rachel said. "Just leave us alone."

"Call me," Reed said adamantly. He picked up the black notebook and tossed it over his mother's head. Brady caught it with one hand, nearly ripping out one of the fluttering pages. He tucked it under his arm and shut the bedroom door behind him. Sounds of the argument between mother and son followed him down the hallway.

Brady got out of there as quickly as possible, though he hated to leave Reed. He'd call him later, when things settled down.

When Brady jumped off the porch and headed to the carport, he saw Dr. Atkinson leaning against his Jag. Brady started to approach him, figuring he'd better ask about the prescriptions before the man saw how upset he'd gotten his wife, but then he heard the doctor's muffled voice and realized he was talking on a cell phone. Brady didn't want to interrupt, and the doctor's back was to him, so he slipped by and kept walking.

A snatch of conversation carried to him anyway.

"You'll get your money," the doctor said. "Yes, but . . . I'm doing all I can, okay? Yes, I know . . . my stepson is supposed to be coming into some money soon, part of a settlement. I'll get you what I owe you. I need a little time. Okay . . . okay, I understand."

Brady ducked behind the hedge until he heard the front door shut. Then he climbed into the Cuda and drove back to Coalmont. Not knowing where else to go, he drove to Tracy Lake. He parked by the hiking trail and pressed the code to listen to his voice mail. Idly, he flipped open Reed's notebook as a recording of Charity's began to play.

"Brady, pick up the phone. Please? I'm sorry, okay? I'm—"

It was a list of suspects, Brady realized. He scanned the next few pages. Reed had compiled a list of suspects, starting with the family members of the dead teenagers. He had a surprising amount of info on each of them.

Jen's brother, Evan. Geez, was he really seventeen now? Charity's brother, Jimmy. Mel's mother . . . the list went on for six pages.

Brady flipped through them and realized he hadn't heard any of the messages he'd just played. He started them again, and the third one stopped him cold. He jerked the Cuda in gear and raced to Nat's house.

He pounded on her front door until she yelled, "Hold your horses. I'm coming!"

She threw open the door, took one look at him and tried to slam it in his face.

"Nat, wait!" He shouldered his way inside before she could stop him. Some of his excitement withered at the stony expression on her face. "We need to talk," he managed.

"I don't have time right now." She brushed past him toward the stairs. He caught her wrist and she reluctantly looked at him.

"Nat, I got the results from the EDR. No one in that car was wearing seatbelts at the time of the crash.

"BRADY!" SHE GASPED HIS NAME LIKE A PRAYER.

He smiled and held open his arms. Without hesitation, she threw herself into them. Brady hugged her fiercely and kissed the top of her head.

"You did it," she whispered against his chest. "You really did it."

Brady pulled back and cupped her face in his hands. For one breath-stealing moment, Nat thought he was going to kiss her, but then he frowned.

"I don't want you to get your hopes up yet. This might not be enough to get them to dismiss the lawsuit. I don't know if your lawyer told you, but civil cases are different than criminal ones because they don't have to prove guilt beyond reasonable doubt. They only have to show a preponderance of evidence, which means more likely than not. They could argue the EDR wasn't functioning properly, though the other data looks in line with what the accident investigators found."

Brady dropped his hands and Nat reluctantly relinquished her hold around his waist. "The EDR recorded the speed upon impact at 90 miles an hour. That's only a couple of miles per hour different than Reuben Layne's estimate."

Nat pushed her hair back from her forehead with both hands and gave him a shaky smile. "No matter what happens with the court case, just to *know* that I wasn't driving . . ." She sighed. "Well, what about Dara? I think she would testify on my behalf."

Brady shook his head. "Hearsay. Only a teenager's word that he ever said it. Besides . . ." His voice drifted off, and Brady stared out the window.

"Besides what?"

He jammed his hands in his pockets and stared at her. "I don't think the jury would believe her. Bobby lived with you. They won't buy that your . . . lover . . . would keep something like that from you."

He tripped over the word, and Nat felt a pang when she saw the way his face scrunched with distaste.

I'm through waiting on Bobby McBee's leftovers, he'd told his mother.

She'd been so elated by his news she'd forgotten the words he uttered a few hours ago. Now they seared her again. Brady thought she was trash, contaminated by Bobby's touch. His stinging appraisal hurt her worse than anything, because if anyone had ever believed in her before, it was Brady.

"You're probably right," she said stiffly.

Even though he'd made it clear he didn't want her back, she couldn't help but wonder what had happened between him and Charity after they left the barbecue. She decided to fish.

"Brady," she said. "I'm sorry I hit Charity—"

He snorted and she caught a hint of a smile before he dropped his head and studied his shoes. "You are not."

She laughed. "Okay, so I'm not. But I am sorry I embarrassed you. I shouldn't have jumped you in front of everyone—"

He waved her off. "I started it. I was out of line. Nat, I—"

"Brady!" her mother exclaimed from the kitchen

doorway. She wiped her hands on her apron and headed toward them. "I didn't hear you come in."

Brady smiled and turned to greet her, leaving Nat to wonder what he'd been about to say. To Nat's surprise, he caught her hand and squeezed her fingers. "Are you going to tell her, or should I?"

Her mother's eyes grew as big as saucers.

"EDR results!" Nat blurted, knowing from the look on her mother's face she expected a romantic announcement and hoping to cut her off before she said something that embarrassed them all.

"Oh." Disappointment flashed in Selena's eyes and Nat might've laughed if she hadn't been so worried that Brady had seen it too. Forget the fact that she was being sued, accused, and stalked; her mother's main concern was reuniting her with Brady.

"The EDR showed no one was wearing seatbelts that night," Brady said. He gave her fingers another squeeze, then released her hand and gave her mother the same 'but don't get your hopes up yet' speech he'd given her.

"It's all going to work out," Nat's mother said, shooting her a secretive smile. "I just know it is."

Uh oh. Nat knew Selena had been on the phone with Brady's mom all afternoon. She could bet those two were cooking up something.

As if to confirm her suspicions, Nat's mother snapped her fingers and started toward the living room. "Come on, you two. There's something I want to talk to you about."

She walked off without waiting on a reply and Nat groaned.

"What is it?" Brady whispered, and Nat shook her head.

"I have no idea. That's what scares me."

Her brother Justin dozed on the couch. In what Nat was sure was another calculating move, Selena hurriedly sat in the recliner. Nat and Brady were forced to sit together on the loveseat.

"I'm going to get to the point," Selena began, and Nat dug her fingers in the soft chair arm. She shot her mother a pleading look, which Selena ignored.

"Brady, I love you like you're my own child," she said. "I was so happy to see you this evening because I can't stand the thought of you and Nat fighting."

Brady shifted. "I'm sorry about that, Mrs. Hawthorne—"

"It's okay," she interrupted. "But I've been talking to your mother this evening, and well . . . we'd like to do something." She held up her hand as if to ward off any protests, but Nat was too horrified to speak. She couldn't look at Brady, but she suspected he felt the same way.

Selena's words came in a rush. "We were talking about old times and how much fun we used to have and we . . . we would like to throw you two a birthday party, like we used to do when you were kids. It doesn't have to be anything major, just cake and ice cream. Maybe a little music. We can have it at the community center, or here or wherever—"

"Mo-*oom*." Nat groaned and put her face in her hands. Her cheeks flamed hot against her palms.

Brady stunned her when he said, "Only if you make me a caramel apple cake like you used to."

"It's a deal!" Selena practically shouted. Justin mumbled something in his sleep and rolled over.

Nat peeked at Brady through her fingers. "You don't have to do this, you know. They *will* survive if you say no."

"It's okay," he said. "But I draw the line at costumes."

To Nat's astonishment, Selena whined, "But that's the best part. We were thinking maybe a Roaring Twenties theme . . . you know, gangsters and flappers. We've all been so tense lately. I think it would be fun."

"That does sound fun," Brady said. "But where do we get costumes?"

Nat couldn't believe he was actually considering it.

"You let Kelly and I handle that," she said. "Just say you'll come."

"I'll come," he said.

"Nat?"

She sighed and shrugged. "Why not?"

Her mother clapped her hands together. "Great! I'm going to call Kelly. We haven't planned a party together in ages. I've got the perfect centerpiece, and we can play all that old music Nat likes . . ."

All that old music Nat liked was from the fifties and sixties, but she didn't bother saying so because her mother wasn't listening. Selena jumped up and practically ran from the room to call Brady's mother.

Nat leaned her head back and smiled at him. "Thanks for humoring her. That was nice of you."

Brady winked. "Are you kidding? Your mother makes the best caramel apple cake in the world. Besides, when she and my mother get together, there's no stopping them."

She couldn't get over how relaxed Brady seemed. Had he broken up with Charity? Maybe it was time for more fishing.

"Tell Charity that I'll play nice if she does," Nat said lightly.

Brady's face remained impassive when he said, "I'll tell her." He stood. "Has your dad heard anything from the lab test on the airbag?"

Nat shook her head. "I don't think so. He called them last night and offered to pay more if they'd put a rush on it, but I don't know when they told him they'd have it ready."

"I'll be right back. There's something in the car I'd like to show you."

He returned with a black notebook. Resuming his seat on the loveseat, he handed it to her.

Nat tried to ignore the fact that his knee was touching hers. "What's this?"

"Reed's list of suspects."

Evan Jacobs.

The name jumped off the first page at her and she glanced at Brady. "Jen's brother? I don't think he could carry off something like that. He's angry at me, but I don't think he could kill anyone."

"Why do you say he's angry?"

Nat frowned and leaned against the cushion. "When I first got out of Cedar Ridge, I had to do some community service work as a condition of my release. I did a speech at the high school. I saw Evan right away. He glared at me from the first row for a few minutes, then stalked out. Bobby drove me to it. When we went back outside, the tires on his car had been slashed."

Brady stared off into space.

"What is it?" she asked, and he sighed.

"I have something to tell you, about who I think is doing all this, but I want you to read through the suspects and tell me what you think first."

"Charity, her brother, and father," she mused, flipping through the pages.

"As far as I know, her old man is still in prison. According to Reed's notes, he's been released, but I haven't had time to check it out. Charity has no contact with him. He was convicted of manslaughter a couple of years ago, killed a guy in a barroom fight. Her brother lives in Hamshire, Texas now."

"Melody's mother." The next name on the sheet

made her glance at him again. "The sheriff? I can't stand him, but he wasn't the man who attacked me in the woods."

"Could it have been Joe?" Brady asked, and Nat frowned.

"Joe who?"

"The sheriff's nephew. Mel's cousin."

"I don't even remember him. Would he attack a stranger?"

Brady shrugged. "Maybe on his uncle's orders. Look, Nat. I found out yesterday that the gun recovered in the woods was supposed to be in the evidence room at the county jail."

"What?" She frowned. "You found out *yesterday*, and you're just now telling me?"

"I'm sorry. So much was going on . . . but anyway, when I was at the jail raising hell about it, I saw Joe Richards. He's a county deputy. I think his nose was broken. Both eyes were black. The TBI guy, Ian Kirby, peeled me off him, but I accused both him and the sheriff."

Nat stared at him, speechless. Despite the gravity of the situation, she couldn't help the thrill she got when she thought about Brady defending her.

His ocean eyes studied her. As if he read her mind, he murmured, "I've always been with you, Nat."

Before she could reply, he took the notebook from her hands. "I'm not sure where this stuff with the wreck fits in. I'm not even sure if I think the same person committed both crimes. I talked to the first cop on the scene, and I think he's solid. I'm betting the person who made the 911 call is the person who staged the scene. It has to be someone in this notebook who figured they'd get more money if you were named the driver."

"Any way to find out who that was?"

"I've got a guy looking, but who knows if they've kept the records that long. I need to talk to Reed, see if he can tell me who was at the party, but his mom threw me out of the house tonight."

"What? His mom threw you out? Why?"

She must've looked like a gaping fish because Brady chuckled. "After I dropped Charity at her apartment, I went to Reed's. We were talking about the case, and his mom was spying on us. When I suggested to Reed that maybe you weren't driving, she overheard. She threw me out of the house and told me not to come back."

Nat made an effort to shut her mouth. She couldn't imagine Brady getting thrown out of anywhere. "Speaking of Reed . . . remember when you asked me about Dr. Atkinson? That's—"

"Reed's stepfather," Brady finished.

"Yeah. I don't know if it means anything, but when I checked the mail, I found his office number listed a couple of times on Bobby's last cell phone bill."

Brady frowned. "Martin Atkinson told me he'd seen Bobby twice on consult. He suggested Bobby might've stolen a prescription pad from his office a couple of months ago. Why would Bobby have called his office after that?"

Nat stared down at her hands. "Who knows? The more I hear about Bobby, the less I think I ever knew about him at all."

Brady jumped up like he'd been jolted from the chair. She'd said the wrong thing again.

"I've got to run," he said. "Call me when you get anything on the airbag."

"Will do," Nat said, but he was already walking away.

The front door shut a moment later. Troubled, Nat parted the curtains and watched until the black Cuda disappeared from sight.

The cordless phone on the coffee table rang and she hurried to grab it before it woke Justin.

"Hello?" She heard breathing over the line, but no one spoke. Nat gripped the receiver. "Who is this? What do you want?"

"I want to finish this," the man said gruffly. "Right now."

CHAPTER 8

"REED? IS THAT YOU?" HIS VOICE ROCKED NAT. IT had been so long since they'd spoken that her mind had filed his voice away with the others from that night, friends she'd never be able to talk to again. It felt like she was talking to a ghost.

"Yeah, it's me." His voice caught, and he cleared his throat.

"Are you okay?" she asked softly.

His muffled sob tore at her. "No," he rasped. "I'm not okay. I haven't been okay in a . . . a long time. Look, Nat, I know I don't have the right to ask, but I need to talk to you. Could you come over?"

Nat blinked. Whatever she'd expected, this wasn't it. "What about your mom? I know how she feels about me."

"She threw Brady out of the house today, and we had this huge argument. She took a couple of nerve pills, so she's probably crashed upstairs. She'll never know you're here."

Nat hesitated, a prickle of warning racing down the back of her neck. She kept seeing Reed's face that day in the mall, mottled with rage and hatred as he hurled curses at her. Could this be some kind of trap?

"Please, Nat."

No, it wasn't a trap. She refused to believe it. This was Reed. Her classmate, her friend, and he sounded like he needed her. For years, she'd prayed for a chance to make things right. Maybe this was her chance.

She took a deep breath. "I'm on my way."

After they hung up, she stared at the doorway for a moment, wondering how she was going to get there. She didn't even have a license anymore. Her parents wouldn't like the idea of her going to Reed's house, not with the case coming up, and Brady would probably think it was some sort of ploy to be near him. She picked up the phone and called Alisha.

"Hey, what are you doing?"

"Getting ready for work. How about you?"

"Do you think you could drop me somewhere on your way to work?"

"Sure. I was about to head out the door, so I can be there in ten minutes or so."

Nat jotted the number to a local cab company on a slip of paper and stuffed it in her pocket, then borrowed Justin's cell phone and watched for Alisha out the window.

When the little Mazda turned in the drive, Nat yelled, "Mom, I'm going with Alisha. Be back soon."

"Oh, okay," her mother called from the kitchen. "Where are—"

Nat closed the door, pretending she didn't hear her, and sprinted down the sidewalk.

"Where are we going?" Alisha asked, when Nat slid into the passenger seat.

"Reed Donally's. It's on the way to the hospital. Turn just before you get to the apple orchard—"

"Reed Donally's! Why on earth are you going to Reed Donally's?"

Nat clicked her seatbelt and sighed. "He called and wanted to talk to me. Please, just drive, and I'll explain on the way."

Alisha frowned, but threw the car in reverse and backed out of the driveway.

Nat repeated the conversation. Alisha didn't say anything for a long moment, merely tapping her nails on the steering wheel. Finally, she said, "I don't like it, Nat. That man is crazy. Do your parents know where you're going? Does Brady?"

"Reed's not crazy. He's hurt, and angry. Who wouldn't be in his situation?"

"He's crazy. Remember, I was standing beside you that day in the mall, when he cussed you up one side and down the other. I've never seen such hatred before. I think he would've killed you if he could've gotten his hands on you. Tell me again what he said to you on the phone."

As Nat recounted the conversation, Alisha's frown deepened into a grimace. "Have you considered the possibility he's suicidal? He could be looking to take you with him."

Nat opened her mouth to protest, but Alisha waved her off. "No, just think about it. He said he wished you both died in that crash."

"That was two years ago. A lot has changed. He's being stalked too, and Brady told him that maybe I wasn't driving that night. He only wants to talk. You're being paranoid."

"And you're being careless."

They argued all the way to Reed's. Nat placed a hand on her friend's arm when they turned into the driveway. "You can let me out here."

Alisha sighed, but slowed to a stop beside the mailbox. Nat got out of the car and shut the door. Alisha rolled down the window.

"Nat, I do not like this. Not one little bit," she said.

"I'll be okay. Go on before you're late for work. I have Justin's cell with me, and I'll call Brady if he gives me any trouble."

Alisha frowned. "You might not have time to call Brady. I'm going with you."

"No, you're not." Nat backed away. "I need to talk to Reed alone, and you'll be late for work. Go on, shoo! And thanks for the ride. It'll be okay."

"Call me as soon as you leave. I want to know you're all right."

"Yes, Mother." Nat gave Alisha a crisp salute. Alisha sighed and gave her a little wave before pulling back onto the street.

Nat stared down the driveway and took a deep breath. Her light mood evaporated when she wondered what waited for her down that winding asphalt drive.

"No turning back now," she mumbled, and slowly walked toward the looming brick house. The afternoon sun beat down relentlessly, making her shirt stick to her back. She twisted her hair off her neck and wished she had a ponytail holder.

A gray Mercedes and a red Jag sat in the carport, but Nat saw no signs of life when she walked up the front steps. It was so quiet, as if even the birds were afraid to sing. Nat's pulse thudded dully in her ears.

"Nat, around here," Reed said, and she nearly screamed.

He glanced at her from the brick walkway, his eyes puffy and red-rimmed, then his wheelchair disappeared around the corner of the house.

Nat pressed a hand to her chest and slowly followed.

Reed stopped by the edge of a sparkling blue pool and sat there, staring into the water. "I was beginning to think you weren't coming."

Nat pushed a piece of hair behind her ear as she approached. "Sorry. I had to bum a ride. I, uh, don't drive anymore."

Reed blew a breath out his nose, and she expected him to say, "Guess what? I don't drive anymore either. Whose fault is that?"

But he didn't. He didn't say anything for a long time. The white patio chair made a long scraping sound against the tile when Nat pulled it out and perched on the edge of it. She stared at his back and wished she could do something—anything—to give him back what he'd lost that night.

"The day they told me I'd never walk again . . . I thought that was the most miserable day of my life." Reed swiveled the wheelchair to face her. "I was wrong. Nat, every night since I last saw you, I lie in my bed and think of the things I screamed at you." A tear streaked down his handsome face. "You were a friend. A good friend. And I talked to you like a dog."

"Reed—" she began, but he shook his head.

"Brady told me there's a chance you weren't driving that night. Nat, I just . . . I just want to say I'm sorry."

"Reed, no," Nat said, shaken. Somehow this was more horrible than to have him shout at her. She jumped to her feet. "Don't apologize to me. What Brady said was right. There's a chance I wasn't driving, but there's a chance I was. I may never know for sure."

"It doesn't matter," he said, his blue eyes fierce. "If you were driving, if you weren't. I had no right. I know you. You'd never hurt anyone on purpose, least of all me and Jen. We were pretty tight back then. It could have been any of us. Hell, it might've been me driving if I hadn't been so drunk."

"It was my car—"

"It was Melody's party. It was her next door neighbors who broke up the party. We can shift this around all we like, Nat, and the fact remains it was only an accident. A stupid, horrible accident."

"The car was going 92 miles an hour," Nat argued, though part of her yearned to believe him, to think it wasn't her fault.

"Yeah, but you might not have been driving. Tony wasn't drinking either. I knew him. If he'd been wanting to show off, you couldn't have stopped him. For all we know, you could've been sitting in the front beside him, screaming at him to slow down. He would've laughed at you and done what he wanted anyway." Reed stared at his lap. "I'm going to call my lawyer and tell him I'm dropping out of the civil case."

"No, Reed—"

"It's the right thing to do. My dad left me money. I don't want the insurance company's." He stared up at her, looking suddenly young and vulnerable. "All I want is my friend back. I didn't realize how much I missed people until Brady started coming around. I've missed you, Nat."

Tears burned her eyes when she leaned over to hug him. His shoulders trembled as he held her.

Nat finally pulled back and brushed a kiss on his cheek. Taking one of his hands in hers, she said, "Reed, it doesn't matter what you do about the lawsuit. I'll always be your friend, no matter what. Don't back out of it because of this. We don't even have any proof."

"My mind's made up." He motioned her back to her chair. "I want this to be over. Maybe the stalker will stop then too."

"I don't understand that," Nat said. "Any of it. Why now? Why you and Bobby? Brady showed me your notebook. It read like you were leaning toward Tony's dad."

Reed rubbed his chin. "Maybe. I don't know. We know he's capable of it. He'd just gotten got out of jail for manslaughter, then dropped off the face of the earth. I called to check on him and found out he's violated his parole. Nobody knows where he is."

"Brady suspects the sheriff." Nat told him about the gun her attacker used and Reed lifted his eyebrows.

"Maybe he and Franklin are in it together," he mused. "The sheriff wouldn't do his own dirty work. We need to get together with Brady and hash this thing out. If anybody can figure it out, he can."

"Just say the word. We can meet here . . ." Nat paused and looked back at the house. "Or we can meet at my parents' house. We'll come get you." She snapped her fingers. "Oh, hey! I don't know if you remember, but mine and Brady's birthdays are a day apart. Our moms have set up this 1920s birthday party. I think it'll be at Coalmont Community Center. No big deal, but there'll be cake, music, dancing and a lot of weird costumes. I'd love it if you would come."

Reed gave her a thin smile. "Ah, I'm not much for

dancing these days."

Nat's face burned when she realized what she'd said. "Reed, I'm so sorry! I didn't mean—"

He held up both palms and laughed. "Joke, Nat. It was just a joke. But to be serious, I don't think I'm ready to be around that many people at once. Not yet. Tell Brady to dance on your feet in my place."

Nat traced the pattern on her chair arm. "There's a new name penciled in on Brady's dance card these days."

"So?" Reed made a face. "He loves *you*."

"He used to love me," Nat corrected.

"Oh come on, Nat." Reed slapped his armrests. "I've seen the way he looks when he talks about you."

"Yeah, well if it's the same way he looks when he talks *to* me . . ." She wrinkled her nose and Reed laughed.

"Pride can be a real bitch sometimes, huh?"

"Can it?" Nat murmured. "It's been so long since I've been proud of anything that I can't remember."

The corner of Reed's mouth quirked. "Yeah. I know what you mean."

Nat tried to smile, but found herself dangerously near tears again. "I've lost him, Reed. He can barely stand to look at me now. I never blamed you for that day at the mall, because I understood what you were feeling. That night ruined my life too. Did I tell you I lost a baby?"

Reed gave her a sharp look. "Brady's?"

A tear slipped down her nose. She wiped it away

with the back of her hand. "No, but he would've treated it like it was. We were going to get married. We could've had a family together."

Reed's chair made a soft whirring sound as he rolled over and placed his hand on hers. "You still can."

"Maybe . . ." Nat sniffed and swiped at her eyes. "Maybe it worked out like it was supposed to for Brady and me. He deserves better."

"Like Charity?"

Nat recoiled, but then saw the derision in his eyes. She laughed. "I don't think so."

Reed laughed too. He rolled toward the end of the pool, where a stack of hand towels laid on a rack. He picked one up and tossed it to her. "Brady deserves to be happy. You do too. He'll forgive you, Nat, but first you're going to have to forgive yourself. We were always a lot alike, you and I, so I'm qualified to tell you what to do here. Get in there and fight for what's yours."

He wheeled back toward her. The soft hum of the wheelchair masked the sound of the patio door opening, but a sudden movement behind Reed drew Nat's gaze. A wild-eyed woman staggered outside in her nightgown, waving a revolver.

Reed's mother.

"You witch!" the woman screamed. "What are you doing here? You've already ruined his life. What more do you want with him?"

She pointed the gun. Something buzzed by Nat's

ear like an angry hornet. The vase beside her exploded in a shower of glass.

"Nat, get down get down get down!" Reed screamed. "Mama, no!"

There was nowhere to go. Nat fell to the ground and scrambled on her hands and knees. A piece of glass from the vase gashed her hand, warm water soaked through the knees of her jeans.

"Nat, get behind me!" Reed shouted as he wheeled frantically in her direction. "Mama, stop it!"

Nat crawled toward him, leaving a bright streak of blood on the white tile.

She dared a glance at Rachel Atkinson. The woman held the gun with both hands and squinted at her.

Nearly three yards separated Nat from Reed. Rachel Atkinson would have one more shot.

Reed ceased his feverish chant for her to stop and instead screamed "Martin!" at the top of his lungs.

BRADY FROZE, HIS HAND LIFTED TO KNOCK ON REED'S front door. Then he vaulted over the porch and raced around the house, spurred by Reed's frantic shouts. He slid to a stop at the corner, stunned by the scene before him.

Reed's wheelchair lay on its side by the pool, its wheels still spinning. Reed was dragging himself across the white tile with his elbows, toward—

Oh, God.

Brady staggered on his feet like a drunk. Nat lay facedown on the white tile.

"Reed, get out of the way!" a woman shouted.

Brady whipped his head to the left and saw Rachel Atkinson standing just a few feet from him, clutching a revolver. She pointed it at Nat.

He launched himself at Reed's mother. The gun fired as he slammed into her. They flew through the air, then crashed into the ground with a thud. Brady landed on top of her, grunting when his elbow cracked against the tile. Even though he heard a whoosh as her lungs emptied, Rachel Atkinson recovered quickly. She bit, kicked and clawed while they grappled for the gun.

They rolled over and over until suddenly the ground disappeared beneath them. Brady sucked in a breath an instant before they hit the water.

Rachel Atkinson wasn't so lucky. Air bubbles hit Brady's face, and she stopped struggling. He shook the gun from her limp fingers. While it sank toward the bottom of the pool, Brady grabbed her waist and kicked toward the surface.

She came up sputtering and choking. Brady dragged her toward the steps and handcuffed her to the aluminum handrail. Gasping, he dragged himself out of the pool.

"What's going on? What are you doing?" Atkinson asked.

Brady glanced up from the warm tile to see Martin

Atkinson run out the patio door. His hair looked wet and disheveled; his feet and chest were bare.

"Mama tried to kill Nat!" Reed yelled.

Atkinson shouted something at Brady, but Brady couldn't answer. He lurched around the side of the pool to the place where Reed hovered over Nat.

She wasn't moving.

Bile rose in Brady's throat while his eyes followed the stark trail of blood from the patio table. He fell to his knees beside her.

Reed's eyes seemed huge and out of place in his chalky face as he tugged Nat onto her back. Brady's vision swam when he saw the bright splash of red on the front of her shirt. He squeezed his eyes shut.

"I think she's okay," Reed said. "She just passed out."

"What?" Brady opened his eyes.

"The blood is from her hands. She was lying on them." Reed gently patted her cheeks. "Nat. Nat, wake up."

She groaned, and Brady's heart surged.

"Neither shot hit her," Reed said, and glanced over his shoulder at his mother. Brady looked too. She stood in the water, crying as she grasped the rail. Atkinson knelt at the edge of the pool beside her.

"I'm so sorry," Reed whispered. "I only wanted to talk to Nat, and I almost got her killed." He exhaled and wiped a hand down his face. "I need to see about Mama."

Brady started to rise, but Reed waved him down.

"Take care of Nat." He yelled, "Martin, come help me!"

Atkinson hurried to the wheelchair, straightened it and pushed it to Reed. He glanced down at Nat.

"Reed, what happened?" he demanded while he hooked his hands beneath Reed's armpits. Brady stood to help. Together, they lifted Reed back into the chair.

"I was just getting out of the shower when I heard all the screaming," the doctor said. "Is the girl okay?"

Nat groaned again. Brady knelt beside her, half listening to the explanation Reed gave his stepfather as they wheeled over to his mother. Nat's lashes fluttered and she stared up at him with dazed green eyes.

"Brady, what are you doing here?"

She tried to push herself up, but then cried out and fell backward, clutching her hand. Her palm gaped open and blood spurted from her little finger.

Brady scrambled to the table and retrieved the white hand towel lying there. It looked clean, so he wrapped it around her hand and squeezed, applying pressure. He helped her sit. "Alisha called me. She was worried about you. I was on the front porch when I heard Reed shouting."

She looked so pale, but she was going to be okay. Relief made Brady almost dizzy. He wanted to wrap his arms around her and never let go.

Nat's eyes widened. "Mrs. Atkinson . . . is she okay?" She jerked her head around and stared at the trio huddled at the steps. "Oh, thank God," she breathed.

Brady pushed to his feet. "Will you be okay for a

minute? I need to call this in."

Nat clutched his sleeve. "No! I don't want to press charges."

"Nat, she tried to kill you."

She set her jaw in that stubborn way of hers. "I don't care. Reed is not going to lose anything else because of me."

"She's a danger to herself and others. Besides, I have to call this in to the county. This isn't my jurisdiction. I have to file a report of what happened in case she decides to file charges against you for trespassing, or against me for assault."

Nat cradled her hand in her lap and stared over Brady's shoulder. "I don't want to hurt Reed."

"I don't want to hurt Reed, either. But his mother needs help. You don't have to press charges, but I'm going to have to call the sheriff."

"The sheriff." Nat scoffed. "A lot of good that will do."

Brady pushed his wet hair away from his forehead. "Yeah, I know. But we have to call him."

She grasped his pant leg with her uninjured hand. "Go explain it to Reed first. Please."

Brady nodded, and left her sitting on the tile while he went to talk to Reed. Reed stared into the pool as Brady talked. The only indication Brady had that Reed even heard him was a terse jerk of his head.

He was in shock, Brady realized. Awkwardly, he patted Reed's shoulder and strode back to Nat.

"I've got to go to the Explorer to call dispatch. Do

you want to come with me?"

Nat nodded, and Brady helped her stand. Rachel Atkinson didn't look up when they approached. Brady stopped, wondering what to do with her. He hated to leave her standing there in the water, but he didn't relish the thought of another fight.

He pulled a chair to the top of the steps. "Mrs. Atkinson, you should be able to slide the cuff up the rail and get out of the water."

She stared blankly at him. For a moment, Brady wasn't sure she even heard him, but then she climbed the steps. She sat in an iron chair and her husband squatted beside her. She pressed her face to Atkinson's shoulder and sobbed.

"Are you okay?" Reed asked softly and extended his hand over his shoulder to Nat.

She clasped his fingers and leaned to brush a kiss on his cheek. "Yeah."

Brady guided her to the Explorer. She closed her eyes and leaned against the fender while he called the county jail. Her pallor worried him. As he held the line for the sheriff, he put his hand on her waist. Her eyes fluttered open.

He motioned his head toward the front seat. "Get in," he said. "You look like you're going to pass out."

He caught the faint, sweet scent of her perfume when she brushed by. She slid into the driver's seat and laid her head against his steering wheel.

The phone crackled to life. "Sheriff Richards."

"Sheriff, this is Chief Simms. There's been an incident at the Atkinson estate—"

"What the hell are you doing there?" Brady winced as the sheriff's voice blasted in his ear. Even Nat heard. She stared at him with worried green eyes.

"Look, I'll explain everything when you get here," Brady replied. "Just . . . hurry."

"Don't be ordering me around, boy," the sheriff warned. "I think I'll be at the city council meeting next week and let the people of Coalmont know how seldom their chief is in his own damn jurisdiction." He slammed the phone in Brady's ear before he could reply.

Brady swore under his breath and snapped the phone shut.

"I'm sorry." Nat twisted to face him. Tears welled in her eyes. Her knees brushed his chest when he leaned in the open doorway and tossed the phone into the passenger seat.

"The sheriff's had it in for me ever since I got the position over Joe," he said. "It's not your fault. I only wish I'd known beforehand what you had planned. I would've come with you."

Nat stared down at her lap. "I-I know, but I've caused you enough trouble lately. It was a spur of the moment thing too. I never thought she'd do that."

Brady shook his head. "She's losing it. All this stalker business . . ." He glanced at the sodden towel wrapped around Nat's hand. "Let me see it again."

She held it out to him and he carefully unfolded the towel. The gaping cut in her palm made his stomach twist. He rewrapped it. "It's almost stopped bleeding, and I didn't see any glass in it, but you're going to need stitches. I'll drive you to the hospital after we finish up here."

"If the sheriff even bothers," Nat grumbled, but a few moments later, sirens screamed up the driveway.

The sheriff bailed out of the cruiser and his nephew, Joe, followed. Mirrored sunglasses hid the bruises under Joe's eyes, but he ducked his head at Brady's stare. Brady frowned and moved in front of Nat.

The sheriff had already spotted her. "You!" He waved a fat finger in the air. "Why is it that whenever there's trouble in this town lately, you're right in the middle of it? What happened here?"

The sheriff's face grew redder and redder while they talked. Before Brady finished explaining, he stormed away. Brady and Nat followed him around the side of the house. Joe trailed behind them.

"Mrs. Atkinson," the sheriff said as he unlocked the cuffs. "Would you like to press charges against Chief Simms?"

Reed's head snapped around. "Are you out of your freakin' mind? If Brady hadn't been here, Nat would be dead."

The sheriff smirked. "You would rather I arrest your mother?"

"We don't want to press charges." Martin Atkinson stepped behind his wife and placed his hands on her shoulders. "I'm glad Chief Simms was here. The situation could've been much, much worse." He looked at Nat. "Young lady, I'm so sorry. Reed said he invited you here. Please try to understand. My wife has been under so much stress lately . . ."

"I don't want to press charges either—" Nat began, and Brady cut her off.

"But Mrs. Atkinson needs help. Maybe you know someone at the hospital . . ."

"I agree," Martin said. "I called my colleague, Dr. Fitzpatrick, while you were around front. He's agreed to admit Rachel immediately."

"No!" Rachel cried. "I can't leave Reed."

"Only for a day or two." Martin patted her shoulder. "I'll take care of Reed."

"So, nobody's pressing charges?" the sheriff demanded. Brady could almost hear the unspoken "so what did you bother me for?" "Where's the gun, anyway?"

Brady pointed to the pool, and the sheriff gave him a thin smile. "Since you're already wet, I guess you can get it."

There wasn't any sense in arguing. Brady dove into the pool and fished the gun from the bottom. He passed it off to the sheriff and took the towel Martin Atkinson offered.

The sheriff took their statements, then Brady drove

Nat to the hospital. He sat beside her while they stitched up her palm and little finger.

When they walked out to the parking lot, Nat glanced down at her shirt. "Do you have something I could change into? I don't want my mom to see me like this."

Brady opened the passenger door for her. "Nat, you have to tell your parents what happened."

"I know. It's just . . . you know my mom. She'll see this and freak out before I can explain."

Brady nodded, remembering the way his heart had stalled when he'd seen the crimson stain on her white shirt. "Yeah," he said slowly. "You're right." He rubbed a hand down his face. "I need to change too. We'll swing by my apartment."

Nat lapsed into silence and stared out the window. She didn't say another word until they walked through his door.

"Nice place," she murmured.

"It's okay," he replied, and strode into his bedroom. Nat tagged behind him.

It seemed wrong, having her here. The air in the apartment suddenly felt pressurized, thick and charged with all the unspoken things between them. The oppressiveness only intensified when she was inside his bedroom. It felt like he was trying to breathe with a plastic bag over his head.

Brady panicked.

He moved to his closet and yanked a T-shirt so

hard he bent its metal hanger and sent it clanging to the floor. He tossed it over his shoulder to Nat, not trusting himself to look at her. Quickly, he grabbed a change of clothes for himself and stalked to the door.

"I'll change in the bathroom," he said tersely, and shut the door behind him. He leaned against it for a moment, willing his racing heart to slow down.

He took his time in the bathroom, but when he emerged, Nat still hadn't come out of his bedroom. He rapped on the door with a knuckle. "Are you okay in there?"

"Yeah," she called back. "No. I'm . . . having a little trouble."

Against his better judgment, Brady opened the door. She shot him an exasperated look over her shoulder.

"That stuff they numbed my hand with . . . it deadened my fingers, too, and I can't get this damn thing unbuttoned."

He searched her face for some sign of duplicity, but saw only frustration.

Woodenly, Brady crossed to her. She turned and he touched her collar. No wonder she was having so much trouble. Dried blood rendered the cotton stiff and resistant. He hoped she didn't see his hand tremble while he tugged the first pearl button free.

But Nat wasn't looking at his hands. He felt her gaze burn into him while he unfastened the second and third buttons. The tan swell of her breasts against the lacy edge of her white bra was almost his undoing.

"Brady," she said, so quietly he might have imagined it. He glanced up and was frozen by the wistfulness he saw on her face.

Dammit. It wasn't fair. Everything he'd ever wanted was just a whisper away, and he couldn't have her.

After she left, he'd buried himself in school, buried himself in work—anything to keep himself so busy he wouldn't think of her. But it never really worked. She lingered at the edge of every conscious thought and haunted his dreams. Nat wasn't just a memory; she lived inside his skin.

Halfway across town or halfway to the moon, he could never run far enough to get away from her.

He thought about what his mother had said, what Reed had said. How easy it would be to believe that he and Nat were meant to be together, to let his temptation for her turn to fate. But that wouldn't be fair to Charity.

It wouldn't be fair to him.

Brady unfastened the last two buttons and left the room.

CHAPTER 9

"ARE YOU GUYS READY?" NAT YELLED UP THE STAIRS.

"Almost," Matt hollered back. "Justin won't get out of the bathroom."

Nat rolled her eyes and suppressed a smile. They took longer to get dressed than she had at that age, and that was saying something.

When she walked past the window, she saw Brady's Explorer turning in the driveway. The sight filled her with a strange mixture of dread and hope. She didn't know how to act around him anymore. Every conversation they had left her feeling confused and frustrated, because whenever it seemed like she was gaining ground, something would happen to slap her down again.

Like that afternoon in his apartment . . . his eyes had burned hot with desire when he'd unbuttoned her blouse, but then his jaw had set and he'd run away from her again. He barely spoke to her all the way home.

Although she'd do anything to win back his trust, she wondered if she was fighting a losing battle. Maybe too much had been damaged in their relationship to ever repair. She hoped not, but she had to face the possibility.

Bobby was dead, but Brady's hurt was still alive and seeking vengeance. Since he couldn't lash out at Bobby, that left her . . . and he wouldn't be happy when he found out where she was going tonight.

He knocked. Taking a deep breath, she opened the door.

His gazed flickered down her body, taking in the dressy black suit and blouse. "Where are you going?" he asked abruptly, though it was clear from his expression he already knew.

She lifted her chin and refused to back down from his glare. "I'm going to Bobby's visitation."

With a derisive snort, he rolled his eyes and leaned against the doorframe. "You can't be serious. After all this . . . after all he did, you're still going to the funeral home?"

He sounded so hurt, so defeated, it was impossible to hold on to her anger. She sighed and tugged on his sleeve, trying to pull him inside. He resisted.

"Come on," she said with resignation. "If we're going to fight, let's not do it on the doorstep. At least come in."

"I don't want to fight," he said, but followed her inside anyway. I just can't figure out what was so damn wonderful about the guy that you can't let go, despite all the things he did to hurt you."

Nat squeezed her eyes shut. "It's not that. It's—

what would people think if I didn't go?"

"Who cares what they think? They're not the ones with a killer after them. Do you realize how stupid this is, parading around when this guy's still on the loose?"

Nat bristled. "Well, you were always the smart one, not me. I'm not asking your permission, Brady."

He scowled and backed her against the wall. "We both know this isn't about appearances. You don't care what people think. You never have."

He placed his hands on either side of her, blocking her in. He was standing too close for her to think clearly. She felt the heat of his body, the heat of his anger, but it was the heat of the desire in his eyes that left her breathless. Even though she knew they were supposed to be arguing, she couldn't concentrate on that, not now.

She hooked a finger in his belt loop, tugging him closer, and was surprised when he didn't pull away. Nat pressed her cheek to his, relishing the feel of his body against hers.

"Promise me—" she said softly. "—that one of these days, you'll quit being mad at me long enough to realize that we belong together."

He pulled back and rested his forehead against hers. She shivered when he twisted his hand in her hair. "I told you a long time ago that we belonged together. Maybe I was wrong."

"Does it feel wrong, when you're holding me like this?"

"No," he admitted, closing his eyes.

"I'm sorry I hurt you. I made a mistake. Please don't punish me forever."

"Punish you?" he mused. "I thought I was punishing myself."

The sound of the twins on the stairs broke the moment. Reluctantly, Brady pulled away. He rubbed the back of his neck and asked, "Who's going with you?"

Nat smiled, encouraged by the lack of anger in his tone. "The Wonder Twins."

Justin loped down the stairs and Brady grinned. "Oooh," he said, feigning a punch at Justin's shoulder. "The Wonder Twins. That should scare the stalker."

Justin laughed and connected a punch of his own. "Better than the Keystone Kops."

"I thought one of the Wonder Twins was a girl," Brady said, winking at Nat.

Justin jerked his head at his brother. "That would be Matt."

"I'm not the one who wears Mom's concealer," Matt retorted.

Justin scowled. "Hey, it's only a little bit. You can't even tell it's there."

"Yeah, I know. It would've taken the whole tube to cover up that zit."

Brady cleared his throat. "If you guys are ready, I'll follow you out. I'd let you ride with me, but I'm still on duty for half an hour and I'd hate to get called out and leave you stranded."

"Why are you going?" Justin asked, then flushed. "I mean, I know you didn't like the guy any more than I did."

"I'm going because of work." He glanced at Nat. "I haven't pegged a good profile on the guy yet, so this is pretty much a hunch. I figured that if he wants revenge as much as he wants us to think he does, there's a chance he might show up at the visitation or funeral to see the results of his efforts."

Nat shivered, and Brady squeezed the back of her neck. "I wish you would reconsider, but if you feel like you need to go, I want to be there with you." He winked. "Just to back up to the Wonder Twins, of course."

On the way to the funeral home, Nat couldn't help but feel encouraged. Brady hadn't said yes, but he hadn't said no either.

"You can quit checking the mirror." Justin gave her a crooked smile while he coasted to a stop at the red light. "He's still back there."

"I wonder if Brady will let me drive the Cuda after he becomes my brother-in-law," Matt commented from the backseat.

Nat refused to be baited. "From your lips to God's ears," she said with a smile.

Still, a shiver of apprehension traced her spine when they pulled into the parking lot of the town's only funeral home. Even with her brothers flanking her and Brady walking behind, she felt uneasy.

She hesitated, lagging behind a step to walk beside Brady. "I promised Dara I'd come," she told him.

He gave her a searching look, then nodded. They walked in silence up the sidewalk.

A group of old men gathered on the front porch of the remodeled Victorian, discussing the Braves and this year's corn crops. Seeing no one she knew, Nat followed the twins inside.

She wondered at the size of the crowd, but it was explained when she saw the placard in the foyer.

> *McBee Visitation, Rm. 1*
> *Metley Visitation, Rm. 2*
> *Hasting Visitation, Rm. 3*
> *Rm. 4—Vacant*

They must've done some remodeling since the last time she visited, because at the time of the accident, they'd had to hold Jen's visitation at the church across the road.

"You okay?" Justin asked, taking her elbow, and Nat nodded.

When they walked down the hall to Room 1, they passed a break room where families could grab a cup of coffee or sample one of the various casserole dishes that people seemed to always bring during these times.

Nat gritted her teeth when she heard Jolene McBee's raucous laughter, and picked up her pace until she was sure she was out of Bobby's mother's line of sight.

People gathered in little groups outside of Room 2, chattering and laughing and straining to hear each other over their neighbors' conversations.

Nat followed on Matt's heels, weaving her way through them and murmuring, "Excuse me."

She felt their stares when they realized who she was. Bobby's murder, and her involvement in the case, had to be the talk of the town.

Suddenly, the crowd cleared. The rest of the hallway looked desolate, and the sight of the open door to Room 1 at the end of it stalled her feet. Closing her eyes, she remembered Bobby's terrified expression, could almost hear him scream at her to run.

Brady's hand brushed her lower back and she took solace in his nearness. Together, they completed the solemn march down the hall.

The room was dusky dark, with only soft illumination around the perimeter of the room and above the gleaming silver casket at the front.

A couple of old women talked quietly on the right, and Dara sat with three teenage girls near the front on the left, but they were the large room's only occupants.

Dara glanced up when they came in. She shot Nat a teary smile and hurried to greet her.

"I'm glad you came," she said, giving Nat a fierce hug.

Nat gave her an extra squeeze before releasing her, then paused to tuck a lock of hair behind Dara's ear.

"Hey, kiddo. How are you holding up?"

"Okay, I guess." She stared at her feet. "Mama's taking it pretty hard."

Nat knew what that meant. Jolene was probably too doped up to stand by now. She suspected as much when Dara called earlier, wanting to know if Nat wanted to help pick out a casket. Jolene had taken the phone away from her and, in a slurred voice, told Nat it wasn't necessary, that she had one in mind already.

Then she'd launched into an incoherent crying jag, telling Nat how hard it was to bury her only son. Nat had been tempted to ask her if it had been half as hard as raising him.

It might've been hardhearted and mean spirited, but she was completely lacking in any sympathy for Jolene McBee. She'd exposed her children to predators and poverty and her addictions until she'd stamped out any innocence they had left. The accident might've hastened Bobby's downfall, but his mother had already set him firmly on the path.

Nat could remember being fifteen and sneaking over to the housing projects to visit Bobby. She often found Jolene laid up in the bed in the middle of the afternoon, sipping wine from a paper cup and reading a tabloid. Bobby and Dara had been responsible for doing their own laundry and cooking their own meals; that is, if their mother hadn't traded all of their food stamps for pills that week.

Bobby had broken her heart the first time he'd come over to her house for dinner. His enthusiastic appetite had raised her parents' eyebrows and later, when he stood in the kitchen with her while she washed dishes, Nat had caught him shoving a piece of cornbread he'd wrapped in a paper towel into his jacket pocket. Embarrassed, he admitted he was taking it home to Dara. Nat had tried to get him to fix Dara a plate from the leftovers in the refrigerator, but Bobby had been too proud. He asked her not to tell her parents, and she'd obeyed his wishes, though she began slipping leftovers out of the house after that.

"Do you want to walk up there with me?" Dara gestured to the coffin, which was, of course, closed.

"Sure," Nat said, and glanced at Brady.

"Go on," he said. "I'm going to sit back here."

The twins sat on the bench beside him, but Nat felt his eyes on her while she made the long walk to the front with Dara.

An 18 X 20 of Bobby on his motorcycle dominated a small table in front of the casket. The photo was a good choice, Nat thought, and figured Dara had probably picked it out. He'd loved that thing, had found the old Indian cycle at the junkyard and painstakingly restored it. His brown hair looked windblown, and his handsome face was defiant and proud enough to put James Dean to shame.

Her gaze dropped to the assortment of smaller photos that surrounded it, and her throat constricted when she picked up a framed snapshot of her and Bobby. His arms were around her and they were both laughing. God, that seemed a million years ago. How she wished things had turned out differently, for both of them.

"He loved you," Dara said quietly. "In his own way, I know he did."

Nat's eyes blurred and she gently set the picture down. "I know."

Hand-in-hand, they walked back to Brady and the twins. They were almost there when they heard a loud sobbing that preceded Jolene's entrance.

She staggered through the door, leaning on a grizzled man in a flannel shirt. Her raccooned eyes widened when she saw Nat.

"Oh, baby!" she cried, and threw herself at Nat.

Nat staggered under the force of the woman's weight and awkwardly patted her back, though she was choking on the fumes of cigarette smoke and cheap hairspray that emanated from Bobby's mother's teased hair.

"What are we gonna do without him?" Jolene sobbed. "Who would do such a thing? Who could hurt our poor Bobby?"

Nat grimaced and tried to extract herself after a moment, realizing Jolene's slurred questions required no answers from her. She finally pulled away and looked at Jolene's boyfriend for help, but caught him staring at her chest instead. Lowering his head, he mumbled something about grabbing a smoke and wandered away.

Disgusted, Nat sat on the bench beside Brady.

Jolene seemed to notice him for the first time. Her dark eyes glittered and she shot Nat an accusing look.

"Excuse me, dear. I haven't met your . . . *friend*."

"Brady Simms, ma'am." Brady offered his hand. "Coalmont Chief of Police."

"Oh." Jolene's eyes widened, and her hand fluttered to the fake pearls around her neck before she seemed to notice Brady's outstretched hand. Instead of shaking it, she grabbed it and pressed it to her ample bosom. "Oh, honey!" she said. "Are you going to find the man who did this to my baby?"

Brady's ears reddened as he tried to reclaim his hand. "Yes, ma'am." He looked at Nat. "I promise you, I'll find the person who did this."

Pacified, Jolene glanced at the twins. "Oh, these must be your brothers," she said, and Justin instinctively leaned back, out of her reach. Matt wasn't so fortunate. He found his face smashed against Jolene's cleavage when she grabbed him in a hug.

"They're adorable!" she said. "So handsome. Aren't they handsome, Dara?"

"Y-yes," Dara stuttered, looking like she wanted to sink through the floor.

"And probably smart. Are you smart?" she asked Matt, who was too busy struggling for breath to answer. "They'll probably be successful like their father. All the Hawthorne men are successful, isn't that right?"

She abruptly released Matt and stared at Justin. He shot to his feet, looking for help.

"I bet you're going to college, aren't you? What are you going to study? Do you have a girlfriend?

"I-I . . . bathroom!" he said, his green eyes panicked. "I need to go to the bathroom. Anybody know where it is?"

Jolene grabbed Dara's wrist and shoved her toward him. She nearly fell over Matt's knees. "Dara will show you."

Wordlessly, Justin grabbed Dara's hand and dragged her down the length of the pew, bypassing the aisle, because that would mean he would have to walk by Jolene.

Fortunately, a man came up and touched Jolene's sleeve. "How you doing, honey?" he asked.

Instantly, she turned on the tears again and fell sobbing into his arms. He comforted her for a moment, then she maneuvered him to the front, where she proceeded to check the condolence cards on the flowers.

Nat pressed her fingers to her eye, feeling the beginning of a headache throbbing behind it. "Matt, are you okay?" she muttered.

"I think she broke my nose."

Brady laughed. They fell silent for a moment, listening to Jolene's loud conversation up front. When Brady spoke again, his voice was sober. "That poor girl. Dara, I mean. She seems like a good kid—"

"She is," Nat replied. "Though I don't know how she's survived."

A man in a black suit walked down the aisle to Jolene. He leaned to whisper something to her and she pointed to Nat. Nat knew what it was about before he even approached her.

"Mrs. McBee?" he said, and Brady stiffened beside her.

"No," Nat said. "Hawthorne. What can I do for you?"

The funeral director looked embarrassed. "Ah, Mrs. McBee . . ." He glanced toward Jolene. ". . . the *other* Mrs. McBee . . . said you were her daughter-in-law. The wife of the deceased."

"We weren't married." Nat shifted uncomfortably. "I assume this is about the bill."

"Yes," he replied, looking relieved she broached the subject first. "If you could come with me to my office, there are some forms I need you to sign. We, ah, generally take care of this during the interview process, but Mrs. McBee . . . the other Mrs. McBee—"

"Quit saying 'the other Mrs. McBee,' " Brady said irritably. "She already told you she wasn't his damn wife."

"Oh, ah . . . excuse me," the man stammered.

Nat stood and smoothed her skirt. "It's okay. Where is your office?"

The director dragged her away almost as quickly as Justin had Dara.

In his office, he showed her the bill, went over the song list and discussed the incidentals. Nat didn't know why he bothered, since Jolene had already made all the decisions. She opened her purse and wrote him a check for $300, which nearly wiped out the account, and set the balance up on installment payments.

Finally, she escaped into the hallway, where a frowning Brady waited. "Are you ready to go? I think the twins are ready to go."

"Yes," she murmured.

"They're outside with Dara." He stalked ahead of her and pushed out the door without bothering to hold it for her.

Matt sat on the front steps, talking to one of the girls who'd accompanied Dara. He looked startled when Brady brushed past.

"We leaving?" he asked, and Nat nodded.

"I'll be in the car," she said, and hurried after Brady.

They found Justin in the parking lot, with his arms around a crying Dara. He saw them coming and held up a finger for them to wait.

Brady sighed and leaned against the Explorer. Nat watched Matt and the girl he'd been talking to join Justin and Dara.

Justin motioned her over a moment later, and met her halfway in the parking lot.

"Do you think Brady could take you home?" he asked. "Dara asked if I could run her by her house to get some clothes. She's going to stay at her girlfriend's house tonight and I don't think her mom is in any shape to drive."

"Are you kidding?" Nat said. "Brady is ready to kill me right now. Can't they call the other girl's parents?"

"Her mom doesn't get home from work until ten."

Nat looked back at Brady and winced. "Okay, fine. Be careful."

"I'll wait to see if he says okay," Justin said.

Nat trudged back to the Explorer and didn't waste time explaining. Brady didn't look like he was in the mood to talk. "Can you take me home?"

He blinked and gave an exasperated shrug. "Get in."

Nat waved at Justin and climbed in the Explorer.

"So, I guess you're hooked for the funeral expense," he said, when he backed out of the parking space.

"I guess."

He glanced at her, his handsome face pained in the glow of the streetlight. "Can I just ask you one thing? What did you see in that guy in the first place?"

The question was asked softly, without malice. Nat gave a shaky laugh. "I don't know . . . maybe myself?"

"You were nothing like him."

"We were both screw-ups. That's for sure. Brady, it may sound like a cop-out, but I don't know. Maybe I saw that he needed me."

"I needed you," he said, and she gave him a tender smile, though he couldn't see it in the dark.

"No, you didn't. You always had it all worked out. What you wanted to do, what you believed . . . I felt like such a mess compared to you."

His voice was tight. "That's how I made you feel? Inadequate?"

"No, you made me feel special. Smarter, funnier, prettier than I am. I guess I thought that one day you'd figure out I wasn't all you thought I was. That I wasn't anything special."

"You're wrong."

Neither of them said anything else until he pulled up in front of her house.

"Well, good—" She froze when he touched her cheek.

His handsome face contorted under the streetlight and his eyes seemed to plead with her, though she wasn't sure what he was asking. She gently brushed a kiss on his cheek.

"Goodnight, Brady," she whispered, and he exhaled before he leaned around her to open the door.

"Goodnight, Nat."

SHE DIDN'T SEE BRADY FOR TWO DAYS, THOUGH HE called her father once to ask if he'd heard anything about the airbag test. Restlessly, she roamed the house, worrying about the stalker, worrying about Reed and Brady, and wondering what she was going to do next.

She even missed her crummy job, because at least it gave her something to do. Her father had begged her to quit, at least until the trial was over, and it hadn't taken a lot of persuasion at the time to make her walk away from minimum wage drudgery, but now she had a funeral to pay for.

Matt passed by her in the hall with the cordless tucked against his ear. Nat could tell by his serious tone and the way he chewed on his thumbnail that he was talking to a girl. She leaned to make kissing sounds into the receiver.

"Ignore that. It's only my sister," he said, scowling at her. "She's a big baby like Justin, even though she's *old*. Twenty-three today. Yeah, you'll get to meet her at the party. You are still coming, right? Great!"

He kept walking and Nat let him go. No point in harassing a fifteen-year-old because his love life sounded more promising than hers.

She flopped onto the couch and thumbed through the latest stack of college catalogs Alisha had brought. Alisha nagged her about going back to college all the time, but it was easy for Alisha. She was smart like Brady. School had never been easy for Nat. She'd gotten her associate degree at Cedar Ridge because it was part of her sentencing. At least college classes were more interesting than high school, which she probably wouldn't have graduated from without Brady's help.

Brady. She couldn't stop thinking about him, and the way he'd looked at her in his bedroom. He still wanted her. It burned in his blue eyes. She was just going to have to convince him to give her another chance. Maybe college would be a good idea. It would show him she was serious about changing her life, serious about changing everything.

She was free. Free from Bobby and his black moods, his jealousy and his fists. Thanks to Reed, she was even beginning to feel free from the heavy burden of guilt she'd carried all these years, but without Brady, it meant nothing.

The doorbell rang and Nat hurried to answer it. She grinned when she spied Alisha through the peephole and threw open the door.

"Happy birthday!" Alisha said, twisting her dark hair up in a scrunchi. "Your present's in the car. I knew you'd be shaking it and banging it around if I brought it in." She strolled into the foyer. "Where is everybody?"

"Matt went upstairs, Justin and Dad are picking up the cake, and Mom and Brady's parents are decorating the community center."

"Don't they need help?"

Nat rolled her eyes. "You're kidding, right? They live for this stuff. They've been at it since yesterday and won't let me near the place. It's a surprise."

Alisha glanced down at her faded jeans and tank top. "Are you sure I wasn't supposed to find a costume?"

"Positive. Kelly found some costume place in Murfreesboro. She's bringing the outfits over as soon as they finish decorating. She said she'd found a dress for me that would knock Brady's eyes out."

Alisha laughed as they walked toward the living room. "So, the plot thickens. I think it's sweet Brady's mom wants the two of you together too."

Nat raised an eyebrow. "Scary is what it is. You should hear her and Mom. I bet they've got a reception hall booked somewhere for our wedding."

"Hey, whatever works." Alisha's dark eyes twinkled. "I was thinking about locking Charity in the broom closet myself. Think the moms will help?"

"No doubt," Nat said, peering out the window. "And speak of the evil duo, here they are." She laughed. "The moms. I like it."

The sound of their giggles preceded Selena and Kelly up the walk. Nat held open the door for them. Although she wanted Brady back too, all this matchmaking made her nervous. If Brady got wind of it, it might push him even further away. The queasy feeling in her stomach intensified when the women beamed at her.

"Only three hours until party time," her mother said. "Are you as excited as we are?"

"I'm not sure that's possible," Nat said warily.

Kelly grabbed her arm and dragged her inside. After a quick hello to Alisha, the moms herded them upstairs to Nat's bedroom.

Kelly thrust a box at Nat. "Open it."

Nat removed the lid and pushed back the tissue. She pretended to shield her eyes from the shimmering, fire engine red material beneath. "Mercy! When you said it would knock Brady's eyes out, I didn't know you meant literally."

The moms looked crestfallen.

"You don't like it?" Kelly asked when Nat lifted it from the box. The beaded fringe hem made a soft clinking sound.

Nat exhaled. "Are you kidding? With the exception of your son, it's the most gorgeous thing I've ever seen. It's perfect! It's . . ." Nat lifted an eyebrow when she held it to the light. ". . . see-through."

"Silk chiffon. Don't worry about the see-through part." Kelly pointed at another box on the bed. "That's what the bloomers are for."

Nat blinked. "Bloomers?"

"I see Paris, I see France . . ." Alisha sang.

Selena coughed. "Ah, don't laugh too much, dear. You have bloomers too. And wigs, and cami-bockers."

"Cami—what?" Alisha was beginning to look pretty nervous herself.

Nat had to admit, the moms' enthusiasm was contagious. They dug through the bags and flung silk stockings, garters and girdles on Nat's bed with glee.

"And this is Alisha's," Selena said, reaching for the zipper on the garment bag. She held up an antique gold dress for inspection.

Alisha squealed. Actually squealed. Nat giggled, unaccustomed to such a show of girliness from her no-

nonsense friend. The dress was flawless: V cut in the front and back with a gold lamé bodice and a black and gold metallic brocade skirt. A gold lamé rose accented the narrow waist. Kelly handed her a cloche hat that was also trimmed in roses.

"Oh, cool! Do I get a hat like that?" Nat asked.

"Nope, this is yours." Selena opened another box, revealing a beaded headband with a billowing red feather attached to the center.

Nat laughed. "You wanted to make sure I was seen, didn't you?"

The moms looked at each other and grinned.

"Well, let's see your dresses," Alisha said, and they laughed.

The nervous feeling fluttered to life in Nat's stomach again. "What's so funny?" she demanded.

Brady's mom wiped mirthful tears from her eyes. "Nothing." She waved her hand at Selena. "You first."

Selena's dress was black, designed somewhat like Nat's with a straight waist and short hem. The moms started laughing again when Kelly reached for her garment bag.

"Ta da!" she said, and held up one of the ugliest dresses Nat had ever seen.

It was some sort of yellow crepe material with a random brown bead design, blouson top and fitted hip band. She could tell in a glance that it would make the wearer look like she was pregnant with triplets.

"So, what do you guys think?" Kelly prodded.

"It's, ah . . ." Nat hesitated, not wanting to hurt Kelly's feelings.

"It looks like an overripe banana," Alisha said, and Nat elbowed her. The moms burst into another giggling fit.

"I'm sorry you don't like it," Kelly said with a wink. "Because I adored it so much I got Charity one just like it, except hers is green."

"Ohh!" Alisha gave Brady's mom a high five. "You moms are bad! And Charity can't say anything because you have the same dress."

Nat shook her head. "I almost feel sorry for her."

Kelly walked over to Nat and touched the side of her face. "No offense to Charity, but I picked out my daughter-in-law a long time ago." She hugged Nat tight. "And I know my son. He loves you. I only want to see him happy."

Nat squeezed her back. "That's what I want too."

"COME ON, MAN," BRADY PLEADED. "YOU HAVE TO COME with me. I've got that sense of impending doom again."

Reed snorted. "I've had enough impending doom lately. What makes you think I want some of yours?" He scratched his chin. "Still, it's tempting . . . the possibility of front row seats to another catfight."

"Come on," Brady said again, shaking the garment

bag. "I even brought you a suit, and a fake Tommy gun that shoots water 150 feet."

Reed laughed. "Well, why didn't you say so? I'm in if I get a water gun. Even if it means I'll look as ridiculous as you."

"What do you mean?" Brady looked down at his black pinstriped zoot suit and wingtips, then grinned up at Reed. "I look *good*."

Reed chuckled and took the garment bag from him. "Yeah, you just keep telling yourself that."

Brady turned his back for Reed to change. "How's your mom doing?"

"Ah, you know. Pretty good. She'll be home tomorrow. She sounded much better on the phone this morning." He paused. "She'd go nuts if she found out I was leaving the house. I'm going to ask Martin to tell her I'm sleeping if she calls."

"I'll protect you." Brady took a shot at Reed over his shoulder with his water gun, hitting him in the back of the head.

"Hey, man! Cut that out. You have a water gun too?"

"You didn't think I'd let you have all the fun, did you?"

"Purple!" Reed grunted. "A purple zoot suit. I'll look like freakin' Barney the dinosaur."

"You whine worse than Charity. She's called me twice this morning, griping about the dress Mom picked out for her. How bad could it be?"

"I can't believe Charity's okay with this party, after what happened at the barbecue."

"She's not, but I told her I was sick of being interrogated." Brady adjusted his white tie in the mirror. "She either trusts me or she doesn't. I'm trying my damnedest to do what's right—"

"At the expense of doing what you want?"

Brady frowned. "I'm not looking for a relationship with Nat."

"So, you don't have feelings for her?"

Brady gripped the edge of Reed's dresser. "How can I not have feelings for her? All my life, it's been Nat. But what I feel for her and what's good for me are two different things."

"Are you sure about that?" Reed asked quietly. "People change, Brady. So she made a mistake. I've made plenty of them, and I can't help but think you're making one now."

"Either she felt it or she didn't, and obviously she didn't. I have too much invested in that relationship to be able to settle for just a little bit of her heart. That may sound stupid, or maybe it's selfish, but I can't help the way I feel. I can't love her like I loved her, and know that I'm just another guy to her. Charity tells me Nat only wants me because she can't have me, and I have to wonder if she's right. Not once in those four years she was gone did she ever contact me. I didn't matter at all until Bobby died and Nat found herself alone. If Bobby was still alive, she wouldn't be here now. She'd be right there with him."

"I think there's more to the situation than you know." Reed wheeled to the dresser and started putting on his tie. His eyes met Brady's in the mirror when he said, "Nat and I talked about the wreck, about what we'd lost. She told me about the baby, and how the three of you could've been a family."

"She said that?" Brady looked at his shoes, swallowing over the sudden lump in his throat. "It's not true, you know. It never would've happened. All Bobby would've had to do was snap his fingers and she'd have been right back there."

"I don't know, man. Since I've been in this chair, I've learned to read people's faces. When Nat talks about you, I see the same regret in her eyes that I see in yours."

Brady exhaled. He really couldn't stand to talk about this anymore. He made a show of glancing at his watch. "Are you ready? Because if we're late, all the water guns in the world won't save us from my mother."

They drove to Charity's apartment. She must've been watching for them because she walked out the door before Brady could go up to get her.

Brady blinked at her lime green and brown outfit.

"Hey, man," Reed whispered. "Does your mom *like* Charity?" He laughed. "Maybe this purple get-up ain't so bad, after all."

Brady hid his smile as Charity stalked toward them,

scowling. "Hey, babe," he said, and brushed a kiss on her cheek.

"Hey, Charity," Reed said cheerfully. "You look great."

"Thanks," she mumbled and slid across the front seat of the Cuda to sit between them.

The easy conversation he and Reed had carried on the way there turned forced and awkward. Brady picked up on a weird vibe between his passengers and wondered again if they'd been lovers. Reed never made eye contact with her, instead making stilted small talk while he stared out the window. Charity seemed flushed and mostly stared down at her hands.

Brady breathed a sigh of relief when they pulled up in front of the community center. He helped Charity out, then hurried to get Reed's wheelchair.

"Ooh!" Reed winced, and grinned at Brady when his mother came over to greet them. He whispered, "Man, if I'd known the twenties were this bright, I'd have brought my shades."

"What are you two laughing at?" Kelly asked.

"Nothing, Mom." Brady fired a shot of water at his dad when he walked by carrying a box of plates.

"Hey, hey, watch it!" Eliot yelled.

"Hi, Charity! And Reed . . . I'm so glad you could make it," Kelly said, reaching to squeeze his hand. "You kids come tell me what you think of our speakeasy."

"All right!" Reed rubbed his hands together. "Bathtub gin, white lightnin' . . . does that mean we get to sample some illegal hooch?"

"Shhhh," she whispered. "The chief of po-lice is right beside you."

"Not tonight." Brady spun his mother around and dipped her. "I brought Reed, didn't I? So, tonight I'm hanging with the thugs."

Jazz pulsed from the walls and as they walked by the big windows, Brady saw some couples already dancing.

"This is great!" Reed said when he wheeled himself inside. "You outdid yourself, Mrs. Simms."

"You did," Brady agreed. He felt like he'd stepped on a movie set. Huge black and white posters of swing dancers covered the wall. A makeshift bar sat in the corner. Smoke rolled from a machine near the door, and Brady peered through the fog before he realized he was looking for Nat. He placed a hand on Charity's waist.

"Oh, Brady. I see Mrs. Laraby over there. I'm going to say hello," Charity said. "Be right back."

Brady nodded and grabbed a handful of chips from a passing Matt's plate. Nat's little brother scowled at him and Reed shot him with his water gun.

Reed grinned up at Brady, then frowned. "What's the matter with you?"

"Just waiting for the sky to fall," Brady said, scanning the crowd. No Nat in sight. He motioned Reed away from the smoke machine. They roamed toward the other end of the room.

"Ah, you forget who you're talking to," Reed said.

"I've had girls fighting over me before. I know what a charge it is. Quit pretending to be so gloomy."

"It's my party, and I'll cry if I want to," Brady said through a mouthful of chips and Reed laughed.

People drifted by to talk to them, then faded away. Brady was watching his mother leading Charity toward the kitchen area when Reed punched his side and pointed at the doorway.

"Holy smokes, Batman. Check it out."

Brady glanced at the entrance. The siren coming through the door froze him in his tracks. Nat's father brushed a kiss on her cheek when she strolled through the door with her brother Justin.

"Talk about drop-dead red," Reed said.

Brady's mouth was too dry to answer him when Nat approached them in her short, shimmering dress. She was talking to Matt and didn't seem to notice them yet. Brady felt a surge of panic when Reed yelled, "Hey, Nat, come here a minute!"

Nat glanced up and met Brady's gaze. Did he imagine the spark in her green eyes when she looked at him? He wasn't sure. He couldn't stop staring at her lips, which were as flaming red as her dress.

"Hey, gorgeous," Reed said. "Why don't you sit in my lap and tell me what you want for your birthday?"

"Well, okay . . ." Brady mimed like he was sitting down. "But people will talk."

Reed tried to shoot him in the back of the head with

his water gun. "Not you, you idiot. I was talking to the Amazing Natasha."

Nat laughed. The smoky sound sent a shiver down Brady's neck. She leaned to peck Reed's cheek. "I'm surprised you recognized me. My mother rouged, powdered, and lipsticked me for an hour. Do I look like a clown?"

"A clown? Darlin', you look incredible. You're the bee's knees, the cat's meow, and the feather in my fedora. See, I have one too. It's just not as big as yours." Reed pointed at his hat, then nudged Brady. "Doesn't she look great?"

"You look beautiful," Brady agreed, and was rewarded with a dazzling smile. He didn't know how long he stood there, staring, but he finally jolted back to himself. "Did you, ah, cut your hair?" he asked, nodding at the sleek black bob.

"No, it's a wig."

"Good," Brady said, and flushed. Why had he said that? But he knew why. He was thinking of the way her hair had been the night they made love, long and curly and flowing down the middle of her back, and how it had felt to run his hands through it.

A strange look flashed in her eyes, and he was afraid he'd insulted her, but she merely laughed again. "Our mothers are fanatics, you know. You wouldn't believe all the stuff I have on with this get-up."

"Yeah, I would." Reed pulled at the flimsy material. "Because I can see most of it."

Nat smacked his hand. She reached for one of her sheer black stockings. Involuntarily, Brady's gaze followed her movement as her fingers tugged the rolled material an inch higher on her tanned thigh.

Once again, Nat caught him looking. "Where's, ah, Charity?" she asked. "Didn't she come?"

"I'm right here," she said icily, and Brady jumped.

CHARITY TUCKED HER ARM IN BRADY'S AND GAVE NAT an exaggerated smile. "I wouldn't miss all the fun. Come on, Brady. I need something to drink."

"Uh, yeah," Brady said, looking like a deer caught in headlights. "Reed, Nat . . . can I get you something?"

"No," Nat murmured, and Reed shook his head.

As she watched them walk away, Reed joked, "She never was one to miss out on any fun."

Nat nodded absently, then jerked her gaze to him. "Oh, God, Reed!" she said through clenched teeth. "Not you too!"

He had the grace to look embarrassed. "So, I wasn't too choosy back in the day. I'm sorry." He shrugged and gave her a devilish smile. "I seem to remember asking you too."

Nat frowned and crossed her arms over her chest. "And just *what* is that supposed to mean?"

Reed's eyes widened and his face flushed almost as red as her dress. "Not that! I didn't mean—" He wiped his mouth with his hand and grinned. "Let me start over. Did I mention you look hot tonight?"

Nat tried to look stern. "Still not off the hook."

"Really, really hot."

She glanced at the couple by the punchbowl and back at Reed. "Does Brady know?"

"Yeah, he knows you're hot."

Nat glared at Reed. "Does he know about you and Charity?"

Reed's smile vanished and he stared down at his lap. "I don't know. But please don't tell him. I really like Brady, and that would be . . . awkward."

"I won't." Nat smiled and leaned to straighten his tie. "She sure shut him down fast, huh?"

Reed snorted. "She may have dragged him away, but I guarantee she's not who he's thinking about right now. You short-circuited his brain in that dress. Check it out."

Nat looked up to see Brady watching them. He quickly looked away.

"Told you so. Listen, Nat. Brady and I were talking earlier, and he thinks you—" Reed stopped in mid-sentence when someone placed a hand on Nat's arm.

"There you are," Alisha said. "I'm sorry I'm late."

"Is everything okay?" Nat asked, remembering the look on Alisha's face when she'd checked her phone messages. She rushed out of Nat's house with a quick goodbye and no explanation.

Alisha's smile looked more like a wince. "Yeah."

Reed cleared his throat. Nat gave Alisha a sly wink and kept talking. Reed cleared his throat again, louder.

"Oh, okay, don't beg." Nat rolled her eyes. "Alisha, this is Reed Donally. Reed, Alisha Walker."

"We've met," Alisha said coolly.

Nat tensed. She knew Alisha didn't fully trust Reed, but she hoped she wouldn't tell him that.

"We have?" Reed squinted at her. "I don't understand how I could forget such a beautiful girl."

Alisha frowned. "You were busy cussing Nat out at the time. At the mall."

A horrified look crossed Reed's face. Nat reached over to squeeze his hand. "But that's in the past now."

"I-I'm sorry," Reed stammered. "I'm sorry that it happened, sorry that you witnessed it. If I could take it back—"

"Reed," Nat said gently. "It's okay."

They lapsed into an uneasy silence. Bleakness chased the sparkle from Reed's eyes, and Nat felt a flash of irritation at Alisha's rudeness. She glanced at her friend and was startled to see she was blinking back tears.

"Reed, excuse us for a minute," Nat said, and grabbed Alisha's arm. She dragged her over to the corner. "What's wrong?" she whispered.

Alisha burst into tears. Shocked, Nat wrapped her arms around her. She'd never seen Alisha cry. Alisha pulled back and swiped at her eyes. "That phone call. It was from my lawyer. The judge denied my custody petition for the boys."

"Oh, honey, I'm so sorry."

Ever since she'd gotten out of Cedar Ridge, Alisha had one goal: to get custody of her two younger brothers from the state. She'd worked like a dog at the hospital and was studying for her RN. It didn't seem fair.

"Did they say why?" Nat asked.

"Um." Alisha blinked and stared up at the lights. "They said the apartment was too small. I told them I was saving for the down payment on a house. The judge said he'd reconsider the petition when I got one."

"Well, see . . ." Nat mustered a smile. "That's not a 'no.' It will happen."

Alisha exhaled. "It's been six years, Nat. Jerome is fifteen years old now. Andre is ten. He probably doesn't even remember me."

Nat hugged her again. "It'll work out. I promise you. You just can't give up hope."

Alisha dabbed at her eyes. "Neither of us can." Nat followed her nod, and saw Brady standing beside Reed. They were both staring.

"I didn't mean to do this here. I wouldn't spoil your party for anything," Alisha said.

"You're not spoiling my party." Nat gave her a crooked smile. "That bitch in the green dress is."

Alisha huffed, then laughed out loud. They watched Charity lead Brady to the dance floor. "God, she looks awful," Alisha said. "Tell you what. I'm going to walk outside a minute, get a breath of air. Then I'm going to ask your man to dance. You hover close and right in the middle of it, I'm going to blink my contact off my eye—"

Nat smiled. "You don't wear contacts."

"So? Brady doesn't know that. I'll tell you to take over until I get back."

Nat rolled her eyes. "Charity will just drag him away again."

"I'll enlist the moms." Alisha stuffed her tissue in the little purse she carried at her side. "You leave Ms. Avocado to us."

She kissed Nat's cheek and slipped outside. Nat wandered back to Reed.

"She okay?" he asked.

"No, but she will be." Nat forced a smile. "Sorry she was so abrupt with you. She got some bad news today."

"What, did Orlando Bloom get married or something? I know how you females are."

"I'm afraid it's a little worse than that." Nat hesitated. "Look, don't tell her I said anything, but Alisha's been trying to get custody of her younger brothers ever since she got out of Cedar Ridge. The judge turned down her latest petition today."

"Where are her parents?"

"Dead. Her mother OD'd when she was a teenager. Her stepfather . . . well, he's the reason she ended up in juvy in the first place. I don't really want to say anything more . . ."

Reed held up his hand. "It's okay. I understand. Think I'll go out and check on her." Nat opened her mouth to protest, and Reed said, "I won't mention anything you told me. Sometimes it's easier to talk to a stranger."

Nat ruffled his hair. "You're a sweetie."

"Shhhh." Reed winked. "Don't ruin my reputation."

As he wheeled away, a strong hand seized hers. For an instant, she thought it might be Brady. She spun around to see her father grinning at her.

"Hey, Birthday Girl. You got a dance for your old man?"

Nat smiled. "Always."

He stepped on her feet when they waltzed, but she didn't mind. Then the music changed and things got wild when Brady's dad cut in to do the Blackbottom with her. He left her breathless with laughter as he shimmied and shook his behind, but she tried her best to keep up. Eliot was like Brady on speed. They got so much applause that they danced the Lindy Hop together next. She caught Brady watching them from the sidelines.

Nat glanced out the window once to see Alisha leaning against the white support column, laughing at something Reed said.

Eliot kissed her hand and doubled over, gasping for breath when the music stopped. "When did we get so old?" he asked her father, who'd grabbed someone's video camera to film them.

"Speak for yourself, old man," Jake replied. "Oh, here we go." He swung the camera around to catch a shot of the huge, flaming cake emerge from the kitchen.

The twins carried it to the bar and eased it down. Jake prodded Nat forward.

"Hey, that's not caramel apple!" Brady protested.

"I've got your caramel apple right here." Selena backed out of the kitchen area clutching the big silver pan with both hands. "It's just too gooey to stick candles in."

Brady hurried around to help her. He gave the cake an appreciative sniff and said, "Now that's what I'm talking about."

He perched on a stool across the bar from her, looking impossibly handsome in the soft glow of the candles. Nat propped against the counter and inhaled the sweet smell of butter cream icing and melting wax. Her heart twisted as memories flashed through her mind of all the other birthdays they'd shared. It felt like old times.

While Reed led the crowd in a rousing, off-key version of "Happy Birthday," Nat smiled at Brady over the cake. To her surprise, he smiled back. When the song ended, he said, "Make a wish, Nat."

You, she thought automatically. *I want you.*

Together, they blew out the forty-six candles on the cake. The crowd applauded when they extinguished them all.

Nat saw Brady's mother nudge his grandmother.

The old woman stepped forward and cupped her hands around her mouth.

"Yoo hoo!" she shouted, and the crowd fell silent.

"Brady, while your mother is cutting the cake, why don't you and Nat have a birthday dance together? I want a picture."

Brady's smile froze on his face. He glanced at Charity, and Nat followed his gaze. Charity's cheeks turned bright red, and her dark eyes shot daggers at Nat.

Nat struggled to keep a straight face. The moms had it figured out. No way could Brady turn down his grandma.

Brady walked over to Charity. Nat's good humor evaporated when he squeezed Charity's hand and leaned to whisper something in her ear.

Nat could imagine what he was saying.

It's only a dance. It doesn't mean anything.

Suddenly, she simply wanted to run. They could force Brady into dancing with her, but they couldn't make him want to. It wasn't the same.

Brady left Charity's side and started walking in her direction. He smiled and held out his hand when a slow waltz began to play. Nat's eyes burned and she tried desperately to blink away the tears before he reached her, but he must've seen them anyway. His smile faded when he reached her.

"What's wrong?" he asked softly.

Nat swallowed and looked at her feet. "Nothing.

You don't have to do this, Brady. I know you don't want to dance with me."

He took a deep breath and placed a hand on her waist. "Sure I do," he said lightly. "It's tradition."

Helplessly, she let him lead her to the dance floor. Brady shocked her when he wrapped his arms around her waist and pulled her close. She'd half-expected him to keep her an arms length away, and almost wished he had. The feel of his warm body moving against hers, the scent of his aftershave, was almost more than she could bear. She slid her arms around his neck and laid her head on his shoulder. The harder she tried not to cry, the more impossible it became. She trembled in his arms.

"Don't," Brady begged hoarsely. "Please don't cry."

Nat jerked her head up straight. His faint stubble grazed her face when she pressed her cheek to his, refusing to look him in the eye. She wanted to deny her tears, but she couldn't speak.

His breath tickled her ear when he hissed, "What do you want from me?"

Tears spilled down Nat's cheeks and she squeezed her eyes shut. She took a deep breath and forced herself to look at him. The pain in his red-rimmed eyes cut her to the quick, and it was a moment before she could speak.

"I want you to forgive me," she gasped. "I want you to love me again. I want this stupid song to play on and on and on because I want you to hold me forever."

Brady made an unintelligible sound through his teeth

and jerked his gaze away from hers. The muscle in his jaw worked furiously while he stared over her shoulder.

"It's not that easy," he growled.

"I know. I understand that. What can I do to show you I'm serious? Tell me what to do, and I'll do it. I'll do anything to get back what we had."

His gaze snapped back to her. "We can't get back what we had. Don't you get it? It can never be the same again."

He dropped his hands, and Nat grabbed one of them. Before she could tell him he was wrong, the window behind them exploded in a shower of glass and fire.

CHAPTER 10

BEFORE NAT COULD REACT, THE SECOND WINDOW dissolved in a glittering cascade of glass. This time, she glimpsed the bottle an instant before it shattered against the floor. A loud whoosh shook the building and the sharp smell of gasoline filled her nose.

Brady seized her hands and jerked her in a wild alley-oop, slinging her as far as he could in the other direction while the gasoline erupted into a lake of fire.

Nat screamed his name when she sailed through the air. Thick, black smoke engulfed the room in the blink of an eye. Nat couldn't see the person she crashed into. They went down in a flurry of arms and legs. Someone stomped on her hand when she tried to scramble to her feet.

Chaos reigned in the darkness. Everyone was screaming and pushing toward the back of the building. Nat got caught up in the crush and at one point the surging crowd lifted her off her feet in their relentless drive toward the exit. She couldn't breathe, couldn't move, and she didn't know where Brady was.

As they pushed her toward the window, Nat recoiled

at the sound of breaking glass, but it wasn't another fire bomb. She saw the hazy outline of a pair of men kicking and throwing themselves at the glass. Her father and Eliot. They started grabbing at the people who weren't pushing through the door and throwing them out the window. Nat gasped for air and found only choking black smoke. She twisted to look over her shoulder as the mob pushed forward, but she couldn't see anything.

Had Brady been consumed in the initial flames?

Her father's hands grasped her forearms and started to lift her.

"No, Daddy!" she protested. "Brady's in there."

"We'll find him," he said, and threw her through the gaping hole like a rag doll. Nat landed on her back in the grass. She lay stunned, gulping in the warm night air like a dying fish.

Again, hands seized her, dragging her away from the open window to keep her from being crushed by the next flying body. Nat blinked up at her brother Justin.

"Are you okay?" he shouted as he grabbed her hand and hauled her to her feet. Nat nodded, and nearly stumbled down the grassy bank.

Numbly, she nodded. She saw her mother and Brady's mother standing a few feet away, clutching each other. Her mother spotted her and clamped her hand over her mouth, bursting into tears of relief.

Nat began to push through the crowd. She lost a shoe but she didn't stop to look for it as she ran. Her mind registered people like snapshots.

Reed and Alisha by the oak tree.

Brady's grandparents and his aunt Elaine on the sidewalk.

Her uncle Scott and his wife, Amy.

She knew where her father and Eliot were, and as she scanned the crowd, the only ones she couldn't find were Brady, Charity and her brother Matt.

The community center's walls shrank and expanded like the sides of some great beast as it belched out great gusts of black smoke.

Oh God, where were Brady and Matt?

She nearly collapsed in relief when she saw Brady hauling Charity through the doorway. One of her brothers ran to help him, though through the haze, she couldn't tell whether it was Justin or Matt.

Sirens screamed in the distance while Nat stumbled toward them. A small huddle of people lurched across her path, their arms linked together like survivors of a plane crash. Impatiently, Nat jostled her way around them.

By the time she got to where she saw them emerge, only Charity stood there.

"Where is Brady?" Nat asked.

Charity must've been as shaken as she looked because she answered, "His dad hustled him around that way." She pointed vaguely up the hill, over Nat's left shoulder. "Your dad's with them. They're trying to take a head count."

"Have you seen my brother Matt?" Nat asked.

Charity paused. "No, I . . . I saw the other one. He was behind me when the thing exploded. Oh, God, you don't think he's still inside, do you?"

Nat didn't answer. She sprinted down the sidewalk.

"Nat, where are you going?" Reed shouted.

"Matt. Have you seen Matt?"

"No, I—"

Nat kept running. She saw some of Matt's friends huddled on the sidewalk. One of them was the girl he'd invited. "Have you seen Matt?" she cried.

The girl tearfully shook her head. "We got separated in there. Justin just ran by, looking for him."

Nat ran to the doorway. She took a great, gulping breath and plunged inside.

There was absolutely no visibility. Gasping and choking, Nat fell to her knees and started to crawl. She pawed blindly in the darkness and screamed her brother's name. A few feet inside, the oxygen disappeared. Nat's head swam and she had the briefest sensation of falling before she blacked out.

"I THINK THAT'S EVERYBODY." BRADY'S DAD RAN A HAND through his hair and stared at the flaming building. "I can't believe we got everyone out."

Brady leaned over, placing his hands on his knees as

he gulped another sweet, clear breath. "Is Jake going to be okay?"

Eliot rubbed a smudged hand over his face. "Yeah, he got burned a little on his back, but it's not too bad. I don't know about Luke Green. He was on fire. I had to chase him down and roll him on the ground. He was standing by the first window."

Brady limped down the hill while he scanned the crowd for Nat. He hoped he hadn't hurt her, throwing her like that, but he reacted as soon as he'd seen what was going on.

He grasped Charity's sleeve. "Hey, have you seen Nat?"

Charity shook her head. "Um, I saw her when she first came out. I think she's with her mother."

"Okay. I'll be right back," Brady said.

He brushed a kiss on her cheek and started around the building.

"Brady!"

He turned to see Alisha running toward him, her face ashen.

"Nat ran back in there."

Even in the mist of the heat pulsating from the fire, Brady felt his blood turn to ice. "She did what?" he shouted. "Why?"

"She's looking for Matt."

"Matt's around front with his mother," Brady yelled, but he was already racing toward the fire.

He held his jacket over his face when he charged

inside.

The oppressive heat struck him like a physical barrier, staggering him on his feet. He screamed her name, but didn't see or hear anything except for the ominous creaking of the ceiling above him. He tripped and fell forward. A piece of glass sliced through his knee, but he scarcely noticed because his hand brushed against something warm. Human.

He fumbled in the pitch black and finally scooped her in his arms. Like a scene in one of those old Frankenstein movies they used to watch, he lurched for the doorway with Nat in his arms.

He heard someone scream when he staggered outside, but he didn't pay any attention. The crowd cleared away when he took a few stumbling steps forward. He laid Nat gently on the grass and felt for a pulse.

She wasn't breathing.

"Oh God, Oh God, please," Brady gasped.

He tilted her head back to open her airway and checked her pulse again.

Nothing.

Fueled by terror, Brady launched a frantic effort to resuscitate her. He zoned out as he went through his CPR routine. Breathing, checking, pumping. Breathing, checking, pumping. The noise of the crowd faded away until there was nothing but him and Nat and the painful thudding of his heart against his ribcage.

Oh God. Breathe, Nat, breathe.

Someone seized his arm and he angrily shook them off. He pinched her nostrils together and huffed another breath into her lungs.

Two of them seized him this time. They clutched his arms and dragged him backward. Brady fought like a wild man until someone shouted, "The EMTs are here. Let them take care of her."

Dazed, he looked up and realized one of the men holding him was his father. Brady nodded numbly and watched the paramedics laboring over Nat.

He shuddered and covered his face with his hands. His father wrapped an arm around his shoulders and held on tight. Brady didn't want his sympathy, because she wasn't gone. She couldn't be gone.

"Hey, we've got a pulse!" one of them yelled.

Brady sagged against his father and bawled like a baby.

He pushed himself to his feet while they strapped Nat to a gurney. He chased them as they loaded her in the ambulance.

"I'm going with her," he said.

"Sorry. No can do," one of them replied. "No passengers."

Brady grabbed the door handle and started to pull himself inside. The burly EMT grasped the back of his jacket. "I said no."

"Pete," the other medic interrupted. "This is Brady Simms—"

"I don't care if he's the pope. We've got to get this

girl to the hospital."

"He's the chief of police."

The burly medic frowned, but released Brady's shirt. "Fine, but he has to sign a waiver."

Brady climbed in the ambulance and the female EMT followed. He dimly recognized her, thought it might be someone he'd gone to school with, but he couldn't recall her name.

He sat on a tiny white stool and watched her back while she leaned over Nat.

"Do me a favor and sign one of those papers on that clipboard," she called over her shoulder.

Brady reached behind him and grabbed the battered white clipboard. He scrawled his name on the bottom of the form without reading it, then resumed his tense vigil.

The EMT turned to smile at him. "I think she's going to be fine, thanks to you. She's breathing much better now."

Relief flooded him. He offered a silent thanks to God before looking up at the EMT. "Thank you . . . Patty," he said, reading the name off her shirt.

"You're welcome. I've got to write some stuff in her chart, so you can move a little closer if you want."

Brady scooted his stool forward and perched by the side of the stretcher. It hurt him to see her lying there like that, so pale and small under the stiff white sheet. He shut his eyes and laid his head against the cool metal rail. He kept picturing her face on the dance floor, how her beautiful green eyes had sparkled with tears when she'd begged him to love her again. Why hadn't he simply told her he'd never stopped loving her, he would probably love her until he died, and he'd wanted to hold her on the dance floor forever too?

He felt someone touch his hair and jerked his head up. Nat gave him a slight, bewildered smile beneath the oxygen mask before her eyes widened. She made a wheezing sound and Brady jumped from the stool. "She's choking!" he cried.

Patty hurried over to her. For a long moment, all he heard was the crackle of the radio and Nat's wheezing. Patty smiled at him over her shoulder.

"Ah, she's not choking. She's laughing." She giggled too, and turned to Nat. "Stop that!" she chided.

"What's she laughing at?" Brady demanded, and Patty giggled again.

"I hated to mention it before, but you got a little, ah . . ." She made a motion with her finger across her mouth.

Brady lifted his hand to his mouth and rubbed. Nat's red lipstick smeared all over his fingers. He gave a startled laugh. Patty moved away from Nat, and Brady resumed his place on the stool.

"You know, you don't look so hot yourself," he retorted. Her black wig sat at an angle on her head, like some kind of small, burrowing animal. He gently unpinned it and threw it in the wastebasket.

A look of pure panic erased the smile from her face.

"Matt," she mouthed.

Brady grasped her slack hand, which was surprisingly cool in his. "He's fine! Just fine, I swear to you. He made it out. As far as we know, everyone did."

Nat exhaled and squeezed his fingers. She closed her eyes again. Brady lifted her hand to his mouth and kissed it. He chuckled when he saw another red smear and wiped his mouth with his sleeve.

He held her hand all the way to the hospital, only relinquishing it when they carried her out of the ambulance and wheeled her into the emergency room. Brady wandered into the waiting room, where he was soon joined by other bedraggled members of the birthday party.

Brady called bureau officer Ian Kirby from the hospital pay phone and explained what had happened. Ian assured him that the TBI was already on the way, along with the ATF. Brady hung up the phone, reassured that the sheriff wouldn't be in control of the investigation.

"Brady!" he heard his mother shout.

She ran to him and checked him over, even making him turn so she could inspect his back. "Are you okay? Are you sure? How's Nat? Where did they take her?"

His father slipped in behind her and placed his hands on her shoulders. He gave Brady a tired smile. "Honey, are you going to give him a chance to answer any of those questions you're hurling at him?"

"I'm sorry," she said, and wrapped her arms around

Brady.

Over her shoulder, Brady spotted Reed and Alisha coming through the double glass doors. He waited until they were in earshot to say, "I think she's okay. She laughed at me in the ambulance, because I had lipstick all over my face."

"Oh, thank God!" Kelly sighed. Eliot clapped his hand on Brady's shoulder. Reed reached up and took Alisha's hand.

"Jake's in the ER too. He's okay. Just wanted to be back there with Nat," Eliot said.

"The twins, they're okay? Both of them?" Brady knew he'd seen both Justin and Matt outside, but he hadn't had time to ask them if they were injured.

Kelly jerked her head at the doors. "They're in the other waiting room down the hall with their mother. Luke is in the ER, and they're checking out a few people for smoke inhalation."

"Charity?" he asked, a little ashamed he was just now asking about her.

His parents glanced at each other.

"I had someone take her home. She didn't want to come to the hospital," his dad said.

Brady felt a stab of guilt for leaving her there. His terror for Nat had taken precedence over everything. He eyed the pay phone and then fumbled in his pocket for change.

"Here." Alisha thrust a cell phone at him.

After five rings, the answering machine picked up. Brady disconnected without leaving a message. With a frown, he asked, "Are you guys sure she was okay? She's not answering."

"I talked to her after you did. She's okay." Reed gave him a faint smile. Probably just pissed. She stomped off when you were doing CPR."

Irritated, Brady asked, "Why? Because I was trying to save Nat's life?"

Reed tugged his ear and squinted up at Alisha. "Ah, I think it was more what you were *saying* while you were trying to save Nat's life."

Brady froze. "What did I say?"

No one, not even his mother, would meet his eyes.

"What did I say?" he repeated. "I don't remember saying anything."

Reed flushed, and finally looked up at him. "Oh, man, you went wild! I was scared you were going to break Nat's ribs or something. You told Nat you couldn't lose her again, that you couldn't live without her . . . stuff like that."

Brady glanced at the solemn faces surrounding him, then sat heavily in one of the padded chairs. "Oh, God," he murmured. He opened the phone and dialed Charity's number again. "Please pick up," he said, when the machine answered. "I'm sorry." He waited a long moment before hitting disconnect and handing the phone back to Alisha, then he slumped forward and placed his hands over his face.

His life was unraveling and all he could do was watch.

Someone sat beside him and placed an arm around his shoulders.

"Never apologize for showing feeling. When you do so, you apologize for the truth."

Alisha offered a sympathetic smile when he looked up at her.

Despite the utter grimness of his situation, Brady smiled back. "Very profound. Fortune cookie?"

"Benjamin Disraeli," she replied. "Want another one?"

Brady sighed. "Sure. Why not?"

She leaned to kiss his cheek. "To thine own self be true." She stood and adjusted her skirt. "I'm going to grab a bottle of water. Anyone need anything?"

"I do," Reed said. "I'll come with you."

As Brady watched them leave, the waiting room phone chirped. Eliot answered it. "Yeah. Hang on a sec." He covered the mouthpiece with his hand and nodded at Brady. "It's for you, son."

Brady took it from him. "Yeah?" he asked tiredly.

"What do you want?"

He could tell by Charity's sullen tone that he'd be digging for awhile to get out of this one. "I wanted to make sure you were okay."

"You mean you care?"

Brady shot an embarrassed look at his parents. His father put an arm around his mother and they walked away to give him some privacy. "Of course I care," he said quietly.

"You've got a fine way of showing it. Brady, what's happened to us? Ever since Nat's been back, you've been a different person."

"It's the case—"

"The case, the case. It's more than just the damn case, and we both know it," she snapped. "You know what she did to you. Are you willing to risk that again?"

"Look, I . . ." Brady winced and rubbed his throbbing temple. "I don't want to talk about this on the phone. Can I come by later?"

"How much later?"

"I don't know. The TBI will want to question us, and I need to see how everyone is doing."

He purposely didn't say Nat's name, but he could almost feel Charity's hostility crackle over the line when she said, "Don't take too long, Brady. I just might not be waiting."

The phone clicked in his ear, and Brady exhaled. His relationship with Charity was collapsing from within like a house of cards, and he hadn't even told her about her brother yet.

He didn't know if he could save their relationship, and worse, he didn't know if he wanted to save it.

He didn't love her. The relationship was too new, and to be honest, he didn't know if he could ever love anyone like he'd loved Nat.

When Charity first asked him out, he wanted to give it a chance. She was pretty and sweet, and he'd reached the point where he'd have done anything to escape his damnable obsession with Nat. Charity had made him feel like a man again, and it'd been nice to feel desired. Important.

Before Nat came back into his life, things between him and Charity had been nice . . . easygoing. No pressure. Now things were boiling over, and he felt like Charity wanted more from him than he could promise at the moment.

But so did Nat.

It ticked him off that she could ask his forgiveness so casually, when their break up had been the singular most devastating event of his life.

I want you to love me again, she'd said.

At least she knew he'd once loved her. She'd never given him that same reassurance, except for a few words whispered the night she spent in his bed.

But still . . . when he thought she was dying, he'd only wanted her back. Unconditionally. Any way he could get her. It might be wrong, it might be stupid, but that's how it had felt. That's how it still felt.

"Hey, Chief."

Brady turned to see the Tennessee bureau investigator, Ian Kirby, walking toward him.

"This is one way to get your birthday mentioned in the paper," Kirby teased.

Brady was wound too tight to joke. "Did you find anything?"

"Arson investigator's on the scene. I talked to an old man who was emptying his trash in the dumpsters across the road. He saw an old pickup slow in front of the community center, but he assumed it was someone attending the party until he heard the glass shatter and the screams."

Brady's pulse quickened. "Did he see the guy's face?"

Kirby sighed. "No. His eyesight isn't much. Shouldn't even have been driving. Got no tag number, either. He said it was blue, but he couldn't give me a make or anything."

"Damn." Brady pinched the bridge of his nose. "Does the sheriff have a blue truck? Or maybe Joe?"

"You really think they're the ones, don't you?"

Brady stared at him for a moment, gauging his reaction, but he couldn't read anything in Kirby's blank expression. "Yeah," he said finally. "I do."

"Nothing registered to either Richards, but the sheriff's sister has a 1986 Chevy Silverado. The title says blue, but it's more rust than anything."

"Any trace of chemicals?"

Kirby shook his head. "Just did a drive by, because I knew you'd ask. Don't have enough to get a warrant on it. You really think someone tried to toast forty people to get at a girl who caused a car wreck four years ago?"

"I think someone was trying to get her and Reed Donally, the other survivor. They were both there. And

I'm surer than ever she didn't cause that wreck."

He filled Kirby in on the EDR results.

"It could be a computer malfunction," Kirby said, but his dark eyes snapped with interest. "Those things were fairly new back then."

Brady also told him his theory about the air bag. "I'm waiting on the results."

Kirby clapped a hand on his shoulder. "That Hawthorne girl is lucky to have you on her side. I want to know when you hear anything. Now, let's get your statement about the fire."

Brady told him what he remembered, which wasn't much.

"Molotov cocktail in Coalmont." Kirby shook his head. "Unbelievable." He closed his notebook and stood. "I've got to talk to the rest of these people. You take care, Chief."

Brady nodded, and glanced at his watch. What was taking them so long with Nat?

Selena Hawthorne opened the waiting room door and scanned the room. Brady jumped up and crossed over to her.

"Any word on Nat?" he asked.

"No, not yet. Have you seen your mom?"

"Not in the last few minutes."

Selena chewed on her bottom lip. "They're moving Jake to a room. I want to go with him, but I'm afraid Nat will need me—"

"Go," Brady said. "I'll be right here. If they tell me anything, I'll come get you."

Her anxious green eyes, so like Nat's, studied him. "You're sure? You don't have to leave or anything?"

"I'm not going anywhere."

"Okay. We're in room 337." She shot him a grateful smile. "Thank you."

She'd been gone about ten minutes when the waiting room door opened. Carla Andrews, the nurse Roscoe was dating, walked inside carrying a clipboard.

"Natasha Hawthorne family?" she called.

"Hey, Carla." Brady touched her sleeve. "How is she?"

"Oh, hey, Brady." Carla smiled. "She's fine. Resting. We're moving her to a room."

"Which one? Her mom is down the hall with Nat's dad. I told her I'd come get her when you moved Nat."

Carla checked the chart. "We're putting her in 315."

"Thanks."

Brady strode down the hall to Jake's room and cracked the door. Jake lay on his stomach, burying his face in the pillow while a nurse applied something to his blistered shoulders. Jake groaned, and Brady took a hesitant step inside. His movement drew Selena's attention. She turned to stare at him with huge, tear-filled eyes.

Brady motioned her over. "They're putting Nat in room 315," he whispered. "Stay with him. I'll go in with Nat."

Jake groaned again, and Selena nodded. A tear slipped down her cheek. "Come get me if you have to leave."

"I won't leave her alone," he said. "I'll take care of her."

Nat's mother squeezed his hand. "I know you will."

Brady hurried back the way he'd come and slipped inside Nat's room. Carla smiled and pressed a finger to her lips. Nat was sleeping.

He watched her hang Nat's I.V. bag. Carla gave a little wave before picking up her clipboard and striding outside.

Brady wandered toward Nat's bed. Her left foot poked out from beneath the thin blanket, and Brady paused to tug the cover over it. He pulled a chair close to her bed and sat. After a moment's hesitation, he removed the shoes from his aching feet and examined the cut on his knee.

He didn't realize how tired he was until he got still. Nat's hands lay atop the white sheets. Brady slipped his hand underneath hers. Her palm was still scabbed from that fiasco at Reed's.

Like a child's, her fingers twitched around his. They were cold. Gently, Brady pulled his hand free and tugged the blanket higher, all the way to her chin, taking care not to tangle her IV line. Then he smoothed her hair away from her cheek.

Nope, he didn't have any pride left at all. Not a shred.

Looking down at her beautiful, smudged face, he only wanted to hold her, to protect her, and forget all the bad history between them. He leaned to kiss her forehead.

Nat stirred. Her eyes flew open, and her body convulsed in a soundless scream.

Brady made a grab for her when she jerked upright. His other hand fumbled for the rail between them. "Nat!" he said. "It's okay."

"Matt," she wheezed. "Matt."

Brady shoved the rail down and crawled in beside her to take her in his arms. "Matt's okay, remember? So is Justin."

Nat sagged against him. "Are you sure?"

"I'm positive. Do you want me to drag both those knuckleheads in here so you can see for yourself?"

Nat made a muffled sound against his chest that might've been a laugh. "No. That's . . . okay. I believe you." Her arm tightened around his waist. ". . . so scared. When Charity said she hadn't seen him, then Matt's girlfriend said the same thing, I lost it."

"Charity said what?"

"That she hadn't seen him. Then Matt's friends said the same thing. I panicked."

Brady frowned. A finger of ice traced its way down his spine.

Had Charity sent Nat back inside that burning building on purpose?

He wanted to believe she'd merely been confused, but he and Charity had seen both boys as soon as he'd gotten her out of the building. Had spoken to both of them.

Troubled, he lay down and eased Nat backward with him. She rested her head on his chest and he tightened his arms around her.

Neither spoke, and in a few minutes Brady felt the sudden heaviness of her head and realized Nat had dozed off again. As tired as he was, he couldn't shut his eyes. He kept replaying the scene after the fire.

Charity had seen both boys. He knew she had.

He was still mulling it over when Nat woke an hour later.

She laughed and rolled over to face him. "Brady, I don't know how you're lying here with me like this." She wrinkled her nose. "I stink."

Brady tweaked her nose and smiled. "The smoke's messed me up. I can't smell anything at all. Besides, it can't be as bad as that summer when we were nine. Remember when you got sprayed by that skunk at the cabin?"

Nat covered her face with her hand and gave a mortified laugh. "How could I forget? Mama scrubbed the hide off me, and I still stank. I remember that first night, they made me eat supper on the back porch." She dropped her hand and smiled. "And you—bless your heart—you got your plate and sat out there with me, anyway."

"Hardest meal I ever had to choke down," Brady admitted with a smile.

Nat swatted at him, but Brady caught her wrist

before she could dislodge her IV. "Easy now!" he said. "Get some rest. I'm too tired to fight tonight. Maybe tomorrow."

He rolled onto his side, and Nat snuggled against him. This time, they both went to sleep.

BRADY JOLTED AWAKE A LITTLE BEFORE DAWN, STARTLED by the beep of Nat's IV. A nurse he didn't know smiled down at him while she changed the bag. Realizing he wasn't supposed to be in the bed, he started to sit up, but she waved him back down.

"It's okay." She shrugged. "I don't mind. Just be up before the doctor comes in at seven."

When she left, Brady gently untangled himself from Nat and sat up anyway. He rubbed his grainy eyes and stared down at her sleeping form. Though the rest of him was chilled, he still felt the imprint of her warm body against his clothes.

He had to talk to Charity. Today.

Brady slipped on his shoes and staggered out into the hall. He was surprised to see his father, a cup of coffee and a McDonald's bag in his hand.

"The nurse said you were awake. I thought you might need this."

Brady gratefully accepted the coffee, but refused the offer of food.

Eliot dug a biscuit out of the bag and unwrapped it. "Oh yeah. Some guy named Mole called the house. Said the station gave him our number when he couldn't get your cell. He's got the tape you wanted, and he'll be at work by seven."

Brady nearly choked on the gulp of coffee he'd just taken. "You're kidding! Oh man, I'd almost given up on that."

"Important?"

"It could be." Brady glanced down at his filthy, rumpled clothes. "Hey, can you or Mom stay with Nat? I need to shower and see this guy. It's about Nat's case."

"Sure." Eliot grinned. "We would've relieved you earlier, but you, ah, looked pretty comfortable."

Brady flushed and looked away. "So, how's Jake?" he asked. "And Luke?"

"Both of them are going to be fine. Jake will probably get to come home today. Luke's burns weren't as bad as I feared. Maybe he will too."

"Good." Brady glanced at his watch. "I'm going to run. I'll have my cell on, so call if anything happens."

Brady phoned Roscoe from his apartment, and was relieved that nothing else seemed to be stirring in Coalmont. For once, he was grateful for a dose of small town inactivity.

Brady patiently answered a barrage of questions about the fire, then took a long, hot shower to scrub the stench of smoke from his body. He was waiting in the courthouse parking lot when Mole arrived at work.

"Are you okay?" the little dark-haired man demanded, as he pulled a briefcase from the passenger seat of his Corolla. "You look like crap."

"Rough night." Brady rubbed his chin and realized he'd forgotten to shave.

"I heard. Everybody heard." Mole popped open the briefcase and handed Brady a cassette. "Sorry it took so long. There was a lot to wade through."

"I know, and I really owe you one. You're a lifesaver," Brady said.

Mole looked embarrassed when he slammed the briefcase shut. "I hope it helps."

Brady stared down at the cassette. "Me too."

FIFTEEN MINUTES LATER, BRADY STOOD OUTSIDE Charity's apartment. He pounded on the door and waited. When she didn't answer, he pounded again. "Charity, I know you're in there!" he yelled.

She opened the door, still dressed in her nightgown. Narrowing her eyes, she crossed her arms over her chest and glowered at him. "It's about ti—hey, what are you doing?" she demanded when he pushed past her and entered the apartment.

Brady didn't say anything. He didn't trust himself to speak. He flopped on the couch and jerked the tape player out of his shirt pocket. Glaring at Charity, he pressed PLAY.

"911, what's your emergency?" the dispatcher asked.

The recording was four years old, but there was no mistaking the next voice it preserved. Her voice was muffled, panicky, but Brady would've known it anywhere.

"Um, there's been a wreck. We saw the lights from the road. Trussell Road. I think it's bad," a teenage Charity sobbed, and hung up the phone.

Brady clicked off the recorder and asked coldly, "So, are you going to tell me what happened, or would you rather wait and explain it to the state police?"

CHAPTER 11

CHARITY GAPED AT HIM, HER PRETTY FACE SUDdenly stricken and pale. "Brady . . . what do you mean?"

He scowled at her. "You mean, what do I know? I know Tony was driving the night of the accident. I know you helped stage the crime scene, and I can bet I know who helped you."

Panic flashed in her eyes. "You can't prove it. You can't prove anything."

"I already did." Brady dug a sheaf of folded papers out of his back pocket and flung them at her. She made no move to catch them. They fell to the floor like a wounded bird.

"Two different forensic tests show Nat wasn't driving. Your 911 call places you at the scene of the accident. Do you have any idea what the penalty is for staging a crime scene?"

Charity pinched the bridge of her nose. "It wasn't like that." She flopped into the recliner across from him and buried her face in her hands. "Mom and Dad were fighting that night. Tony was the only one who could do anything with Daddy when he was like that."

"So?" Brady prompted.

"So, my brother Jimmy and I went looking for Tony. We found him at Melody's party, but he didn't want to come with us. He was begging Nat to let him drive her car. Then Mel's mom said the neighbors had complained about the noise and the party started breaking up. A bunch of people decided to go to the Pearl's Diner for breakfast, and everyone started piling into cars. Nat told Tony he could drive them to the diner. Jimmy and I were supposed to follow them and pick him up at Pearl's."

Brady shifted on the sofa. "What happened next?"

A tear slipped down Charity's cheek. "Oh, Brady, it was awful. We were right behind them, but Tony kept going faster and faster. He lost control going into that curve and started sliding. The car seemed to flip forever. Jimmy nearly wrecked, too, trying to stop. We ran down to help them. There was so much blood . . ." She rubbed her forehead. "Jimmy freaked out. Bodies were scattered everywhere. Tony was hanging out the driver's door. He was already dead. Jimmy dragged him out on the grass and tried to do CPR, but Tony's chest was crushed. Jimmy was afraid they would sue our parents, so he tugged Nat across to the driver's side and belted her in."

Brady stared at her in disbelief. "Nat was alive, Charity. Your brother was dead. How could you let her take the blame for that?" He jumped to his feet and paced the narrow living room.

Charity stood too. She held her palms out, entreating him. "We thought they would all die. You didn't see them."

"What about the trial? You could've come forward then."

"I couldn't," she said weakly. "I was so scared. Haven't you ever been scared, Brady?"

He stopped pacing and glared at her. "Not scared enough to let an innocent person be punished for something I did." He pushed his hand through his hair and gave a harsh bark of laughter. "You made me apologize to you for working on Nat's case, and you knew. . ." He shook his head. "Do you know how guilty I've felt about all this?"

She studied her fingernails. "Not guilty enough to tell me you were investigating it."

"I wanted to be sure. I didn't want to hurt you. I've suspected a while now that Tony was the driver, but I didn't know about you until this morning." He laughed again. "Some cop I am, right? All this searching, and you've been under my nose all along. God, how do you even sleep at night?"

Anger sparked in her brown eyes when she jerked her head up. "I hate Nat," she said through clenched teeth. "I've always hated her. She's caused me nothing but trouble. If you're waiting for me to say I'm sorry, forget it. She shouldn't have let him drive that night."

"I can't believe you," Brady snapped. He was resisting a mighty urge to throttle her. "Did you and Jimmy also kill Bobby McBee? Are you behind these attacks on Nat and Reed?"

The defiant look on Charity's face vanished, washed away by shock. "How can you ask me that? You know I couldn't do that."

Brady fingered a picture of himself and Charity that sat on her bookshelf, then knocked it off into the garbage can. "I don't know you at all."

"I was in that fire too!" Charity yelled, and Brady turned on her.

He stalked toward her, backing her against the entertainment center. "Did you send Nat back into that burning building?"

"Of course not!"

They stood so close his breath moved her hair. "You told her you hadn't seen Matt."

"Her brother? I didn't say that. I saw both twins as soon as we got out."

Brady brushed his hand against his mouth. For a moment, he simply stared, stunned to see the monster beneath her pretty façade. "You really did it. You really tried to kill her."

"No! She's lying. She's only trying to get you back. As many times as she's hurt you, do you really believe her over me?"

"Anytime."

The word seemed to echo in the small apartment. Suddenly, Charity's face went from defiant to fearful. She reached for him, and Brady flinched away from her touch.

"You don't have to tell anybody," she said desperately. "What's done is done. I can't give Nat back the time she served. You can get the civil case thrown out without involving me, can't you? You owe me that much."

Brady frowned. "I don't owe you anything. I've already called Ian Kirby. Expect a visit from the TBI this morning."

He turned, picked up his tape recorder and stalked out the door.

Back inside his car, Brady opened his wallet and stared down at his badge. He had one more stop to make. He shoved his troubled thoughts aside as he slammed his Explorer in gear and drove to the mayor's house.

He found Mike in the back yard, sitting on the ground surrounded by Go Cart parts. Mike slapped a skinny white knee in disgust and threw down the part he was holding. He looked up when Brady strode across the yard to him.

"Boy, where've you been?" Mike demanded. "I was worried about you after I heard what happened at the community center. I just got off the phone with your old man and he said you were okay." He peered at Brady from beneath his bushy brows. "You *are* okay, aren't you?"

Brady squatted beside him and picked up the part

Mike had discarded. He forced a smile and said, "No. No, I'm not. I need to talk to you." With his free hand, he fished a piece of paper out of his front pocket and handed it to Mike.

"What's this?" Mike frowned at the paper and pulled it away from his face to read it.

"My resignation."

Mike shot him a startled look over the top of the page. "What? Why? Is this about your FBI application?"

Brady stared at him blankly. He'd been looking forward to this birthday for two years, when he'd finally be old enough to apply to the FBI, working hard to build the background he'd need for the time when he could finally apply to the bureau. The dream that had driven him for years had ceased to be important after Nat had blown back into his life. He shook his head. "You know about the McBee case I've been working on?"

"The murder case?" Mike grunted. "Helluva way to break you in. How's it going? Are you making any progress?"

Brady snapped a part in place and tightened the screw. "Maybe. I don't know." He briefed Mike on the investigation, where it pointed, where it had led. "That's why I'm resigning. I haven't been able to focus on anything but this case. All I know is, I have to protect Nat. Things are moving so fast that I've not had time to worry about anything else. I'm neglecting my duties as police chief."

Mike snorted. "Which are what, holding Roscoe's

hand while he sits in the school zone looking for speeders? Brady, nothing else is going on. Coalmont ain't exactly New York City. You're working a murder case that occurred in your jurisdiction. I'd say you're doing exactly what you're supposed to be doing."

Brady grabbed a wrench and strained to loosen a bolt on the motor. "Yeah, well, the sheriff doesn't think so. He's been threatening to call a special city council meeting."

Mike ripped the resignation letter in half and tossed it over his shoulder. "You leave Boss Hogg to me."

"But..."

Mike grinned. "I do not accept this resignation."

"But I might have to go out of town for a few days," Brady protested.

"So go. We can hold down the fort." Mike scratched his hairy calf. "This girl . . . she must mean a lot to you, huh?"

Brady paused, weighing his words. In the end, he simply stated the truth. "She means everything."

Mike clamped his shoulder. "You gotta take care of her then. Go take care of your witness. You leave the rest to me."

※ ※ ※

NAT SAT ON THE PORCH SWING, LISTENING TO THE dull whack of Justin lobbing baseballs at the target he'd painted on the side of their father's outbuilding. The scent of fresh apple pie drifted through the kitchen window, making Nat's stomach rumble, but she was too content to move. The breeze that stirred the leaves carried the promise of cooler weather to come.

"I think Nat's outside," she heard her mother say.

The back door swung open, and Brady walked out.

"I found her," he called over his shoulder. He stood there for a moment, shifting from one sneaker to the other.

His eyes had stolen the color of the stormy summer sky behind him. Even in a white t-shirt and faded jeans, he took her breath away.

He ambled over to the swing, and she moved her feet so he could sit beside her.

"How are you?" he asked, reaching to squeeze her hand.

"Okay. Still coughing, but I'll live."

"There's something we need to talk about," he said, and his troubled expression made her heart do a crazy little dance in her chest.

"Is it that bad?" she joked, but couldn't quite muster a smile. "Did you get the DNA tests? They were on Daddy's fax when we got home."

"Yeah." He leaned back in the swing and crossed a leg underneath him. Sunlight played on his golden hair. "But I have more than that. I know who set you up, Nat." He took a deep breath. "It was Charity. Charity and her brother Jimmy. They staged the accident scene."

Nat wrinkled her nose and shot him a puzzled smile. Surely she hadn't heard him right. "What?"

Brady pulled a small recorder out of his pocket and played the 911 tape.

"Is that her?" Nat stammered. "Are you sure?"

"I confronted her, and she confessed."

The implication of what he'd said finally began to sink in. Nat covered her mouth with a shaky hand. The tremor spread down her arms until she was quaking all over.

Brady pulled her into his arms, against the warmth of his chest. "I'm so sorry," he murmured. "I'm sorry you were punished for something you didn't do. I always felt something was wrong about the seatbelts. I should've figured it out sooner."

"Are you kidding?" Nat hugged him. She spoke in a rush, unable to contain the giddiness bubbling in her chest. "Ever since that day with Dara, I've been so hopeful, but I never really let myself believe. Don't you realize what you've given me?"

She pulled back and clasped his face in her hands. His stubble tickled her palms as she gave him a dopey grin. His brow furrowed, and all at once, she saw so much in those blue eyes. Confusion, fear, desire.

Trust me, Brady, she begged silently. *I swear I'll never hurt you again.*

She leaned to kiss him.

CHAPTER 12

BRADY'S HANDS SHOT UP AND CIRCLED HER wrists. In one smooth motion, he twisted his head and gently pushed her away. He jumped up and paced in front of the swing.

"Something you said at the hospital got me to thinking," he said briskly, as if nothing had just happened.

Nat turned away so he wouldn't see the tears burning her eyes. "What?" she muttered over the lump in her throat.

"Pack your bags. We're going to the cabin to stay until your trial date."

Startled, she jerked her gaze to him, her tears forgotten. "What?"

Brady grimaced and stared out at the lawn. "This whole investigation, we've been reacting instead of acting. I want to play on the other side of the ball for awhile. If we go to the cabin, I won't have to worry that you're in danger, and maybe I'll have time to go over all the evidence and figure out who's doing this. Kirby told me he checked out Jimmy Franklin. He's working on an oil rig in Alaska, and he's got an alibi for all the attacks." He slapped his knees. "But anyway . . . nobody other than our families knows about the cabin. You should be safe there."

Nat made an effort to shut her gaping jaw. "What about Reed? I'm worried about him too."

Brady shook his head. "I called his house. This time his stepfather answered and chewed me out for putting Reed in danger. He threatened to sue me, and he wouldn't let me talk to Reed. He seems to think Reed is safe enough as long as he hides in that house. There's not much I can do without his permission." He glanced up at her. "What do you say?"

Nat exhaled and climbed out of the swing. "I say I can be ready in ten minutes."

Her shoulder brushed his when she walked by. Even that small contact sent shivers through her. Three days, alone at the cabin with Brady. They'd shared so many good times there. At the cabin, he wouldn't be able to run. He'd have to listen to her, and maybe if he did, he would understand.

This felt like her last chance, and she wasn't going to let it slip away.

Brady followed her inside. He sat at the kitchen table to talk to her mother while Nat ran upstairs to pack.

Nat tugged an overnight bag from the top of her closet and started throwing clothes in it. As she rifled through her dresser drawers, her hand hesitated on a folded square of silver silk. She pulled the nightgown from the drawer and held it to her face.

Brady would remember the gown—she was sure of it—but was it fair to play on his memories like that?

"They're my memories too," she said softly, and tossed it in the bag before she could change her mind. All was fair in love and war. The trouble was, she wasn't sure which of the two she was about to get into with Brady.

Nat skipped downstairs. Brady took the bag from her hand and she hugged her mother goodbye.

"You two be careful," Selena said as she released Nat and hugged Brady too. "Have you told your mother?"

Brady nodded. "I went over there first. Remember, don't tell anyone outside of the immediate family where we're going, no matter what. I'll be checking in with everyone who needs to hear from me."

Selena nodded, and walked them outside to Brady's Cuda.

Like a little kid, Nat waved to her mother until they drove out of sight, then she leaned back against the leather seat and stared at Brady.

She was really alone with him, would be alone for the next three days. The flutter in her stomach was part anticipation, part fear. She couldn't blow this.

Brady must've mistaken the reason for her stare. "I'm making sure no one is following us," he explained.

Nat glanced out the windshield and realized they

were heading in the wrong direction. She chuckled when he went through a series of complicated turns and side roads. "Don't you think you're being a little paranoid?" she teased.

Brady didn't return her smile. If anything, his frown deepened. "I haven't been paranoid enough. You almost died, Nat, because of me."

Nat felt a surge of tenderness for him. Brady was so responsible, such a perfectionist. Always ready to bear the weight of the world. This time, she wasn't going to let him. "Wrong. I lived, because of you."

Brady filled his cheeks with air and slowly exhaled as he glanced in the rearview mirror. He flipped on the radio and scanned until he found an oldies station.

So, he didn't want to talk. Too bad.

"What will happen to Charity?" Nat asked, slipping off her sandals and tucked her leg beneath her.

Brady shook his head. "I'm not sure. Staging a crime scene is a felony. She was underage at the time, but I don't know if that will help her. The court won't look lightly on it, especially since there were deaths involved and an innocent person was incarcerated."

"What if I don't want to press charges?" Nat asked.

Brady nearly ran off the road when he jerked his head around to gape at her. "What?"

Nat twisted the beads on her bracelet, struggling to find the words to explain it to him. "I'm tired of living my life around that one night," she said finally. "So many lives were destroyed in the space of a few minutes. I wasn't the only one who was hurt. Charity lost someone too. Punishing her won't bring back Tony, or Jen or Mel. It won't give Reed back his legs, and it won't give me back the two years at Cedar Ridge. Like Reed said, I want this to be over. Seeing Charity suffer won't give me any satisfaction."

Brady swallowed, then nodded. "That's pretty big of you, considering. But I don't think you'll have any say in the matter. The state will take up the investigation."

"Will you see about it? If I have to testify, I'll be glad—"

"Nat, I need to tell you something. Charity doesn't deserve your help. I think . . ." He hesitated, shooting her a troubled look. "I think she tried to kill you."

"What?" Once again, he'd caught her off-guard.

"The fire. Something you said at the hospital made me realize it, and I questioned Charity about it. What did she tell you outside the building?"

Nat shook her head, confused. "Nothing. I asked if she'd seen Matt. No one had. Not his girlfriend, not his buddies—"

"Charity saw Matt. And Justin. We talked to both of them as soon as we made it out. We heard him say he was going around front to look for your mother. I think Charity told you that, hoping you would react like you did."

Stunned, Nat opened her mouth, then shut it again.

Two different people had tried to kill her in the same night. If *that* wasn't an attention grabber, nothing was. But maybe it hadn't been two different people . . .

"Do you think Charity and her brother, or Charity and her father, could be behind this all?" she asked.

Brady's brow furrowed. "That's what I thought at first, but Jimmy Franklin is working in Alaska. He has a solid alibi for all the attacks. We still don't know where Charity's father is, but she denied having anything to do with it. At least on that one point, I think she was telling the truth." He shrugged. "But what do I know? I never dreamed she was capable of any of the things she did. I guess I'm just a chump. People lie all around me and I never see it until it slaps me in the face."

Nat caught the bitterness in his voice and knew, in part, the statement was directed at her too. So, that was his problem. Brady's ego had been nicked yet again by a lying female. She longed to tell him about Bobby, and why she'd left, but she knew that in his current state of mind, he'd slam the door in her face yet again. Everything in Brady's world was so neatly drawn, so black and white. Even if he did listen to her, she wasn't sure whether her explanation would make a difference.

Instead of rising to the bait, she shut her eyes. The Brady she loved was still beneath the caustic exterior. He still cared, or he wouldn't be here. She had to hold onto that, and not let his defensiveness discourage her. He had every right to be angry, every right to be bitter. She was going to have to find a way to break through the wall he'd built around himself.

Maybe the best way to do that would be to keep him talking. The trouble would be avoiding all the little landmines she seemed to step on every time they had a conversation.

Nat adjusted the vent on the air conditioner. "I'm worried about Reed. I don't like leaving him behind."

"What else could I do?" Brady said tersely.

Pow! She stepped right on that one. He'd taken her comment as an attack. Brady was spoiling for a fight. Nat doubted there was anything she could say that wouldn't provoke him, but she stumbled on anyway.

"Should I have Alisha go check on him?" Nat asked.

"No. Reed's mother is home now, and God knows how she reacted to news of the fire. She could go off like she did on you that day and hurt Alisha."

Nat gave a humorless chuckle. "And that was Rachel Atkinson on Valium. Can you imagine her without medication?"

"What are you talking about?" Brady asked, when he turned onto the interstate.

Nat waved her hand dismissively. "Nothing. That day Reed called, he told me it was safe to come over because his mom had taken a couple of Valium and gone to bed. Valium is a depressant, usually mellows you out. I remember when Bobby took them—"

Nat froze. Damn, she'd done it again.

Brady gripped the steering wheel so tightly his knuckles shone white. "I know what Valium is," he said curtly.

They lapsed into an uncomfortable silence that lasted halfway to Alabama. Brady finally spoke to her again after he stopped to refuel the Cuda.

"Are you hungry? There's a burger place across the road."

"Sure," she said brightly, though she wasn't sure she could swallow a bite right now.

She let Brady lead the way into the garishly painted restaurant. She didn't even glance at the menu, knowing she didn't want anything. She ordered the same combo Brady did and handed the cashier a twenty to pay for both meals before he could protest.

"Dr. Pepper?" he asked, grabbing the paper cups from the tray.

She nodded. He wandered off, leaving her to wait on the burgers. She heard the dull chug chug of the ice machine behind her, but didn't turn to watch him fill their drinks. For the first time, she despaired of ever making things right between them. Even with Charity out of the picture, even with everything else happening around them, she couldn't change the fact that she'd broken his heart. He seemed determined to make her pay.

Brady returned just as the cashier shoved the tray across to Nat. He took it from her and led her to a booth.

He ate with grim determination, hunching over his

burger in a way that discouraged any attempt at conversation. Nat managed to shove down a few greasy fries, but couldn't muster any enthusiasm for her burger.

Brady finished quickly, and leaned back to inventory her side of the tray. When he spoke, his voice was wary, but gentle. "You need to eat. You've been through a lot lately, and you have to keep up your strength."

"I'm eating," Nat said, and poked another fry in her mouth to emphasize the point. She winked and swallowed. "I just can't keep up with you."

To her surprise, he gave her a faint smile. "Okay, then, Slowpoke. I'm going to use the restroom while you finish up."

As soon as he walked out of sight, Nat spread open a napkin. She tore off a third of her burger and tossed on a handful of fries, then quickly deposited them in the trash before he returned.

"All I can handle," she said, and shoved the tray across to him. "You want the rest?"

Brady frowned at the tray, then shook his head. "Guess we're on our way, then."

The mood seemed a little lighter for the rest of the trip. Nat even coaxed a smile from Brady when she sang along—loudly—with Frankie Valli on the radio to "Walk like a Man."

They arrived at the cabin fifteen minutes later. Nat hugged herself when she climbed out of the car and stared over the sparkling blue lake. Though it looked a little worse for wear these days, and the yard needed mowing, the cabin was probably her favorite place in the world.

They carried their bags inside and and Brady went back outside to mow the lawn while Nat changed the linens on the beds.

After she finished, Nat went to the kitchen to do a quick inventory of the cupboard. She was pleasantly surprised to find them well-stocked. Apparently, her parents had kept coming here after she'd left with Bobby. She recognized Justin's favorite canned pasta, and the name brand peanut butter Matt insisted upon. It might not be gourmet, but they wouldn't starve. They'd have to make a trip out for perishables, but not tonight.

The buzz of the mower grew louder and she peeked out the window at Brady. He straightened over the ancient push mower. Nat got a cheap thrill when he tugged off his shirt and tossed it on the hood of the Cuda. For a long moment, she simply stared. He was so perfect. His lean, tan torso glistened with sweat in the late afternoon sun. She watched the muscles in his back and shoulders bunch while he fought against the tall grass.

As if he sensed her staring, he jerked his head around. Nat ducked beneath the kitchen window. She cupped her hand over her mouth and giggled, hoping he hadn't caught her ogling him.

Getting back to work, she brewed a pot of sweet tea and set it in the refrigerator to chill. Then she swept the hardwood floors and gave the place a quick dusting. She was finishing up when she heard the mower shut off. Moving quickly, she grabbed a couple of glasses from the cabinet, rinsed them and threw in some ice cubes. Grateful the tea was cool, if not chilled, she filled the glasses and met Brady on the front porch. He was wiping his face with the T-shirt he'd retrieved from the Cuda.

He accepted the glass from her and breathed a "thanks" before he took a seat on the edge of the porch. Propping his back against one of the cedar posts, Brady crossed his long legs out in front of him. He drained half the glass in two long swallows.

"Ahhh, that was good," he said with a sigh.

Nat found herself staring at his chest. Then her gaze swept downward, marveling at his sculpted abs.

"I know what you're thinking," Brady said, and she jerked her eyes back to his, flustered.

I bet you don't. Nat hid her smile behind her glass. *Or you'd be running halfway back to Tennessee by now.*

"I know it's not a big yard, but that tall fescue is something else. I don't know what our dads were thinking when they planted that stuff."

Nat snorted. "I'll tell you what they were thinking. They were thinking they didn't have to worry about it because they had cheap child labor around. That's probably the only reason my parents had Justin and Matt. They were the next generation of lawn mowers."

Brady laughed. The sound was so sweet to her ears, so relaxed and genuine. "Hey, you're probably right," he said, and gulped down the rest of his tea. He started to push himself up, but Nat grabbed his arm.

"You want more tea? I'll get it."

"Sure. Thanks."

Nat went inside to pour him another glass, feeling some of the tension that held her rigid evaporate. She was actually a little hungry. Opening the cupboard, she withdrew the jar of peanut butter and grabbed a tablespoon out of the silverware drawer.

When she returned, Brady was rummaging in the trunk of the Cuda. Nat sat on the porch and ate a spoonful of peanut butter, watching him emerge with a cardboard box.

She ignored her mother's chiding voice in her head as she stuck the spoon back in the jar and extracted another bite. She and Brady had done this all the time when they were kids, walked around with a spoon and a jar of peanut butter. Their mothers had fussed, but then eventually gave up and simply bought a separate jar for the adults.

The box made a dull thud when Brady dropped it on the porch beside her, and Nat realized it was full of files. "This is all I have on the accident, and the murder investigation. Maybe I'll finally have time to go over it," he explained.

He took the spoonful of peanut butter Nat offered and stuck it in his mouth. He held it like a lollipop as he extracted the first stack. They swapped it back and forth for a few bites. Their childhood ritual, something she'd once thought nothing of, now seemed intimate. Sexy.

She wondered if Brady felt it too, because he shoved the files aside, leaned against the post, and looked at her.

She stared back at him, afraid to speak, afraid to move, afraid that whatever she did would bring back the tension between them.

Brady looked away first, and stared down at the thin row of weeds closest to the porch that the mower hadn't been able to reach. He nearly fell off the porch when he leaned to pluck something from the ground. Nat reached out to grab him. He laughed and clutched Nat's wrist to right himself. Triumphantly, he held up a four leaf clover. For a moment, he twirled it between his thumb and forefinger, then placed it in her hand.

Nat smiled as she stared down at it. "Ever since we were kids, you've always given me your four leaf clovers."

Brady grinned. "You always got in more trouble than me. I figured you needed them worse."

Some things never changed, she supposed.

Brady's smile lingered for a moment, and she wished she could read his mind. Then he turned away and scrounged a pencil from the bottom of the box. As he laid the top file across his lap and opened it, Nat realized she'd been dismissed.

She sat there for a moment, content to merely watch his blond head bent over the files. Then she collected their glasses and took them inside.

Walking down the hall to the bedroom her parents usually shared, Nat opened one of her mother's romance novels and placed the clover inside.

Staring down at its perfect petals, she decided—literally—to press her luck.

BRADY POURED OVER THE TRIAL TRANSCRIPTS, JOTTING notes on a yellow steno pad. He strained to see in the gathering darkness, but hated to risk losing his place by getting up to turn the porch light on. There had to be some clue in all this paperwork.

He didn't look up when the screen door banged shut.

"Oh good grief," Nat said, and Brady winced at the sudden burst of light when she flipped on the switch. "Is that better?"

"Thanks," he replied, and scratched another note in the margin about Jen's brother, Evan. He'd been questioned but not charged in a school arson incident.

"Why don't you take a break?" Nat asked. "I think I'll go for a swim."

"I didn't pack my suit," Brady murmured distractedly.

She laughed. "Neither did I."

Brady's nerve endings jolted to attention and his eyes flew upward of their own volition. Nat stood on the edge of the porch, wearing a short white robe. She gave him a seductive smile over her shoulder and skipped down the steps.

Even though the rest of her soon disappeared in the shadows, his gaze followed her white robe down to the water's edge. He watched it spill onto the dock, and heard a splash when she jumped in.

The pencil in his hand snapped in half.

Why did she have to bait him like that? What did she want from him?

I want you to love me again, her husky voice echoed in his head.

"Stop it," Brady muttered, squeezing his eyes shut.

Big mistake.

Images flashed behind his eyes, an erotic movie created by his own feverish desire. Images of Nat swimming naked in the cool, dark water of the lake, her skin as pale and smooth as marble in the moonlight.

All he had to do was go to her.

She would welcome him into her arms, into her bed. But would he find any solace there from the doubts that plagued him?

Need for her throbbed within him, as relentless and savage as a toothache.

All he had to do was go to her.

Brady shoved the files back in the box and stood, staring into the darkness. His heart pounded against his ribs and a fine sheen of perspiration beaded his upper lip, even though his mouth was completely, utterly dry.

His heart pleaded with him like a doomed man

might beg for his life, but Brady knew if he took one step toward that dock, he might as well run to it, because he would be lost.

It was all or nothing with Nat.

In the end, that's what decided it. He didn't want her body if he couldn't have her heart, and he couldn't give her any more of himself without losing his soul. He grabbed the box of files and stalked into the cabin, kicking the door shut behind him.

NAT GRASPED THE EDGE OF THE DOCK. THE HOT TEARS streaking down her cheeks were a stark contrast to the chilly water enveloping her body.

He wasn't coming.

Once again, she'd made a fool of herself. If he'd meant to punish her, to reduce her to begging, she hoped he was happy. She hoisted herself onto the dock and jerked on her robe.

She stared at the blazing lights of the cabin and sat down on the edge of the dock, dangling her feet in the water while she wrung the moisture from her hair.

The weathered gray board on which she sat bore hers and Brady's initials, but it felt like they were the initials of another couple, a young boy and girl who might've been something great if only the girl hadn't screwed up and ruined both their lives. She remembered the day a twelve-year-old Brady had carved them there, only hours after they'd shared their first kiss.

Nat sat on the dock until she was reasonably sure she wouldn't burst into tears at the sight of Brady's face, then she slowly stood and trudged to the cabin.

With a heart heavy with trepidation, she tugged open the door and slipped inside. Brady sprawled in the faded recliner, glowering at her. He'd changed clothes, and his hair looked wet and disheveled, like he'd just stepped from the shower. Her resolve not to push things any further crumbled at the fiery look in his eyes. She couldn't bear for him to hate her.

Helplessly, she spread her hands out to her sides. "Brady, don't be like this. All this distance that's come between us has gone far enough. Can't we talk about it?"

His lip curled, and he stared at the wall. "This was a mistake, coming here with you."

"Brady, I—"

"I've been trying to help you, and all you do in return is throw yourself at me. I think I've made it clear how I feel."

Stung, Nat lifted her chin, fighting the tears that burned her eyes. "Yes, you've made it abundantly clear. You win, Brady. I give. You don't have to worry about me 'throwing myself' at you anymore."

"Oh, really?" His fists clenched in his lap. "Is this part of plan B? Dammit, Nat, you were the one who left me. You are the reason we're not together. I would've waited on you forever. Now you stare at me with those big sad eyes and make me feel like a heel. If you really care about me, stop using me." He shook his head and repeated, "I never should've come here with you."

Resentment boiled in her at his tone. "Then leave!" she snapped. "This was your idea, so don't twist it around like it's some master plan of mine. I'll be all right by myself."

"Who needs me, right?" Brady jumped to his feet, his eyes glittering with fury. "Certainly not you. You want to talk? We'll talk. You can say anything you want to me, but first I have just one question for you. Did that night we spent together mean *anything* to you?"

Defeated, Nat slumped against the wall and covered her face with her hand. "How can you ask me that?" she whispered. "It meant everything to me."

Brady picked up a throw pillow and clenched it to his chest. "You've got a funny way of showing it. You lied to me, Nat. That night in my bed, you told me you loved me too. Were you saying it to spare my feelings, or because that's what you thought you should say, or what?"

"I meant it."

Rolling his eyes, Brady stared at the ceiling.

"It's not what you think!" she cried. "Bobby—"

Brady scowled. "I don't want to hear anything about that bastard."

Nat pointed at him. "You said you'd let me talk. I didn't go back to Bobby because I loved him. You don't know what he put me through."

Brady gave a derisive laugh and hurled the pillow at the couch. He stalked toward her, waving his hands in the air. "You keep *saying* that, but I know how you were with him. He treated you like dirt, but you'd always crawl back to him." He shook his head, expelling an angry breath. "You've even got his name tattooed on your chest."

Nat recoiled, and Brady gave her a bitter smile. "Yeah, I saw it that day at the picnic. And it wasn't there the night we made love."

Was that what all this was about?

Brady opened his mouth, and Nat held her palm up in front of his face. "Just shut up. Don't say a word until I get finished. If you still want to hate me then, fine, but you're going to let me have my say."

Brady nodded tersely, his lips set in a thin, grim line.

Nat pushed her damp hair back from her forehead. "I went back to Bobby because I thought I owed him. He came to visit me a couple of months before my release. He told me he was sorry for the way he treated me."

Brady laughed. "And you believed him?"

"He wanted to make things right between us before he died."

"What do you mean, died?"

"He told me he was going to kill himself."

Brady crossed his arms over his chest. "Oh please. That was a sympathy ploy, a way to get back in your pants. Bobby loved himself too much to commit suicide. If he'd really wanted to make things right between you, he would've told you the truth about the accident."

Brady's comment stung, because she recognized the truth in what he said. Maybe Bobby had manipulated her yet again, but at the time, she had believed him. What she had done, she had done with the best intentions.

"Do you have his medical records in that stack of files?" Nat asked quietly.

"No."

"No. Well, let me tell you what you'd find in them. The wreck broke Bobby's pelvis. It smashed his right femur. They had to put in an artificial hip and piece his leg back together with rods and pins. He might not have been confined to a wheelchair like Reed, but he came close. Whatever else Bobby lied about, I know he suffered. When he talked to me, he was strung out and desperate, wasted on pain pills. I thought I'd caused that wreck, and I felt like I owed him. So, I begged him not to kill himself. I promised if he could hold on, I'd take care of him when he got out."

"Why you?" Brady demanded. "He had family. Why couldn't they take care of him?"

"You met Bobby's mother." Nat pushed a hand through her damp hair. "He never knew who his father was. Jolene is an addict too. He'd have to hide his pain medication to keep her from taking it or selling it on the street. He and Dara were raised in hell. Both were physically—and I suspect sexually—abused by the men she dragged in and out of their house, though Bobby never came right out and admitted it. Other than a grandmother in a nursing home, he didn't have anybody but me. You can condemn me all you like, but try to put yourself in my shoes. You're much more heroic than me. What would you have done?"

Brady perched on the sofa arm, his handsome face troubled. The fire in his eyes dimmed. "Why didn't you tell me?"

"I've tried."

"I mean, back then."

"Because you wouldn't have let me go, and I felt like it was something I had to do."

"No," he said softly. "I wouldn't have let you go."

Nat shook her head, feeling drained. Hopeless. "And you keep bringing up sex. There wasn't any. I was Bobby's nurse, his maid—even his punching bag—but I wasn't his lover anymore. He had so much nerve damage from all those surgeries . . ." Nat rubbed the bridge of her nose. "The drugs he took probably didn't help either, but you couldn't tell him that. He went to doctor after doctor, more worried about his inability to have sex than the fact he could hardly get out of bed in the mornings. Yet another reason for his anger and frustration. If you don't believe me, get his file. It's all there."

Brady slowly pushed himself to his feet.

Nat started toward her bedroom, then turned back

to face him.

"One more thing, and please don't take this as another of my pathetic attempts to 'throw myself' at you. I just thought you might like to take a closer look at my tattoo."

Her hands trembled while she untied the sash of her robe.

MODESTLY CLUTCHING THE RIGHT SIDE OF THE ROBE closed, Nat peeled back the left side to reveal one perfect breast, and the tattoo etched above it.

Brady stared speechlessly at his own name.

She jerked the robe closed. Her cool monotone cracked when she said, "I got it a few months after I got out. The idea was Alisha's. She has her brothers' names tattooed over her heart. She said she put them there as a reminder that if you love someone, and keep them near your heart, you can't really lose them. Guess we've proven what a crock that is, right?"

Tears streaked down her cheeks and she impatiently swiped them away. "If I could go back, I would change it all. I was so scared, and so guilty. I know it's no excuse, but I did what I thought was right at the time. I'm sorry I hurt you. I'm sorry for so many things. The night I came to you . . . I meant every word I said. I love you, Brady. I never stopped loving you. I'm sorry I made you doubt that."

She stared at him, as if waiting for a response, but Brady stood rooted to the floor, unable to move, unable to breathe. Nat gave him a sad smile and started to turn away.

Her movement freed him.

He was never going to let her walk away from him again.

CHAPTER 13

BRADY LUNGED FORWARD AND GRABBED HER wrist. He caught a glimpse of her startled green eyes when he spun her around, making her robe flare open, but then he had her in his arms. His hands clutched at her hot, bare back as he crushed his mouth to hers.

For an instant, she stiffened. Then her arms snaked around his neck. Her fingers twisted in his hair, urging him closer, deeper. Her tongue met his thrust for thrust, sending delicious, savage sparks racing through his nerve endings. He jerked the robe off her shoulders and she released him just long enough to let it fall to the floor.

Heat from her bare body burned through his clothes, into his bones, enveloping his senses in a hazy, red cloud of desire. They stumbled backward, and Brady smacked painfully into an end table. He heard a crash when he knocked over the lamp, but he wouldn't let go of her.

He couldn't.

They missed the couch and tumbled into the floor. Brady rolled over, pinning Nat on the faded blue rug.

"I love you!" she gasped, and the sight of her beneath

him, naked and glorious and wearing his name above her heart, was almost more than he could bear.

She was his. She was really his.

He tore at his clothes, anxious to rid himself of any barrier between them. Her hands were everywhere, grasping, tugging, trying to help, and the desire in her eyes moved him more than any physical act ever could.

She was his.

As feverish as he felt, he shivered when skin met skin. He nudged her thighs apart and groaned when Nat's fingers clasped around him, guiding his tip inside her. Before he could lower himself, Nat jerked her hips up to meet his, taking all of him inside her in one savage, liquid stroke.

Stars exploded behind Brady's eyes when she closed around him, hot and dark and silky. For a moment, he couldn't even see her. Then his vision cleared and the tension became unbearable. He began to thrust.

Nat locked her legs around his waist, and the fervor with which she matched his pace nearly drove him over the edge. The dull throbbing in his groin gathered power like a developing storm. It coiled tighter and tighter until he thought he'd die from the exquisiteness of it all.

Sweat trickled into his eyes and Brady squeezed them shut, trying to think about baseball, trying to think about anything to delay his release, but when Nat screamed out his name and her muscles spasmed around him, he lost all control. Her nails dug into his back hard enough to bring blood as the world exploded around him.

Brady collapsed on top of her, burying his face in the soft, damp hollow of her neck and shoulder. "I love you," he whispered. "I love you so much."

Nat's arms tightened around him. His muscles quivered like he'd just competed in a triathlon, and he wasn't sure how long he lay there before realizing he was probably crushing her. He pushed himself up on his forearms, but Nat grabbed him and pulled him back down.

"Not yet," she said softly.

Brady gave her a long, lingering kiss, then shifted so she wasn't bearing his full weight. He slipped an arm beneath her to circle her waist and lay his head against her breast. Her thundering heart made him smile while she stroked his damp hair.

For a while, they simply lay there, clutching each other but too spent to speak. Then Brady propped up on an elbow to stare at the tattoo. He laughed and traced his finger over the letters.

A perfect, rosy nipple sprang to attention, and Brady bent to kiss it. "I feel so stupid. I saw the 'B' and I saw the 'Y', but not for one second did it occur to me that it was my name."

"And that's why you were so grouchy at the barbecue?"

Brady's face flushed, and he grinned. "Yeah, that's why I was so grouchy at the barbecue. I didn't mean it, what I said to my mother. You're mine, Nat. It drove me crazy to think of another man's name on your body." His grin widened and he shrugged. "But now that I know it's mine, I kinda like it."

Nat rolled her eyes. "Is that right?"

"Yeah." Brady glanced at the tattoo again, then frowned at the jagged white scar running alongside the 'B.'

"Hey, what happened there?" he asked.

"Let's not talk about it right now," Nat said, and the sudden change in her tone made Brady glance up.

"No more secrets," he said. "What happened?"

Nat sighed and twisted a lock of his hair around her finger. "About a month after I got it, Bobby caught a glimpse of it, but he knew exactly what it said. I woke up one night to find him standing over me with a pocket knife. He said he was going to cut it off me. I fought him off before he could do much damage though."

Brady swallowed hard and laid his head back on her chest. He tightened his arms around her. "As long as I'm alive, no one will ever hurt you again."

He should've known. He should've come for her. Brady wondered what else she had suffered at Bobby's hands.

DAWN FOUND THEM SITTING ON THE DOCK, WRAPPED up in a blanket while they watched the sun rise over the lake.

Nat smiled and kissed the top of his shoulder. "You know you're in love when you hate to go to sleep because your life is better than a dream."

Brady slid his hand down her bare back. "Most people wouldn't consider your life during the past few weeks a dream."

"I'm here with you." Nat snuggled against him. "I can make it through anything with you beside me." She glanced at the faded initials beside them and smiled. "I was thinking last night about our first kiss. Do you remember?"

"Vividly." Brady tightened his arm around her waist. "I was sitting here, minding my own business, skipping rocks across the lake when you sat beside me and said, 'Kiss me, Brady. A real kiss, like Daddy gives Mama. I thought we could practice on each other, for when we get ready to kiss other people.' "

Nat flushed, wishing she'd never said that to him. She wished she'd realized even then how he felt about her. To break the awkward moment, she pretended to be cross. "You took your sweet time in doing it too. I thought you were going to say no."

"To you?" Brady smiled. "When did I ever say no to you about anything? I was only trying to catch my breath." He trailed his fingers over her shoulder. "I remember what you were wearing. That yellow bathing suit with daisies on it and pink shorts. Your nose and forehead were sunburned and peeling, your knees were scraped, and I thought you were the loveliest thing I'd ever seen."

"You remember all that?" Nat asked, her eyes misting.

"How could I forget? It's still one of the greatest days of my life. Do you want to hear what else I remember?"

"Sure," she said softly.

"You got all mad at me, impatient as ever, and you braced your arms to push yourself into the water. I was afraid you were about to get away, so I reached out to touch your face."

Brady stared into her eyes, just like he had that day, and lowered his blond head to brush his lips against hers. He kissed her softly at first, then more insistently. As his tongue began a tentative exploration, Nat felt a shiver of déjà vu, and she was glad to the depths of her soul that she'd shared that moment with him.

Abruptly, Brady pulled away and grinned at her. "Then you jerked away from me so fast I nearly fell off the dock. You accused me of doing it before, of kissing—" Brady frowned and shook his head.

"—Tanya Mullins," Nat supplied, making a face. "She had the hots for you in seventh grade."

"Tenth grade too," Brady said, and dodged the swat Nat made at him. "Do you remember what I told you?"

"You told me you hadn't kissed Tanya or anybody else, nor did you want to, and I believed you because you never lied about anything." Nat wrinkled her nose and grinned. "It's just that you kissed so *good*. You still do." She pressed her hand to the back of his neck and tugged his mouth down to hers.

The kiss was long and sweet, and made her toes curl.

Brady laughed when he pulled away. "You're only saying that to keep me from throwing you in like I did that day." He feigned like he was going to toss her in the lake and Nat screamed.

"Please, no," she begged. "It's too early. Too cold." She lifted her eyebrows suggestively. "But I could go for a nice . . . hot . . . shower," she said, punctuating each word with a kiss on his throat.

Brady exhaled. "That sounds better than the cold one I took last night."

Nat giggled. "You did?"

He made a face. "Lot of good it did me. I kept thinking about you, swimming around out here naked . . . you sure you don't want me to throw you in?"

"Hmm umm," she pleaded, standing. "Please don't. I'll wash your back."

"Well, what are we waiting for?" Brady stood and swept her in his arms. He carried her all the way back to the cabin.

After their shower, they split a can of fruit cocktail and went back to bed. Nat woke nearly seven hours later to find Brady's side of the bed empty.

For one paralyzing, heart-stopping second, she thought, *What if it was just a dream?*

But then she spotted the wet towels and discarded clothes on the floor and smiled. She slipped on his T-shirt and went to find him.

Brady sat on the living room floor, clad only in a pair of faded jeans. Files and legal pads covered the coffee table in front of him, and he was taking notes with a broken pencil. He looked up with a smile.

"There you are, sleepyhead. I was about to roll you out of there. I'm starving. If you feel like it, I thought we could run to town, get a few things. Eat something that didn't come out of a can."

"Ooh, that sounds good. I wonder if that Mexican restaurant is still on the square." Nat slipped behind him and sat on the sofa. Grasping the back of his neck, she gently began to knead. He groaned and leaned his head forward, giving her access. Nat smiled when she saw her fingernail marks on his back.

"It has to be the sheriff and Joe," Brady said. "I think they're in it together. Joe's doing his dirty work. I know the sheriff couldn't chase you through the woods. But I called Ian Kirby while you were sleeping and got him to do a little checking up for me. Joe has an alibi for the fire bombing. He was responding to a drunk and disorderly in Beersheba at the time." He leaned back and draped an arm across her knee. "I got Kirby to check on Reed too. He slipped him my cell number when he went to question him about the fire, and he also said Reed's stepfather had hired a security guard to stay at the house while he's at work."

Nat sighed. "Good. I'm afraid the killer will come

after Reed when he can't find me."

"You know, that's one thing that's bugged me. You've had direct attacks. The woods, the fire—"

"The fire could've been meant for him too," Nat said.

Brady shook his head. "I don't think so. We didn't know he was coming until the last minute. That fire was aimed at you. Why isn't the killer coming after Reed as hard as he is you?"

An uneasy feeling settled in the pit of Nat's stomach. "Maybe he figures Reed has nowhere to run."

"WHAT IS IN THERE?" NAT DEMANDED, AND MADE A grab for the shopping bag in Brady's hand.

"Huh uh." He snatched it away and held it just out of her reach. "Let's get the groceries put up first."

He smiled at her, knowing it was driving her crazy. Nat was not a patient person, and she'd been hounding him ever since they'd left the mall.

"I sat outside that store for twenty minutes with my eyes closed feeling like a dork. I think I've waited long enough," she pouted as she shoved a half-gallon of orange juice in the refrigerator.

Brady kept the bag at his side until they finished putting everything away, then he motioned Nat toward the living room. He sprawled on the couch and pulled her into his lap. Placing the bag in her hands, he said,

"It's your costume."

One of Nat's eyebrows shot up. "Costume?"

He caressed the inside of her knee and smiled. "Blame it on that old drive-in theater in town. Ever since I was in ninth grade, when Dad brought home that wreck of a Cuda and said we were going to rebuild it, I've had this fantasy."

Nat traced her fingers along his jaw line. Her green eyes sparkled with mischief when she said, "I might regret asking this, but what sort of fantasy?"

"Me and you in the back of that thing, making wild, hot monkey love."

Both eyebrows shot up this time. For a moment, she looked stunned, then she giggled. "*Monkey* love?"

Brady grinned and rubbed his hands together gleefully. "Oh yeah."

Nat shook her head and laughed again. "Brady Simms, I'm shocked at you. I never knew you were such a pervert."

"All ninth grade boys are perverts," he said. "And I'm sure I'm not the only one who had that particular fantasy, but tonight, I get to live it."

"And the clothes?" she asked, holding up the bag.

He gave her a stern look. "It's a detailed fantasy. They're not exactly right, but close enough. Now; are you going to get ready so I can take you to a movie I'm not going to let you watch?"

Nat rolled her eyes and smiled. She grabbed the bag

and wandered into the bedroom. A few moments later, Brady grinned when he heard her shriek.

"Good grief, Brady!" she yelled. "You didn't tell me I was a *hooker* in this fantasy."

Twenty minutes later, she still hadn't emerged from the bedroom. The anticipation was killing him. "C'mon," he pleaded. "We're going to be late."

"What does it matter?" she answered through the door. "We're not watching the movie anyway. Sheesh, I finally understand the power of Britney Spears."

The door creaked inward, and Nat slowly emerged. Brady felt like he'd taken a blow to the gut.

She patted her hair, which was wild and curled, and said, "Hey, since we were going for high school, I thought I'd do the hair and make-up too." She pursed her red lips and winked. "Does this do it for you?"

Brady opened his mouth to speak, but all that emerged was a groan. He wet his lips and tried again. "That does it for me so well I might not let you out of this cabin."

His erection throbbed painfully tight as he took in the thigh-high black stockings, short black skirt and white shirt tied just above her navel. She'd left the top three buttons undone, allowing the black lace push-up bra and swell of her cleavage to peek through.

"It's a good thing you said drive-in," she said. "Because I am *not* getting out of the car in this get-up."

She walked up to him, enveloping him in a cloud of

perfume and hairspray that smelled as sexy as sin. She slipped her hand underneath the hem of his T-shirt and hooked a finger in his belt loop, tugging him close.

"Well, come on, lover," she whispered huskily. "I didn't get all undressed for nothing." Brady groaned against her neck, sliding his hands beneath her skirt to cup her buttocks. He pulled her up hard against him and attacked the little spot just below her ear.

Nat gasped and leaned her head back. "Mmm . . . no fair. You know I can't handle that."

He smiled. Tonight wasn't going to be about 'fair.' He might not have known much about what he was doing that first night they'd spent together, but he was a quick learner. Tonight wasn't just about him and his fantasy. He wanted to make her as crazy as she'd made him all these years.

"Let's go," he said, giving her butt a gentle squeeze.

It was hard to keep his eyes off her as he drove to the drive-in. He didn't mean to touch her, but one of his hands stole over to caress her thigh. Her eyes danced as she took his hand and flung it back in his lap.

"What do you think, I'm easy or something?" she asked with mock indignation.

Staring at her in that scant outfit, Brady had to laugh. "Well, you *look* easy," he admitted.

Nat glowered at him and folded her arms under her breasts, purposely popping even more of her cleavage into view. Brady nearly put the Cuda in a ditch.

"My daddy warned me about guys like you, and drive-ins."

Brady rolled his eyes. "Yeah, I can see how much good that lecture did. You're here, aren't you?"

She gave him a seductive smile, her glossy red lips shimmering in the glow of the streetlights. "Yeah, but I'm in the front seat. You don't think I'll give it up without a fight, do you?"

Brady laughed. "God, I hope not."

She leaned over and teased his earlobe with her teeth. "You want me in that backseat, you'll have to convince me," she whispered.

"I like a challenge."

As he coasted to a stop at the ticket booth, she pulled back and tried to adjust her clothing. Her efforts at modesty were in vain. The pimply face teenager inside still gave her a double-take when he reached to take Brady's money. Brady leaned forward to block his view.

"Hey, man, what kind of car is this?" the kid asked, his eyes still seeking Nat over Brady's shoulder.

"It's a 1970 Cuda."

"Sure is hot," the teenager said, handing Brady his change.

Brady smiled and pulled away. He trailed his fingers over Nat's knee as he drove through the field, searching for an empty spot near the back. "You know he wasn't talking about the car, right?" he said.

Nat laughed. "What do you expect? He's a teenager, and I'm sitting here practically naked."

"Not as naked as you're gonna be."

"You sound awfully sure of yourself."

Brady parked and twisted around to look at her. "Not as sure as I'd like to be. See, I've never taken a girl to a drive-in before. Maybe you could help me out with something, just to let me know if I'm on the right track."

Most of the security lights winked out, and the movie flickered to life on the screen. Nat slid a little closer to him. "I'll do my best," she said.

"Those things your father was warning you about . . . did he tell you I might try this?" He pushed back her hair and trailed kisses from her ear down her throat.

"Yes," she gasped . "I think he mentioned that."

"Hmm . . . interesting," he said, and undid another button on her blouse. Slowly, he tugged the material open to reveal the swell of her breasts inside the lacy black bra. He trailed his fingertips over the soft mounds, then ran his thumb down the crevice between them. "How about this . . . did he warn you I might try this?"

"Definitely," she said, as his fingertips slipped beneath the lace to rub one hardened nipple. She moaned. Brady glanced around. The dark tinted windows were already fogging up. He lowered his head and kissed the tops of her breasts.

He smoothed a palm over her knee, then slid it up her thigh, stopping on the lacy edge of her stocking. "And this?"

"I don't think that came up," she said in a breathy little voice that made his pulse spike.

"Then it must be okay," he said, and moved it higher. He tickled her through her panties. They were already damp.

He forgot any attempts at inane conversation, charged at the proof that she wanted him as much as he wanted her. He caressed her through the silky material, then slipped a finger inside the edge. Inside her.

"Brady," she said, and pulled him to her in a hard kiss. He shifted his hand, then stroked her clit with his thumb. In a few moments, he had her jerking, panting for breath against his mouth. Her gasping little moans were driving him insane.

Her hands abandoned his face. Her nails dug into his shoulders as she squirmed against his palm. Their noses bumped in the dark as they alternately kissed and struggled for breath.

"Don't stop," she begged. "Please don't stop. Right there. Right . . ."

Brady pressed his mouth against hers, muffling her cry as she came.

"Let's get in the backseat," she said a moment later.

He couldn't resist a dig. "Thought you weren't getting back there without a fight?"

She smiled and ran her finger along his jaw. "Change of plan. But the fight's not over yet. It's my turn to make you beg."

With that, she crawled between the seats, and she didn't have to ask him twice to join her. Brady tried to pull her onto his lap, but she pushed his hands away and reached for his belt.

He didn't know about the begging part—he was too incoherent to beg—but she soon had him at her mercy, driving him to the edge as she knelt in the floorboard and ravished him with her tongue and that sweet mouth.

When he didn't think he could take anymore, he smoothed a hand over her hair and rasped, "Come here. Please, come here."

Nat crawled into his lap. She gave a shuddering little sigh as she impaled herself on him, then she rode him hard. Brady touched her face, then grasped her hips. Together they found a frantic rhythm that soon sent them both over the edge.

She collapsed against him. For a long time, neither of them moved. Brady wasn't sure he could have if he wanted to.

"So," she asked, nuzzling his neck. "Did the real thing measure up to your fantasy?"

He laughed. "Babe, no high school boy could've ever imagined anything like that. That was a million times better than I'd imagined it would be, and I had high expectations at fourteen." He cleared his throat and squeezed her. "I love you, Nat."

"I love you too. Please tell me this is it, that nothing will ever come between us again. I can't lose you again."

The vulnerability in her voice touched him. "You'll never lose me," he said, hugging her close. "I swear it. Nothing will ever tear us apart again."

After the movie was over, they went back to the cabin. During the ride, Nat inflamed him again with a few brazen caresses and dirty little comments she whispered in his ear. By the time they stumbled back into the cabin, giggling and clutching at each other like a couple of drunks, Brady was ready for the double feature.

NAT TUGGED OUT OF HIS GRASP. "HUH UH, NOT YET. This hairspray is killing me, so first I'm going to take a shower—alone, because I can't trust you, Monkey Man."

"Aw, c'mon. I'll be good," he promised, but the bulge in his pants promised something different.

Nat wrapped her arms around his neck and kissed him soundly on the lips. Brady slid his hands underneath her skirt, grabbed her hips and ground her against him.

She laughed and pushed him backward onto the couch. "See what I mean? But good things come to those who wait, and I promise you a surprise when I get out."

"Oh, yeah?" he asked, his blue eyes dark with desire.

She winked. "Oh, yeah. So be a good boy and sit right there until I'm finished."

She kicked off her high heels and placed a foot on the recliner. While Brady watched, she slowly rolled one of her stockings off and threw it to him. He caught it one-handed, his eyes never leaving her. She followed suit with the other, and reached for the buttons on her shirt.

"Nat, you're killing me here," he murmured, when she slipped it off her shoulders and let it fall to the floor. She bent to give him a flash of her black thong as she picked the shirt up.

"Aw, man, oh!" Brady grabbed a throw pillow and buried his face in it when she straightened and gave him a sultry look over her shoulder. He peeked over the top of it and grinned. "You'd better lock the door behind you."

Nat smiled and unfastened her skirt. It fell around her ankles. She stepped out of it and kicked it toward him. Then she reached behind her to unfasten her bra. As she slid it down her arms, he growled, "You'd better run."

Nat squealed and threw it at him when he launched himself from the couch. He chased her to the bathroom. She slammed the door in his face and barely got it locked in time. She leaned against the door, panting, while he pressed against the other side.

"I love you, Nat," he whispered through the crack.

She giggled. "I love you too, Brady."

"Then for God's sake, hurry up."

She tried. Nat soaped, lathered, and rinsed in record time. A few minutes later, she hesitantly opened the bathroom door, expecting him to pounce.

Clutching her towel to her chest, she followed the sound of the radio to the bedroom. Brady clamped his hand over his eyes when she walked in.

"I'm going to take a shower too," he said, quickly moving past her. "I've waited this long, guess I can wait a few more minutes."

She laughed. "You're so deprived."

He dropped his hand and smiled at her from the doorway. "Every minute I'm away from you is a minute too long."

Nat smiled to herself when she heard the bathroom door shut. She dropped the towel and yanked on one of Brady's T-shirts.

She moved around the room, setting things up, and just as she heard the shower cut off, she realized she'd forgotten the most important thing. She ran to the living room and rifled through the CDs in the entertainment center until she found what she was looking for.

Spinning on her heel, she found Brady standing in the doorway watching her, clad only in the white towel swathed around his narrow hips.

"So, what's my surprise?" he asked, advancing on her.

"It's time for a Nat fantasy."

His laughter was so genuine and happy it made her heart twist. He made a grab for her and she danced out of his reach.

She'd put him through such hell, but she intended to spend the rest of her life making up for it.

"What?" she asked lightly. "You think you're the only one who has fantasies?"

He lunged for her again. This time he caught her and drew her up close. Still damp from his shower, he smelled of Irish Spring and Crest. She placed her palms against his bare chest and smiled.

"I'm listening," he said.

Nat slipped her arms around his neck and twisted a lock of his blond hair with her finger. "In my fantasy, I have super powers."

Amusement sparkled in his blue eyes. "Why does that not surprise me?"

"Are you game?"

The corner of his mouth quirked. "Lead the way, Wonder Woman."

She took his hand and tugged him toward the bedroom.

Brady stopped by the bed, watching Nat as she moved toward the dresser. He lifted an eyebrow when she turned to reveal the silk scarf in her hands.

She rolled her eyes and crossed the room to him. "Don't you dare give me that look, mister. Not after your fantasy."

As she stretched to tie the scarf over his eyes, he pressed his face against the soft cushion of her breasts and slipped his hands beneath the hem of her T-shirt to run his hands over her bare buttocks. Her skin felt feverish, but Nat's skin always felt like that, as if the fire inside her burned hotter than in other people.

"Pretend you're home, in your old room." She led him to the window and slid it open. A breeze ruffled against his skin, but his shiver was more from anticipation than the cool night air.

"When I was in Cedar Ridge, after lights out, I'd lie on my bunk and pretend I could make myself invisible. I'd slip past the guards, out the front gate . . . and I'd find my way to you." He felt her heat against his back, but she didn't touch him when she whispered, "Tell me what you smell."

Feeling a little awkward, Brady said, "I smell the approaching rain, the scent of the honeysuckle outside the window . . ." Suddenly, the spicy, oriental fragrance of her perfume filled the air, as clean and sharp as if she'd sprayed it in front of his face. Even though he was blindfolded, Brady closed his eyes and inhaled. "I smell you."

She feathered a kiss along the nape of his neck and moved away.

"I don't want you to see me yet," she said. "I'm watching you stand there, and I ache to be in your arms, but I don't know how you'll react. So, I'm going to seduce you."

With just those words, spoken in that husky voice of hers, his tremor became a quake.

He heard the click of the CD player, then their song filled the room, the song that had imprinted itself on his heart the first time they'd made love. Brady lost himself in the fantasy. Suddenly, it was like he'd stepped back in time to the days after her trial, days when he'd been so afraid for her, had longed so deeply for her.

"Nat," he breathed, and reached blindly for her.

His fingertips brushed against satin, and he knew, as surely as if he'd seen it, that she'd changed into the silver gown she'd worn their first time together.

She melted into his arms. His hands skimmed the smooth material on her hips as she pressed herself against him. Slowly, they swayed together. Brady leaned his head back as she kissed a trail of fire down his throat. He stroked her damp hair and she pressed her ear to his chest. If she meant to listen to his heartbeat, she was getting an earful.

"I'm sorry I hurt you," she whispered. "Living without you was like living without my soul."

Finally, her mouth found his. Her kiss, hesitant at first, grew needier, more demanding. Brady's hands slid up to cup the fullness of her breasts in his palms.

She left him panting, throbbing, aching for her.

"Nat," he gasped. "Let me see you."

She reached to untie the blindfold. The love in her green eyes closed around his heart like a fist. Brady swept her in his arms and carried her to the bed.

Lightning flashed and rain beat against the cabin's tin roof as he stripped the beautiful gown from her body. He made love to her slowly, gently, trying to convey everything he felt for her in his touch, his kisses, because it was more than words could say. His love for her enflamed him, consumed him. Living without her had been like living without his soul.

As they lay in each others arms afterward, Brady stroked her bare stomach and said, "You know, we haven't used any sort of protection."

Nat stiffened. "I can't believe I haven't thought about that at all." She clutched his hand and whispered, "A baby. How would you feel about that?"

Brady kissed the top of her head. "I'd love it, but I hope it doesn't happen right now. Not with the killer still out there. I want to marry you as soon as possible, and I want babies, but I need to know you're safe first." He smiled and tucked a lock of hair behind her ear. "But after that, yeah. I can't think of anything that would make me happier."

"Can you imagine how our moms would react?"

Brady chuckled. "Our moms aren't the ones I'm worried about. Your dad is. Hey, I wonder if he'll sell me that wooded lot across from Mom and Dad's? That would be a perfect place to build a house."

"Yes, it would," she said softly, and Brady hugged her close.

He wanted to make all her dreams come true, but first he had to catch a killer.

Brady closed his eyes and drifted off to sleep.

The chirp of his cell phone jarred him awake. Brady squinted at the clock and was a little surprised to find it was

4 a.m. He fumbled for the phone before it woke Nat.

"Yeah," he mumbled.

"Brady?"

He jerked upright at the sound of Ian Kirby's voice and glanced at Nat's sleeping form. "What's going on?"

"I hate to call you at this time, but I thought you'd want to know. I don't have any details yet, but there's been a shooting at the Atkinson residence."

"Who is it?" Brady demanded. "Is it bad?"

Kirby cleared his throat over the phone. "Well, they called me, so you know what that means . . ."

Brady's stomach clenched. He did know what that meant.

If the sheriff had called in the state investigators, someone was dead.

CHAPTER 14

"DAMMIT."

That one word, spoken hoarsely in the dark, woke Nat as suddenly and completely as if someone had dashed a pitcher of ice water on her.

Brady sat on the edge of the bed with his head in his hands.

"What is it?" She brushed her fingers against his back and he trembled beneath her touch. She jerked upright, clutching the sheet around her breasts. "Brady, talk to me."

He reached behind him and grasped her hand. "There's been a . . . shooting. At the Atkinson house. Ian Kirby just called."

"Reed?" she gasped.

"I don't know. Kirby didn't know any details yet, but it's not a good sign he was called there."

Nat jumped out of bed and yanked on her clothes. Wordlessly, Brady flipped on the light and did the same. By the time they stepped onto the front porch, she was shaking, but it had little to do with cool morning air.

She hugged herself while Brady locked the front door and watched the billowing white fog rolling off the lake. She clamped her eyes shut, squeezing out hot tears that seemed to ice instantly on her cheeks.

Please, God, let him be okay.

Brady's warm arms encircled her, shutting out the cold. She clung to him for a moment, pressing her face against the warm hollow of his throat.

"We'd better go," he said softly.

She stared up into his red-rimmed eyes and nodded. They hurried to the Cuda and climbed inside.

Brady clutched her hand all the way home, not even releasing it to change gears. The ride home was much like the trip there. Neither spoke, and this time even the radio seemed intrusive.

Nat stared out the windshield and pictured Reed's handsome face. Who would do this? What kind of monster would get any satisfaction from harming him? In school, everyone loved Reed. Senior year, he'd won so many class superlatives he'd had to pick one and decline the others he won so the rest of the boys could get awards too. He was voted most popular, most athletic, most everything. He even gave Brady a run for most likely to succeed, because everyone thought Reed was going to be an NFL star. He picked most athletic, and a few months later, that dream had been stolen from him. Now someone might've stolen everything.

When they pulled into Coalmont city limits, Brady

cleared his throat. "I'm going to drop you by your dad's house."

"I want to go with you."

Brady stroked the top of her hand with his thumb. "If it is him—if he is dead—I don't want you to see it. I promise I'll call you the second I know anything, but right now, my main priority is keeping you safe. Who knows how Reed's mother is taking it?"

Nat shivered when she remembered the look in Rachel Atkinson's eyes that day at the pool. If Reed was dead, his mother would never survive it.

When they pulled into Nat's driveway, she was surprised to see Justin and Alisha on the patio, eating breakfast.

Brady put the car in park and went around to open her door. He gave them a little wave before taking Nat's hands in his. "I love you," he said softly, and bent to kiss her.

"I love you too," Nat said, ignoring the hoots and clapping from the patio. "Call me."

She stood in the driveway and watched until he drove out of sight before she trudged up the steps.

"Well, now," Alisha said with a grin. "Looks like your little getaway did some good. How long did it take you guys to, ah, work things out?"

"The first night." Nat sunk into a chair beside Justin.

She should've gone with him.

"Exactly how long?" Alisha asked, winking at Justin. "Six, seven hours, maybe?"

"No fair!" Justin yelled.

Nat frowned. "About five hours. Why?"

Alisha yanked a piece of paper from her purse and scanned it.

"Still me!" she crowed, and jumped up to do a little dance. "I'm the closest. Pay up, Matt!"

Distracted, Nat glanced at them. "You two *bet* on us?"

"We all did," Justin replied as he dug out his wallet. "Well, everybody but Dad. He said he didn't want to think about it." He slapped a ten on the table beside Alisha, and said, "*Jus*-tin. I'm Justin. Don't forget I've already paid you."

Alisha snatched up the ten and gave Nat a sheepish grin. "Hey, blame it on Reed. He started it. We were talking at the party, and he said all you guys needed was two or three hours alone. I figured it would take a little longer, because Brady's so stubb—hey, what's wrong?" she asked, as tears began to rain down Nat's face.

BRADY'S STOMACH ROLLED WHEN HE PULLED INTO THE Atkinson driveway and saw all the vehicles. The sight of the EMTs rolling a body bag out the front door made him dizzy.

He had failed Reed.

Nat had said maybe the killer figured Reed had

nowhere to run, and it looked like she'd been right. Some friend he was. He'd left Reed here defenseless.

The sheriff and Joe prowled around downstairs. The sheriff saw Brady and yelled, "Boy, what the hell are you doin' here?"

Brady ignored him and sprinted up the stairs, following a girl in a TBI jacket. She turned at the top of the stairs and held out a hand to stop him. "Hey, you can't come up here," she said.

"Tess, it's okay," Kirby said. "I called him in."

"Kirby, what—" Before Brady could get the question out, a commotion at the end of the hall interrupted him.

"I want to see her, dammit! I want to see my mother," Reed bellowed.

He was trying to charge through a pack of bureau officers who were spread out in front of him like an offensive line.

Brady jerked his gaze around to Kirby, who shook his head.

"The shot almost decapitated her, Brady. He doesn't need to see that," he whispered.

Brady shook his head, stunned. Rachel Atkinson was dead.

Moving quickly, he stalked down the hall and pushed himself into the middle of the fray. Reed was sobbing, swinging wildly at everyone who approached him. Brady caught one of his fists and was nearly clocked by the other before an officer grabbed it.

"Reed!" he shouted. "It's me, Brady."

Reed's eyes flew open, and the relief in them twisted Brady's gut. "Let go of him," he told the cop, then Brady did the only thing he could think to do. He wrapped his arms around Reed and hugged him tight. Reed clutched him.

"They won't let me see my mama, man," Reed wailed against his shoulder. "I just want to see my mama."

"She's already gone," Brady said gently. "The ambulance was loading her when I pulled up."

"Take me to her then," he pleaded. "Take me to her right now. She can't be dead." His head sagged against Brady's, and he whispered. "She's all I have. I don't have anyone now."

"You have me, and Nat. We—"

"Let me help him. I'm a doctor." Martin Atkinson pushed through the crowd and before Brady could react, he plunged a needle into Reed's arm. Horrified, Brady let go of Reed as Atkinson yanked it back out. Reed screamed a rash of obscenities at his stepfather.

"Why did you do that?" Brady demanded. "He was okay."

"He is not okay," Atkinson stormed, turning his black eyes on Brady. "What are you even doing here?"

Reed went wild in the chair, cursing and flailing at everyone in reach.

"He'll be all right in a second," Atkinson said, and almost instantly, Reed's chin dropped. His breath hitched in and out like a crying child's.

"What did you give him?" one of the officers demanded, as Brady took control of Reed's chair. He left Atkinson talking while he pushed Reed down the hall to his bedroom. Not knowing what else to do, he lifted his unconscious friend from the chair and laid him on top of the rumpled bedspread.

He grasped Reed's wrist and took his pulse, which seemed steady and normal, then pulled out his cell phone to call Nat. She answered the phone on the first ring.

"It's not Reed. It's his mother," he said quietly.

"His mother? What happened?"

"I don't know yet."

"I'm on my way," she said. "Reed will need—"

"Reed's knocked out. Atkinson gave him a shot. Just stay where you are until I figure out what's going on." Brady hung up before she could protest and went down the hall in search of Kirby.

Atkinson stood in the hall beside a crying boy who looked to be about nineteen. The doctor's dark eyes flashed at Brady, but he was talking to Kirby as he said, "I've already told the sheriff all this."

"Well, now I want you to tell me," Kirby said, flipping the page in his notebook. "What happened?"

"I finished my shift at the hospital at midnight, but I got stuck in the emergency room working a car accident. I got back here at about 2:30, and spoke to Jason." He nodded at the crying boy.

"Who is he?" Kirby demanded.

"He's my security guard," Atkinson answered. "I hired him to watch the house while I'm at work. We were talking while I unlocked the front door. I punched in the code to the burglar alarm, but I was tired and must've hit a wrong number. I dropped my keys and was fumbling around for them when the alarm went off. It's ear-splitting, and I'd just got the damn thing shut off when we heard the shot. We ran upstairs, and found her—" Atkinson's voice cracked and he covered his face with his hands.

Jason the security guard awkwardly patted his shoulder.

"This is all my fault," Atkinson sobbed. "The alarm must've scared her to death. Have you figured out what happened, investigator? Did the gun misfire, or did she drop it or what?"

"What was she even doing with a gun?" Brady asked. "You saw what condition she was in a few days ago. Why in the hell would you give her a gun?"

"Don't you dare judge me," Atkinson said. "Rachel was doing much better after she got out of the hospital. She was terrified of this stalker, a man that none of you have been able to catch. She agreed to lock the gun up after Jason started working for us. I thought she was doing better. I guess I was wrong."

"What are you talking about?" Kirby asked. "What hospital?"

"Mrs. Atkinson had some sort of manic episode here a few days ago," Brady explained. "She tried to shoot Nat, but I disarmed her. Nat didn't want to press charges, but Dr. Atkinson promised he'd take his wife to get help."

"I did. Check her records, ask Reed. She was doing a lot better."

"Are you sure about the time it happened?" Kirby asked, directing his laser stare at the security guard.

The boy was so startled he hiccupped. "Uh, yes, sir," he stammered. "It was around 2:35, because I'd just gotten off the cell phone with my girlfriend. She was griping about having pulled a double shift because Mary didn't show up for work."

"Did you call her, or she call you?"

"I called her . . . sir."

"Let me see the phone."

As Kirby examined the phone, he asked, "Who called 911?"

"I did," Jason answered. "Dr. Atkinson was trying to help Mrs. Atkinson."

"You don't have any blood on you," Kirby observed.

Atkinson's eyes narrowed. "Because I didn't touch her. You saw the body. It was obvious there was nothing I could do to help her."

Kirby nodded and snapped his notebook shut. "Come on, Brady."

They left Atkinson standing there while they walked down the hall to Reed's mother's bedroom.

Brady wasn't prepared for the sight of that room. Blood pooled on the floor and spattered high on the wall and ceiling. Its coppery scent made him nauseous. Fingerprint dust coated everything.

"So, what do you think?" he asked Kirby.

Kirby sighed. "I think Atkinson's one cold bastard, but I think he's telling the truth. I know that kid back there. His dad was a state trooper, and I don't think Jason would lie for anybody. I talked to Reed first. He heard the alarm go off, then the gunshot just after it stopped. By the time he got out of bed and to his mother's room, Atkinson had the door locked and the police were on their way."

"You don't think it could've been an intruder?"

Kirby shook his head. "No. The bullet caught her right above the collar bone and exited high in the back of her head. I've had my boys in here with lasers. It's not for the record yet, but going by spatter and the entrance and exit wounds, I'd say the bullet was fired from the ground. I figure it happened pretty much like he said. She freaked when the alarm went off, jumped out of bed and dropped the gun."

Brady squatted by the edge of the bed and pointed at two parallel marks on the wood floor. "What are these?"

Kirby shrugged. "I dunno. Wheelchair scuffs, maybe?"

Brady frowned. They looked too narrow to be wheelchair scuffs to him. "I thought Reed wasn't in here."

"He wasn't. Must be old marks. I swabbed them

and took pictures, but I don't think they're anything."

The girl Brady had followed upstairs stuck her head in the doorway. "The doctor's time checks out. A couple of nurses and a security guard at the hospital back up his story."

Kirby shook his head. "Looks like that's that, then. I think this is just a stupid accident."

Brady nodded. He thought of Reed, and wondered if his friend could withstand the fallout from another stupid accident.

NAT PACED THE LIVING ROOM, GLANCING AT HER WATCH for the thousandth time. It was nearly eight o'clock. Where on earth was Brady?

At last, the yellow beams of his headlights sliced up the drive. She drummed her fingers against the window casing while she watched him park. He climbed out of the car, dragging a black duffle bag with him.

Her father smiled up at her from the living room floor, where he lay sprawled watching TV. "Uh oh. Looks like Brady's going to get an earful."

"He deserves it," Nat retorted.

She crossed into the foyer and yanked open the door before Brady could knock. She meant to yell at him, but one look at his tired face made her clamp her mouth shut. Instead, she threw her arms around his neck and hugged him.

"That's letting him have it!" Justin said through a mouthful of popcorn.

Nat jerked her head around to glare at her brother, who smiled and nudged his twin.

In a squeaky falsetto, Matt piped, "Why, I'm so mad at you, I could just . . . kiss you!"

The boys dissolved in laughter. Nat released Brady and took a menacing step toward them.

"Daddy, turn your head!" she yelled, and made a rude gesture at the twins.

Brady caught her waist and dragged her back to him. He kissed the back of her head and murmured, "You're mad at me?"

Nat pressed her cheek against his chest. "I've been worried about you. Why didn't you call?"

"I went to the lab with Kirby. He pulled some strings with the coroner and they're already working Rachel Atkinson's autopsy. Nothing's final yet, but it looks like they're going to rule it as an accidental shooting."

Nat released a breath she didn't realize she was holding. "So, it wasn't the stalker?" she asked leading him into the living room. Picking up a throw pillow, she hurled it at Matt before plopping onto the loveseat and dragging Brady down with her.

"No." Brady sighed. "Do you believe, after all that happened that day with you and Reed, Dr. Atkinson let her have access to a gun? Then this morning he came home early from the hospital and accidentally set off the alarm while talking to the security guard. Looks like she grabbed the gun, jumped out of bed, dropped it and shot herself in the throat."

"That poor woman," Nat whispered.

Brady stretched his arm across the back of the loveseat and Nat snuggled against him. "How is Reed?" she asked.

Brady's voice caught when he said, "Not good."

For several moments, they sat in silence. Brady stroked her arm and hugged her a little tighter. "I feel so bad for him, Nat. He looked so relieved to see me and I couldn't do anything to help him. He was begging to see his mother, and they didn't want to let him. She looked . . . she looked horrible."

Nat glanced up at Brady. "Did they ever let him see her?"

Brady frowned. "No. He got a little wild, but I think I could've handled him. Before I could calm him, Atkinson charged in there and jabbed him with a hypodermic. Knocked him out cold."

"Hmm," Nat's father said. "Wasn't that a little drastic?"

Brady leaned forward, his elbows on his knees. "I thought so. Something about Atkinson . . . it's not right. He's a cold fish, for sure. I admit, I wondered if he was trying to keep Reed quiet about something, but Kirby said he'd already interviewed Reed. All Reed could tell them was that he heard the alarm go off and the gunshot a few seconds later. The police were on their way, and Atkinson had the door locked by the time Reed got himself out of bed and down the hall."

"That poor kid," Jake murmured.

Brady nodded in agreement and squeezed Nat's knee. "Any word about the civil trial?"

"My lawyer sent the evidence to the other lawyer and the judge, but he says I still have to be there in the morning at eleven."

"Brady, have you eaten?" Jake asked. "Selena saved you some supper."

Justin grinned. "You mean that plate of stuff in the fridge? Oops. Nobody said it was Brady's."

Nat rolled her eyes and stood. "He's lying. He didn't eat your food, but it wasn't from lack of trying." She grabbed Brady's hand. "Come on. I'll heat it up for you."

Just inside the kitchen entrance, Brady tugged her to a stop. Pressing her against the side of the refrigerator, he gave her a long, hard kiss.

"Um." Nat smiled. "I've missed you today."

"I missed you too," he said, stroking her cheek with his thumb. "And your dad's just going to have to kill me, I guess, because either I'm staying here tonight or you're going home with me. I don't intend to spend another night without you."

Nat laughed. "I don't think that will be a problem. We're not seventeen anymore, you know. Dad's mellowed a little since then."

"I don't know," Brady said. "I was sort of glad he wasn't here when I announced I was taking you to the cabin."

Nat's eyes widened. "They bet on us! All of them except Daddy. On how long it would take us to, ah . . . get together when we were alone."

Brady shot her a look that was part mortification, part amusement. "You didn't tell them, did you? Mr. Willpower caved after, what, three or four hours?"

Nat smiled and kissed the soft spot just below his ear. "It wasn't about willpower. It was about true love conquering all."

He leaned forward to kiss her again, but pulled away when the basement door opened. A blast of warm, fabric softener-scented air preceded Nat's mother into the kitchen. Bracing a laundry basket against her hip and cradling a cordless phone with her free hand, she saw Brady and grinned.

"He's here, Kel," she said, and set the basket of towels down just inside the door. "Uh huh. Okay." She covered the mouthpiece with her hand. "Your mom wants to know where you're going tonight."

"He's staying here," Nat said, and slipped beneath Brady's arm to extract a plastic wrapped plate from the refrigerator.

"He's staying here," Selena repeated, and Nat rolled her eyes at the barely suppressed glee in her voice.

Selena handed Brady the phone. "She wants to talk

to you, hon."

With that, she winked at Nat, retrieved her basket and headed down the hall. Brady sat at the kitchen table. Nat felt his stare while she punched in two minutes on the microwave's timer and poured him a glass of tea. When she set the glass in front of him, he grabbed her hand and kissed the inside of her wrist.

"Yeah, Mom," he said softly, burning Nat with his propane blue gaze. "We worked it out. I'm happy. I love her more than anything."

Silly, joyful tears stung Nat's eyes, and she brushed them away. Brady tugged her into his lap and kissed the top of her shoulder.

"Okay, I will. I will." He laughed. "I love you too. Bye." He pressed the end button and laid the phone on the table. Nuzzling the back of Nat's neck, he said, "Mom sends her love. And an order to check your mother's e-mail. She says she's found the perfect wedding dress for you."

Nat giggled. "I'm surprised they haven't already bought it. I expected to find one spread across my bed as soon as I got home."

"Well, we weren't gone the whole three days."

Nat stacked the dishwasher while he ate, and then they rejoined the rest of the family in the living room. At about 9:30, Nat said, "Daddy, is it okay if Brady stays here tonight?"

"Sure," Jake said, not taking his eyes from the TV.

She yawned and, with faked nonchalance, stood and clutched Brady's hand. "Well, we're going on up. Goodnight, everybody."

Jake glanced around at them, his blue eyes narrowing. Brady gulped audibly beside her and grabbed his duffle bag. The twins merely gawked.

Selena smiled and laid a hand on the back of Jake's neck. "Goodnight."

Although Nat felt like running, she casually climbed the stairs with Brady on her heels. As soon as they reached the top and turned the corner, he pushed her forward. "Go, go, go!" he whispered.

Once inside her room, he shut the door and locked it behind him. He leaned against it and laughed. "Man, I hate that look. Your dad can look at me like that, and it's like my guts just wither up and die. I'm a grown man now—I'm even armed—and your dad makes me feel like some little sixteen year old punk. I'm just hoping when we have a daughter, I can nail that same drop dead stare."

He made a practice face at Nat, and she giggled. "You're going to have to do better than that," she said, and unbuttoned the first two buttons of her blouse.

"Um, let me help you with that." He slowly unfastened the rest of the buttons and slid it down her arms. Placing his hands on her bare shoulders, he grinned and surveyed the room. "You know, this might be another one of my fantasies. Spending the night in the forbidden lair. Nat Hawthorne's bedroom. It smells so good in here, just like you."

He pulled her close and Nat sighed when he slid his hands down her bare waist and cupped her hips.

"Oh wait," he said with a grin. "Before I get you completely undressed, I want you to try something on."

Nat raised an eyebrow. "Don't tell me you have another one of your . . . costumes here."

Brady slung the duffel bag on the bed and unzipped it. "Are you kidding? I'm afraid to even *think* about costumes in your dad's house." He tossed a heavy vest at her. "Try it on, see if it fits. You're wearing it tomorrow."

Nat frowned. "Is this what I think it is? A bulletproof vest? You're joking."

Brady sat on the edge of the bed and tugged off his shoes. When he looked up at her, the playfulness had vanished from his eyes. "I'm dead serious. I don't know what we'll get into at that trial tomorrow, and I'm not taking any chances."

CHAPTER 15

NAT GLANCED AROUND THE NEARLY EMPTY COURTroom and shifted in the hard chair. Brady rubbed her cold fingers.

"Relax, babe," he whispered. "This will all be over within a minute."

Nat nodded and tried to smile, but her stomach churned when she remembered how horrible it had been to be seventeen years old and sit in this very courtroom—maybe even in the very chair in which her father now sat—and feel like her life was over. But this time, because she'd been a minor at the time of the accident, her father was the one on trial. He leaned on the mahogany table, talking to the insurance company's lawyer.

Anger flashed over her like a lightning strike when she recalled how Bobby had sat across the courtroom from her at the criminal trial, offering her sympathetic smiles when he'd known the whole time she was innocent.

Would he have even come forward if the prosecutor had won his motion to try her as an adult?

Not likely.

She'd thought nothing he could do would hurt worse than when he'd denied their baby, but this betrayal did, because it was all about money. Her first lover, and he hadn't given a damn what happened to her.

Nat closed her eyes and tried to banish all thoughts of Bobby. She was tired of living in the past. What mattered was here and now, her future with Brady. She would never have to feel alone again.

She smiled at him, and he gave her a reassuring wink. How she loved him!

Her heart swelled just looking into those guileless blue eyes. They would be all right. Reed would be all right too. It broke her heart to think of how he must be hurting, but he would never have to feel alone again, either.

"All rise for the Honorable Henrietta Blake, presiding," called the deputy, and Nat forced her attention to the front of the courtroom.

Judge Blake entered through a side door, crossed in front of the bright red Tennessee flag and ascended the dais. She settled into a high-backed leather chair and adjusted her glasses. "You may take your seats."

Brady nudged her and whispered, "None of the plaintiffs are here. That's a good sign."

Nat nodded, but she was still too wired to feel relief.

"Mr. Scoran," the judge said. "I understand you wish to file a motion?"

"Yes, your honor." Jake's lawyer hastily stood. "We file a motion for a continuance based on new discovery."

Wayne Breely, the lead council for the plaintiffs, rose halfway to his feet. Breely was painfully thin, with a receding hairline and skin the color of bread dough. He shot an apologetic look at Scoran and cleared his throat. "May we approach, your Honor?"

The lawyers huddled in front of the judge, whispering fervently. They conferred for nearly ten minutes before Scoran's head popped up like a turtle's. He flashed Jake a smile before returning to the defense table.

"Motion to dismiss, your Honor," Breely said.

With a crack of the gavel, the trial was over. The judge called a recess for lunch, and Scoran walked back over to Breely.

"What just happened?" Nat's mother asked her, and Nat leaned over the rail to ask her father.

Jake stood and pushed his chair in. "I'm not sure, but Scoran looks like a kid at Christmas."

"Sorry about that, guys," Scoran said when he returned to the table. "Good news. Really good news. They've decided to settle for the amount of damages they're entitled to in the original policy." He shot Jake an apologetic glance. "They could've kept the lawsuit going, suing you for negligence because the Franklin boy was driving your car, but in light of Natasha's wrongful conviction and the other evidence, they didn't think they could get more than that in front of a jury."

"So, it's over?" Jake asked.

Scoran flashed them an impossibly white lawyer

smile. "It's over."

Jake exhaled. "Thank you."

"Thank him." Scoran jerked his thumb at Brady. "Good work, Chief."

They shook hands and, with a wave, Scoran disappeared into the sea of three-piece suits and uniforms exiting the courtroom.

Jake pushed through the gate and joined them. He held out his hand to Brady, who grinned and clasped it. Instead of shaking hands, Jake pulled him into a hug.

Nat's eyes misted when her father said, "Thanks, son. For everything. I can't tell you what it means to me to see her happy again." Jake pulled back and smiled. "Now let's go get some lunch. It's on me."

Nat slipped her hand in Brady's when they left the courtroom. Following her parents' lead, they threaded through the crowd to the rear exit.

Nat shielded her eyes against the bright sunlight. She felt hot and slightly ridiculous in the Kevlar vest, and opened her mouth to tell Brady she was going back inside to slip out of it when a commotion in the parking lot drew her attention.

The sheriff bent halfway inside a battered blue pickup, arguing with the driver while a deputy leaned on the fender and watched. Nat couldn't make out what they were saying, but it was obviously a heated discussion.

The sheriff leaned back, his pudgy face red with exertion, and Nat caught a glimpse at the boy behind the wheel.

Jen's brother, Evan.

His dark eyes burned with hatred as he stared directly at her, then Brady took a protective step in front of her. Evan's tires squealed when he roared out of the parking lot.

"He still hates me," Nat said brokenly. "Brady, why does he still hate me?"

Brady's voice was quiet and reassuring as he herded her toward the car. "Jen's family wasn't part of the lawsuit. He may not know what's going on, and who knows what the sheriff told him. You can call his grandmother and talk to her when we get home."

Nat climbed in the back seat and Brady crawled in behind her. She fished his cell phone out of his shirt pocket to try Reed again. The answering machine picked up on the second ring. She pressed the end button instead of leaving another message.

Jake glanced at them in the rearview mirror. "Call Eliot and Kelly. Tell them to bring the boys and meet us at that steak place on Fifth Street."

Brady punched in the number and rested his hand on Nat's knee while he talked to his father. He placed his next call to Ian Kirby, who told him Rachel Atkinson's body hadn't yet been released for burial.

"When we get back to your house, we'll swap cars and run out there," Brady said. "I know Atkinson doesn't like either of us, but surely he wouldn't keep us from seeing Reed at a time like this."

At the restaurant, Nat tried to smile and act cheerful, but worry for Reed and Evan overshadowed her happiness. The look in Brady's eyes told her he wasn't buying her act for a minute. He leaned to whisper, "Just a few more minutes and we'll go check on him, okay?"

"Hey, no whispering!" Eliot said as he attempted to spear a cherry tomato. He flashed them a grin. "So, when's the big day?"

Nat scoffed. "What big day? Brady's not even asked me yet."

Brady laughed and wiped his mouth with his napkin. "I haven't had time to get a ring yet, but it's coming." He twisted in his chair to face her and reached to tuck a lock of hair behind her ear. "I can promise you, I'll never let you go again."

Brady's mother leaned to whisper something to Eliot. He smiled and nodded, then she cleared her throat.

"Nat," she said. "I'm not sure you would want this, and it's okay if you don't, but I thought I'd ask."

She tugged her engagement ring off and slid it across the table to them. "This ring has been on my finger for twenty-five years, and in my family for well over a hundred. It belonged to my great-great-grandmother, who gave it to her eldest daughter, who decided that it should be passed on to each firstborn daughter." Kelly smiled and twisted her napkin. "As you know, I was never able to have a daughter of my own, so I figured the tradition would die with me, or at least skip a generation, but sitting here looking at my son looking at you—a girl I've known and loved her whole life—I feel like it should be yours . . . if you want it."

"But no pressure," Eliot joked, and Kelly elbowed him.

"No pressure," she said. "If you don't like it, I can save it for my first granddaughter."

"It's lovely," Nat said over the lump in her throat. "I would be honored to wear it."

Brady reached over and picked up the ring. "Well, this isn't exactly how I'd planned it, but like Mom said, it feels right."

He slid out of his chair and, in the middle of the crowded restaurant, he took a knee.

Nat's heart leapfrogged when Brady looked up at her with shining eyes. "Ever since I've been old enough to know anything, I've known I love you. I remember one day when we were six. You said you were going to marry the red Power Ranger when we grew up, and I thought, 'Nope, she's mine. She just doesn't know it yet.' "

A startled hiccup of laughter escaped her. Nat cupped her hands over her mouth and blinked back tears while Brady grinned at her and rubbed his chin.

"I guess what I'm trying to say, Nat, is that in all my memories, you've been right there beside me. When I'm an old man, I want to look back and have my whole life be like that. Will you marry me?"

"Yes!" she said.

Her hand was shaking so hard it took him two tries to slip the ring on her finger. Applause broke out all around them when he kissed her.

When Nat looked around the table, both their mothers were crying. Even her father had red-rimmed eyes.

Selena linked her arm through Jake's and sniffed. "Jake, as much as I loved your proposal, I think Brady beat you."

"Showoff," Jake grunted, but he was grinning when he looked into Nat's eyes and that only made her cry harder.

"Stop that," he laughed, and swiped at a tear of his own. He cleared his throat and looked at Eliot. "Man!" he said softly. "You'd better bring a crowbar to the wedding, because I don't know how I'll ever let go of her to give her away."

They spent the next two hours at the restaurant, only to return home and get caught by Nat's grandparents. Alisha dropped by on her way home from work, and it was dark by the time company left and Nat and Brady were able to slip away.

"Bye." Nat kissed her mother's cheek on her way out the door. "Don't expect us back tonight. We're staying at Brady's apartment."

"We are?" Brady asked when Nat pulled the door shut behind them.

She straightened his collar and winked. "We are. I want to celebrate our engagement later without you worrying about Daddy hearing us."

"Thank you!" Brady pulled her close and nuzzled her neck.

Nat laughed. "Later, gator. We need to get to Reed's."

As she pushed him away, her hand brushed his shoulder holster.

"Do you have to carry that?" she asked softly. "I don't want to upset Reed."

"I don't either, but with everything that's been going on, I'm not going anywhere without it."

On the way to Monteagle, Brady said, "I want to get married as soon as possible, but would you mind waiting a little while to let Reed regroup? I want him to be in the wedding."

"Yeah?" Nat smiled. "That would mean a lot to him."

"It would mean a lot to me too."

Lights blazed at the Atkinson house.

"Well, looks like somebody's home." Brady put the car in park. When he touched the door handle, a pair of bright headlights swung in behind them, blocking them in.

Nat winced in the glare, and a door slammed.

"Stay here," Brady said, and jumped out of the car.

A muffled voice said something to Brady and Nat saw him pull his gun.

The world moved in nightmarish slow motion. Nat screamed when she saw the baseball bat come round. It struck Brady's arm and the gun went flying. The second swing caught him in the ribs and Brady crashed against the driver's door. Nat climbed the seat of the Cuda like Jackie Kennedy going over the back of that convertible, fueled by terror and moving on instinct.

The windshield burst into a spider web of cracked glass.

Nat screamed again and fumbled for the door handle. The door opened and pitched her into the asphalt driveway.

She stumbled to her feet and raced through the yard, but her attacker was right behind her. He tackled her just inside the carport. The impact knocked the wind out of her, and before she could regain her breath, fingers dug into her shoulder and flipped her onto her back. Nat stared into the glassy eyes of Evan McAlister.

"You think you got away with it, doncha?" he slurred, blasting her with a rush of beer breath. "You killed my sister."

His hand pressed against her throat, his thumb burrowing painfully under her jaw.

"I . . . didn't," she gasped. "Don't . . . do this."

"I heard about the trial, how your cop boyfriend fixed things for you." His fingers tightened, closing off her windpipe like a bent straw.

Spots danced before her eyes. Consciousness began to bleed away.

Suddenly, the vise around her throat relaxed and Nat wheezed for breath. Evan cursed and lurched to his feet. Blue lights danced across his flannel shirt, and he aimed an off-balance kick at Nat's head. Stars exploded behind her eyes when he connected.

Voices. She heard someone in the distance yelling for an ambulance, but she couldn't move. Brady. Was Brady okay?

Footsteps thudded by the carport, only a few feet away, and Nat would've screamed if she could've made any sound at all.

"Joe, what the hell is going on?" Martin Atkinson demanded in a coarse whisper.

"That McAlister kid went nuts, attacked Simms. Uncle Pete saw him trailing the Cuda through town, figured something was up, and we followed him here."

"The girl?"

"Looks like Simms was alone."

Nat tried to make a noise, alert them to her presence, but Martin Atkinson's next words stopped her cold.

He hissed, "You have to get them the hell out of here before you ruin everything. Reed's not dead yet."

"Joe!" the sheriff bellowed from down the drive. "Quit gabbing and find that kid. Be careful, he might be armed. Simms is wearing a holster, but I don't see his gun. Doctor, give me a hand here!"

After their footsteps pounded away, Nat forced herself to her knees.

What was she going to do? Was the sheriff part of this?

The world swam crazily as she crawled to the porch. She had to find a phone.

Nat dragged herself up the steps and dared a look back. The sheriff and Martin Atkinson huddled over Brady. He didn't appear to be moving.

She stifled a cry and scuttled forward. The front door stood halfway open. She grasped the edge of the door and pushed herself inside.

Crawling across the floor, she realized she was going to have to stand if she hoped to see a phone. She clutched at the edge of the white leather sofa and pulled herself upright. A cordless phone lay on the end table.

Her stomach churned as she leaned over the sofa arm to reach it. She hit the talk button and held it to her ear. When Nat didn't get a dial tone, she held it back and looked at it. The low charge light pulsed once, then twice.

The phone was dead.

A strangled cry escaped her lips and she became aware of a dull plop-plop sound. Blood dripped from her head to splatter on the white leather.

Horrified, she glanced over her shoulder. The movement made her dizzy, and it took her a second to focus on the blood trail she'd left behind.

There had to be other phones in this house. Reed had a cell phone, and she had to get out of here before Atkinson got back. She stumbled toward the elevator and hit the up button. The doors swung open.

Her knees shook so hard she could barely stand as

she hauled herself inside.

Once on the second floor, Nat gave another cry of frustration. A row of closed doors greeted her. Which room was Reed's?

She lurched down the hall, trying doors and searching for phones. She threw open the door to the last room and nearly fell backwards at the sight that greeted her.

Reed lay on his bed, staring sightlessly at the ceiling.

"Noooo!" she moaned, and staggered toward him. Brown pill bottles littered the white sheet in front of him. One gummy red capsule stuck to his bottom lip. A glass of water lay overturned on the floor, like it had slipped from his slack hand.

"Reed!" she cried, and shook his shoulders.

His blue eyes rolled like marbles and tried to focus on her. "Nat?" he mumbled. "Is that you?"

"We've got to get out of here!" she said, scanning the room. Reed's wheelchair sat against the opposite wall. Atkinson had wanted to make sure he couldn't escape. She didn't see his phone anywhere.

"Reed, I have to call for help. Where's your phone?"

"Martin," he groaned.

"Okay." She squeezed her eyes shut, trying desperately to think. Brady would come for her. She only had to keep them alive until he got there.

Swaying precariously, she crossed the room to his wheelchair. If she could get him onto the elevator, maybe she could lock them inside until help arrived.

Reed's cell phone lay in the seat.

The bedroom door swung open when she picked it up. Martin Atkinson grinned at her from the doorway.

"Miss Hawthorne," he said. "I do believe you have the worst timing of anyone I've ever seen, and you've made a mess downstairs."

Nat's breath caught in her throat, but she figured her only chance was to pretend she didn't know about him.

"We've got to call an ambulance," she cried, flipping open the phone. "Reed's dying."

Atkinson crossed the room and grabbed the phone out of her hand. "Yeah, I know." He glanced at his watch. "And taking his sweet time about it too."

He pulled a gun from the back waistband of his pants. Brady's gun, she realized.

Tossing Reed's phone out into the hall, Atkinson fished another out of his pocket and pressed in a number.

"Where are you?" He rolled his eyes at Nat and smiled, like he didn't have a .45 pointed at her chest. "You've got the boy? Has anyone seen you with him? Fantastic. Bring him back to the house. We've got a new plan."

"You took a nasty hit, didn't you?" he asked cordially, leaning to peer at Nat's forehead.

She jerked away from his touch and the room spun at her sudden movement. She had so many questions, but all she could think to ask was, "Why Bobby?"

"You know, I've wanted to ask you that very thing," he said, and perched on the edge of Reed's bed.

Reed wasn't moving at all. His head lolled against his shoulder, and anxiety pierced Nat's chest. If she didn't get help soon . . .

Atkinson sat there chattering like they were old friends. "Bobby was such a greedy little punk, and you're a bright, attractive girl. I have to say, Simms is a much better match for you, although I'm sure all that nobility gets tiresome too." He smiled. "What was the question? Oh, you wanted to know why I killed McBee. It was his fault. We had a good thing going. He sold prescription drugs for me on the street. Well, at least he did until he started taking more than he sold. I gave him an allotment, but he kept needing more and more. Addiction is such a nasty thing. The very substance his body craved ended up destroying him."

Nat leaned on the arm of the wheelchair. "The drugs didn't destroy him. You did. I was there, remember?"

Atkinson rolled his eyes. "If you want to get technical about it, Joe did, but I still don't see how it was much of a loss either way. Do you know anything about magic?"

"What?" Nat frowned. "Are you crazy?"

Atkinson laughed. "Crazy? Please. Sweetheart, I'm the smartest man you'll ever meet. See, I was a magician back in college. The greatest trick of a magician is to keep your audience focusing on one thing so they don't see you doing another. The stalker plan was brilliant. Not only do I get rid of McBee, who had become quite a bother to me, I get rid of Rachel and Reed, and leave everyone else chasing a man who doesn't exist. The sheriff is easy—I'm not boasting about fooling him—but I have your 'Boy Wonder' running in circles too. I never really intended to kill you, by the way. Just wanted to make it look good. But you kept getting in my way."

Nat gestured at the bed. "Was Reed in the way too?"

Atkinson smiled. "Yes. With him out of the way, all Rachel's life insurance—all this—belongs to me. The poor kid didn't have anybody else."

The cell phone in Atkinson's hand chirped. "Yeah?" He shook his head. "Well, come on up here." He pulled a pair of surgical gloves out of his pants pocket and slipped them on.

In moments, Nat heard footsteps in the hall, then Joe Richards shoved Evan inside. The boy stumbled and fell by the foot of the bed. He glanced up at Nat, his face slack with terror.

Joe's eyes widened when he saw Nat. "What's she doing here?" he demanded. "What are we going to do now?"

Atkinson shot him between the eyes.

CHAPTER 16

BRADY WAS DROWNING, SUCKING IN GREAT MOUTH-fuls of cold, black water. He sank deeper and deeper. Why couldn't he move? Nat was here somewhere; he could hear her screaming.

A voice seeped into his consciousness, crackling and hissing. Unintelligible at first, then growing louder. Brady struggled to concentrate, willed his eyes to open.

He winced in the burst of bright light and squinted at the face hovering over him.

"Don't try to talk," she advised. "We're almost there."

"Where?" he tried to ask, but then he knew. The hospital. He was in an ambulance. The screaming was a siren, the crackling and hissing, a scanner.

Where was Nat?

He tried to sit up, and gagged when a white-hot pain stabbed through his side.

"Nat!" he asked. "Where's Nat?"

Patty leaned over him, pressing him back onto the stretcher. "Don't worry. I'll have someone call her as soon as we get to the emergency room."

"No!" He groaned, teetering on the edge of panic. "She was with me."

Patty frowned. "Are you sure?"

"Let me out of here."

"Hang on just a second, okay?" Patty hurried around him and had a hushed conversation with the driver.

Gritting his teeth, Brady sat up and gingerly felt for his phone. His right arm ached. He glanced at the ugly purple knot above his wrist and remembered the rage on Evan's face when he swung. Did he have Nat? Was she lying somewhere hurt—bleeding?

He called Roscoe. "Where are you?"

Roscoe paused. "The sheriff's summoned us all to Monteagle to look for that McAlister boy. Where are you?"

"In the back of an ambulance." Brady cradled the phone against his shoulder and yelled, "Where are we, Patty?"

She cast a dismayed look over her shoulder and hurried toward him. "Harper Farm Road, but you need to lie back down."

"Harper Farm Road," he told Roscoe and dodged her attempt to take his phone. "Come get me."

Five minutes later, Roscoe pulled the ambulance over. On Brady's orders, Roscoe helped him out of the ambulance despite the heated protests of Patty and the other EMT. Brady vomited in front of the police car.

"Can't you see he needs to get to the hospital?" Patty asked. "He's in no condition to—"

"I've got to find Nat," Brady said, and hauled himself in the passenger side of the police cruiser.

Half a mile from the Atkinson estate, they met the sheriff heading in their direction. He flashed his lights and Roscoe pulled over.

"What are you doing?" Brady protested. "I have to find her."

"Just a second." Roscoe reached for the door handle. "We need to tell him she's out there."

The sheriff pecked on Brady's window. "What the hell are you doing? You need to be at the hospital."

"Nat. Nat was back there. I have to find her. No telling what McAlister will do to her—"

"He's alone," the sheriff interrupted. "I saw him in my headlights when I pulled up. He bolted like a deer, and he was alone."

Brady swallowed hard and tried to tamp down his panic. "She could be hurt."

"Did you have a gun with you?" Richards asked.

"Yeah. McAlister knocked it out of my hand."

"So, he might have it?"

"He might. I don't know. It could be lying in the driveway."

"I didn't see it there." The sheriff rubbed his face. "Okay, here's what we'll do. Roscoe, you go help my men in the woods. I'll take Simms back to the scene and look for the girl."

The sheriff would never be able to keep up in a footrace

with Evan, Brady realized. He nodded at Roscoe. "Go."

The sheriff grunted as he fell in the driver's seat. "You okay, boy?" he asked, peering at Brady in the glow of the interior light.

"I'm fine." Brady closed his eyes, fighting back another wave of nausea. "Or I will be," he corrected. "As soon as we find her." He opened his eyes a moment later and said, "Thank you. You probably saved my life, showing up when you did."

The sheriff gave him a half-smile. "Don't be thanking me yet. You look like crap. I might've just postponed it a little."

"How did you know McAlister was going to attack us?"

"Saw the kid following you in town. After this morning, I figured he was spoiling for a fight, so I thought I'd better keep an eye on him."

They reached the Atkinson estate and Brady waved the sheriff off when he came around to help him out of the car. Together, they walked around the Cuda. Brady retrieved a flashlight from the glove compartment and asked, "When you pulled up, where was McAlister?"

"Over there, by the carport."

Brady shone the light around the concrete pad. When he scanned the second time, the sheriff yelled, "Right there."

He stooped over a dark stain and stuck his fingers in it. Rubbing his fingers together beneath his nose, he glanced up at Brady. "Blood," he said. "And here's some more."

Someone screamed inside the house.

For a split second, they stared at each other, then they both took off. Each step Brady took felt like it was slicing him to the quick, but he gritted his teeth and charged forward.

Blood. He saw it everywhere. On the door, on the hardwood floor in the living room.

A male voice cried out and Brady jerked his head around, trying to find the source. The sheriff pointed at the baby monitor on top of the television.

They had to be in Reed's room.

EVAN JERKED BACKWARD, CRACKING HIS HEAD AGAINST the footboard of Reed's bed. "What are you doing?" he shrieked. "What's happening?"

Atkinson swung the gun around, pointing it at his chest. Suddenly, Evan looked so young and scared. Nat saw Jen in his eyes.

"No!" Nat cried. "Leave him out of this."

Atkinson laughed. "Are you kidding? He's the new star of the show. I was going to set Joe up as the killer, but Evan is a much better suspect, considering how the sheriff saw him running from the scene after assaulting the chief of police." He glanced at Reed and shook his head. "But if I'd known he was coming, I wouldn't have shoved all those pills down Reed. Could've just shot him like the rest of you." Atkinson wrinkled his nose. "It's overkill, don't you think?"

"You're a monster," Nat whispered.

"And I'll never get away with it, right? Is that all the clichés, because I really want this business to be over with. Guess you're next, hon. Then poor Evan here will put an end to his rampage by killing himself." He smirked. "The rest of us will just have to pick up the pieces and do what we can to get on with our lives. I, for one, think I'll grieve in the Bahamas." He pointed the gun at Nat. "It's been a pleasure, Miss Hawthorne."

"CALL FOR BACKUP," THE SHERIFF CRIED, BUT BRADY was already charging up the stairs. He stumbled halfway up and had to grab the rail to keep from falling backward. The sheriff passed him, tossing a walkie talkie in his direction. "You ain't even armed. Get your ass back down there."

Brady flipped on the radio and said, "Backup, backup. We need backup at the Atkinson house."

"On the way," Roscoe's voice crackled back.

The sheriff reached the top of the stairs and turned the corner. He sounded a million miles away when he yelled, "Drop it!"

Martin Atkinson whirled at the sound and opened fire.

Without even a glance at each other, Nat and Evan charged him. They tumbled into the hall in a wild flurry of arms and legs.

Where was the gun?

Nat could hardly see anything in the melee. She snatched a handful of Atkinson's dark hair and yanked his head back.

Brady scrambled for the sheriff, unable to take his eyes off the fight at the end of the hall. Warm blood seeped through the knees of his pants, pooling beneath the sheriff's body. His dark eyes stared sightlessly at the ceiling. Brady pried his revolver out of his hand.

Brady didn't know who the hell to shoot at.

"Run!" Evan shouted at Nat. "I think I have him."

But she couldn't move, trapped under their weight. A burst of gunfire exploded above her, and for a moment, all three of them froze.

Atkinson shoved Evan's limp body aside and pressed the barrel of the gun to Nat's forehead.

Nat squeezed her eyes shut. She froze when a second blast ripped through the hall, and she gasped as it lifted Atkinson halfway off her.

"Nat!" Brady screamed. "Nat, are you okay?"

She tried to answer, but all that emerged was a desperate huff of breath. He stumbled down the hall, falling on his knees as he drew near her.

He took her face in his hands. "Baby, baby, are you okay?" he babbled, his frantic blue eyes scanning her for injury.

Numbly she nodded, and he crushed her against his chest.

"Reed!" she said. "Reed needs help."

Brady released her and pressed his fingers to Atkinson's throat to make sure he was dead. Then he staggered toward Reed's bedroom. He nearly tripped over Joe's outstretched legs.

Evan groaned. Nat bit back the cry in her throat and scrambled over to him. A gaping wound savaged the front of his chest. She pulled his head in her lap and his eyes fluttered open.

"Did you get him?" he whispered, and she nodded blindly.

He coughed and a trickle of blood snaked from the corner of his mouth. To her astonishment, he smiled.

"Jen."

Nat's breath caught. "Honey, it's me, Nat. Just hold on. Help is on the way."

"No. Behind you," he said softly.

Nat jerked her head around, but saw nothing in the dark hallway.

Evan smiled again, and he was gone.

Nat sat rocking in the hallway, so numb she couldn't even cry. She couldn't move even when she heard the sirens screaming outside, even when the paramedics and cops pounded up the stairs. She didn't move until Brady knelt beside her and took her in his arms, and she didn't cry until they told them at the hospital that Reed was going to be okay.

EPILOGUE

Three months later

BRADY GOT DOWN ON HIS KNEES ON THE LAB floor and braced the dummy.

"Okay!" he yelled.

Ian Kirby pushed off the wall with his feet and slid on the creeper until he was in front of the dummy. From flat on his back, he fired off a shot, catching the dummy in the chin.

He rolled off the creeper they'd recovered from the Atkinson garage and stared at the black marks on the floor. "Sonofabitch," he muttered. "That's how he did it. My shot was just a little high, but we've got this nailed. Atkinson doped his wife on Valium, got Joe in place and set himself up with an alibi."

"Can you imagine how long Joe had to wait?" Brady mused. "I bet he lay there for a couple of hours, and he only had one shot." He stared at the dummy. "But what I don't get is how he got off a shot like that at that time of the morning in a dark bedroom."

"We found a pair of night vision goggles in Joe's truck. I don't know if it was the craziest plan I've ever seen, or the most brilliant." Kirby grinned. "And he would've gotten away with it too, if it hadn't been for you meddling kids."

Brady snorted and carefully laid the dummy in the floor so he could stand and examine the slug in the retainer wall. "Did he set her up or what? The tox report from the day she took a shot at Nat revealed high levels of amphetamines in her system. She was wired, and thinking the whole time she was taking a relaxant. After that fiasco at the pool, who would doubt the jumpy accident scenario?"

Brady squatted to examine the dummy again, tilting back what was left of its head.

"Should I be jealous?" a husky voice asked.

Brady grinned up at Nat, who stood in the doorway in a long black trench coat watching him with sparkling green eyes.

"Stop it." He groaned and clutched his ribs as he stood. "It still hurts to laugh."

"Are you coming to the wedding Saturday, Ian?" she asked, while Brady crossed to join her.

"Wouldn't miss it for the world," Kirby replied.

Brady slid his arms around Nat's waist and kissed her cheek. "Me either. Are we through here, Kirby?"

"Yeah, we're done. Take this beautiful lady to lunch. I'll write it up."

When they walked out of earshot, Nat leaned into Brady and smiled. "Lunch isn't exactly what I had in mind."

"Oh, yeah?" Brady punched the button for the elevator.

"Oh, yeah," she purred, pressing her palms against his chest.

"Ow," Brady said, and pulled away.

Nat frowned. "What do you mean, ow? What's the matter with you?"

"Nothing."

"Something." She touched his chest again and he flinched. Placing her hands on her hips, she said, "Brady Simms, what exactly did you guys do last night at that bachelor party?"

"Reed told me you'd be nosy. I can't tell you about my bachelor party. It's guy stuff."

Nat leaned close to nip his ear and whispered, "Not even for a Scooby snack?"

Brady's eyes narrowed. "Have you been watching cartoons with Kirby?"

"What?"

He laughed. "Never mind. You were saying?"

With a secretive smile, Nat untied her coat. She gave him a flash of thigh-high stockings and short skirt before the elevator doors opened and she shot out into the lobby.

"Hey, no fair," he complained, running ahead to open the door for her.

"You bought the outfit," she reminded him while they crossed the parking lot.

Brady unlocked the passenger door of the Cuda for her. Nat slipped off her coat and tossed it in the back seat before brushing a kiss on his mouth and climbing inside. Her scent perfumed the cold air around him.

Grinning, Brady shut the door and hurried around to his side.

"Where are we going?" she asked while he slammed the car in gear.

"I thought we could go someplace private, so we could, uh, negotiate."

Nat slid her hand down his thigh. "I do hope we can come to terms," she said. "I'd hate to have to . . . hold out."

Brady groaned. "You wouldn't do me like that, would you?"

She merely smiled.

He drove out in the country, past the old strip pits onto a narrow gravel road. Once he was fairly certain they wouldn't be disturbed, he pulled off the side of the road and turned off the ignition.

"Brady, it's cold," she complained as she crawled in the back seat.

"I'll keep you warm," he promised, sliding in behind her. He pulled her into his lap and nuzzled her neck. "Now, what were we talking about?"

She smacked both hands on his chest and grinned when he yelped. "We were talking about that."

"It was supposed to be a surprise for our wedding

night, but I told Reed you'd never be able to keep your hands off me for three whole days."

Nat rolled her eyes and Brady laughed.

"Help me out here," he said, and Nat helped him skin the shirt over his head.

"Oh, Brady!" she said, when she spotted her name tattooed over his heart.

He brushed a wave of dark hair out of her face. "Do you like it?"

"I love it," she said softly.

"After we ditched the old guys last night, Reed and I went to that tattoo place in McMinnville. He said I was cheating by not spelling out the whole thing, but Natasha is such a long, long name . . ."

Nat laughed and swiped at her eyes. "Oh you! You're going to make me cry and ruin my mascara."

Brady smiled at her. "Your name's been written inside my heart forever. I figured I might as well put it on the outside too."

"Is that right?"

He nodded. "A very wise, very beautiful woman once told me that if you keep something near to your heart, you can never lose it. I'm banking on that."

Nat laughed through the tears streaming down her cheeks. "Forever," she whispered.

"Forever." With a wink, he said, "Pinky swear?"

Nat hooked her little finger in his and inclined her head to kiss him.

Paint *it* Black
Michelle Perry

DEA agent Necie Bramhall thinks she knows a thing or two about revenge. She's devoted her life to bringing down the drug lord father who abandoned her. When she finally captures him, she thinks she'll be able to put her painful past behind her. What she doesn't realize is that she's created a brand new enemy. A deadly enemy.

Maria Barnes is beautiful, ruthless, and driven by a lifelong jealousy of the half-sister she's never known—the daughter their father could never forget. Her hatred for Necie spirals out of control following their father's arrest, and Maria vows to destroy everything Necie holds dear . . . starting with her marriage and her family.

When her daughter is kidnapped, new revelations reveal the man she always perceived as her greatest enemy might be the only one who can save her from her half-sister's wrath. And now her father is behind bars . . .

ISBN#1933836008
ISBN#9781933836003
Jewel Imprint: Emerald
US $7.99 / CDN $9.99
May 2008
www.michelleperry.com

IN ENEMY HANDS

MICHELLE PERRY

How hard could it be to kidnap a pampered little rich girl?

Especially if you're bounty hunter extraordinaire Dante Giovanni, who normally prowls the underworld in search of the most vicious criminals. Piece of cake, Dante thinks, when reclusive businessman Gary Vandergriff offers him a cool half million to bring home his estranged daughter, Nadia.

Enter Nadia.

His first meeting with her is stunning; both literally and figuratively. He foils an attempt on her life, and falls immediately under her spell. It's not gonna be hard duty, Dante thinks, keeping her safe from the Mexican drug lord infuriated by her stepfather's expanding meth operation. He'll take her out of harm's way, no problem, get her back to her father, and enjoy the ride along the way. Everything is great.

Until he delivers her into Enemy Hands.

ISBN#1932815473
ISBN#9781932815474
Jewel Imprint: Emerald
US $6.99 / CDN $9.99
Available Now
www.michelleperry.com

For more information
about other great titles from
MEDALLION PRESS, visit

www.medallionpress.com